RUMPOLE OF THE BAILEY

Horace Rumpole, barrister at law, sixty-eight next birthday, with a mind full of old murders, legal anecdotes and English verse and an unsurpassed knowledge of blood and typewriters, takes up his pen to entertain others like himself who have found in British justice a life-long subject of harmless fun. In these six stories Rumpole reconstructs some of his triumphs and disasters in the Courts of Law.

Library of Congress Cataloging-in-Publication Data

Mortimer, John Clifford, 1923–
  Rumpole of the Bailey / John Mortimer.
    p.   cm.—(Eagle large print)
  Originally published: Harmondsworth; New York:
Penguin Books, 1978.
  ISBN 0–7927–1532–2
  ISBN 0–7927–1531–4 (pbk.)
  1. Rumpole, Horace (Fictitious character)—Fiction.
  2. Detective and mystery stories, English.   3. Lawyers—Fiction.
  4. Large type books.   I. Title.   II. Series.
[PR6025.07552R8 1993]   92–43129
823′.914—dc20   CIP

British Library Cataloguing in Publication Data available

This Large Print edition is published by Chivers Press, England, and Chivers
North America, 1993.

Published in the U.S. by arrangement with Sterling Lord Literistic, Inc. and in
the British Commonwealth with Penguin Books Ltd.

U.K. Softcover ISBN 0 7451 3456 4
U.S. Softcover ISBN 0 7927 1531 4

Photoset, printed and bound in Great Britain by
REDWOOD PRESS LIMITED, Melksham, Wiltshire

Rumpole of
the Bailey

John Mortimer

CHIVERS PRESS

For Irene Shubik

CONTENTS

CONTENTS

RUMPOLE OF THE BAILEY

RUMPOLE AND THE YOUNGER GENERATION

I, Horace Rumpole, barrister at law, 68 next birthday, Old Bailey Hack, husband to Mrs Hilda Rumpole (known to me only as She Who Must Be Obeyed) and father to Nicholas Rumpole (lecturer in social studies at the University of Baltimore, I have always been extremely proud of Nick); I, who have a mind full of old murders, legal anecdotes and memorable fragments of the *Oxford Book of English Verse* (Sir Arthur Quiller-Couch's edition) together with a dependable knowledge of bloodstains, blood groups, fingerprints, and forgery by typewriter; I, who am now the oldest member of my Chambers, take up my pen at this advanced age during a lull in business (there's not much crime about, all the best villains seem to be off on holiday in the Costa Brava), in order to write my reconstructions of some of my recent triumphs (including a number of recent disasters) in the Courts of Law, hoping thereby to turn a bob or two which won't be immediately grabbed by the taxman, or my clerk Henry, or by She Who Must Be Obeyed, and perhaps give some sort of entertainment to those who, like myself, have found in British justice a life-long subject of harmless fun.

When I first considered putting pen to paper in this matter of my life, I thought I must begin with the great cases of my comparative youth, the 'Penge Bungalow Murder', where I gained an acquittal alone and without a leader, or the 'Great Brighton Benefit Club Forgery', which I contrived to win by reason of my exhaustive study of typewriters. In these cases I was, for a brief moment, in the Public Eye, or at least my name seemed almost a permanent feature of the *News of the World*, but when I come to look back on that period of my life at the Bar it all seems to have happened to another Rumpole, an eager young barrister whom I can scarcely recognize and whom I am not at all sure I would like, at least not enough to spend a whole book with him.

I am not a public figure now, so much has to be admitted; but some of the cases I shall describe, the wretched business of the Honourable Member, for instance, or the charge of murder brought against the youngest, and barmiest, of the appalling Delgardo brothers, did put me back on the front page of the *News of the World* (and even got me a few inches in *The Times*). But I suppose I have become pretty well known, if not something of a legend, round the Old Bailey, in Pommeroy's Wine Bar in Fleet Street, in the robing room at London Sessions and in the cells at Brixton Prison. They know me there for never pleading guilty, for chain-smoking small cigars, and for quoting Wordsworth when they least expect it. Such notoriety will not long survive my not-to-be-delayed trip to Golders Green Crematorium. Barristers' speeches vanish quicker than Chinese dinners, and even the greatest victory in Court rarely survives longer than the next Sunday's papers.

*   *   *

To understand the full effect on my family life, however, of that case which I have called 'Rumpole and the Younger Generation', it is necessary to know a little of my past and the long years that led up to my successful defence of Jim Timson, the 16-year-old sprig, the young hopeful, and apple of the eye of the Timsons, a huge and industrious family of South London villains. As this case was, by and large, a family matter, it is important that you should understand my family.

My father, the Reverend Wilfred Rumpole, was a Church of England clergyman who, in early middle age, came reluctantly to the conclusion that he no longer believed any one of the 39 Articles. As he was not fitted by character or training for any other profession, however, he had to soldier on in his living in Croydon and by a good deal of scraping and saving he was able to send me as a boarder to a minor public school on the Norfolk coast. I later went to Keble College, Oxford, where I achieved a dubious third in law—you will discover during the course of these memoirs that, although I only feel truly alive and happy in Law Courts, I have a singular distaste for the law. My father's example, and the number of theological students I met at Keble, gave me an early mistrust of clergymen whom I have always found to be most unsatisfactory witnesses. If you call a clergyman in mitigation, the old darling can be guaranteed to add at least a year to the sentence.

When I first went to the Bar, I entered the Chambers of C. H. Wystan. Wystan had a moderate practice, acquired rather by industry than talent, and a strong disinclination to look at the photographs in murder cases, being particularly squeamish on the fascinating subject of blood. He also had a daughter, Hilda Wystan as was, now Mrs Hilda Rumpole and She Who Must Be Obeyed. I was ambitious in those days. I did my best to cultivate Wystan's clerk Albert, and I started to get a good deal of criminal work. I did what was expected of me and spent happy hours round the Bailey and Sessions and my fame grew in criminal circles; at the end of the day I would take Albert for a drink in Pommeroy's Wine Bar. We got on extremely well and he would always recommend 'his Mr Rumpole' if a solicitor rang up with a particularly tricky indecent assault or a nasty case of receiving stolen property.

There is no point in writing your memoirs unless you are prepared to be completely candid, and I must confess that, in the course of a long life, I have been in love on several occasions. I am sure that I loved Miss Porter, the shy and nervous, but at times liberated daughter of Septimus Porter, my Oxford tutor in Roman Law. In fact we were engaged to be married, but the engagement had to be broken off because of Miss Porter's early death. I often think about her, and of the different course my home life might have taken, for Miss Porter was in no way a girl born to command, or expect, implicit obedience. During my service with the ground staff of the R.A.F. I undoubtedly became helplessly smitten with the charms of an extremely warmhearted and gallant officer in the WAAFs by the name of Miss Bobby O'Keefe, but I was no match for the wings of a

4

Pilot Officer, as appeared on the chest of a certain Sam 'Three-Fingers' Dogherty. During my conduct of a case, which I shall describe in a later chapter which I have called 'Rumpole and the Alternative Society', I once again felt a hopeless and almost feverish stirring of passion for a young woman who was determined to talk her way into Holloway Prison. My relationship with Hilda Wystan was rather different.

To begin with, she seemed part of life in Chambers. She was always interested in the law and ambitious, first for her widowed father, and then, when he proved himself unlikely Lord Chancellor material, for me. She often dropped in for tea on her way home from shopping, and Wystan used to invite me in for a cup. One year I was detailed off to be her partner at an Inns of Court ball. There it became clear to me that I was expected to marry Hilda; it seemed a step in my career like getting a brief in the Court of Appeal, or doing a murder. When she proposed to me, as she did over a glass of claret cup after an energetic waltz, Hilda made it clear that, when old Wystan finally retired, she expected to see me Head of Chambers. I, who have never felt at a loss for a word in Court, found absolutely nothing to say. In that silence the matter was concluded.

*　　　*　　　*

So now you must picture Hilda and me twenty-five years later, with a son at that same east coast public school which I just managed to afford from the fruits of crime, in our matrimonial home at 25B Froxbury Court, Gloucester Road.

5

(A mansion flat is a misleading description of that cavernous and underheated area which Hilda devotes so much of her energy to keeping shipshape, not to say Bristol fashion.) We were having breakfast, and, between bites of toast, I was reading my brief for that day, an Old Bailey trial of the 16-year-old Jim Timson charged with robbery with violence, he having allegedly taken part in a wage snatch on a couple of elderly butchers: an escapade planned in the playground of the local Comprehensive. As so often happens, the poet Wordsworth, that old sheep of the Lake District, sprang immediately to mind, and I gave tongue to his lines, well knowing that they must only serve to irritate She Who Must Be Obeyed.

'Trailing clouds of glory do we come   From God, who is our home; Heaven lies about us in our infancy!'

I looked at Hilda. She was impassively demolishing a boiled egg. I also noticed that she was wearing a hat, as if prepared to set out upon some expedition. I decided to give her a little more Wordsworth, prompted by my reading the story of the boy Timson.

'Shades of the prison house begin to close   Upon the growing boy.'

Hilda spoke at last.

'Rumpole, you're not talking about your son, I hope. You're never referring to Nick...'

'Shades of the prison house begin to close? Not round our son, of course. Not round Nick. Shades of the public school have grown round him, the thousand-quid-a-year remand home.'

Hilda always thought it indelicate to refer to the subject of school fees, as if being at Mulstead

6

were a kind of unsolicited honour for Nick. She became increasingly business-like.

'He's breaking up this morning.'

'Shades of the prison house begin to open up for the holidays.'

'Nick has to be met at 11.15 at Liverpool Street and given lunch. When he went back to school you promised him a show. You haven't forgotten?'

Hilda was clearing away the plates rapidly. To tell the truth I had forgotten the date of Nick's holidays; but I let her assume I had a long planned treat laid on for him.

'Of course I haven't forgotten. The only show I can offer him is a robbery with violence in Number 2 Court at the Old Bailey. I wish I could lay on a murder. Nick's always so enjoyed my murders.'

It was true. On one distant half term Nick had sat in on the 'Peckham Billiard Hall Stabbing', and enjoyed it a great deal more than *Treasure Island*.

'I must fly! Daddy gets so crotchety if anyone's late. And he does love his visits.'

Hilda removed my half-empty coffee cup.

'Our father which art in Horsham. Give my respects to the old sweetheart.'

It had also slipped my mind that old C. H. Wystan was laid up with a dicky ticker in Horsham General Hospital. The hat was, no doubt, a clue I should have followed. Hilda usually goes shopping in a headscarf. By now she was at the door, and looking disapproving.

'"Old sweetheart" is hardly how you used to talk of the Head of your Chambers.'

7

'Somehow I can never remember to call the Head of my Chambers "Daddy".'

The door was open. Hilda was making a slow and effective exit.

'Tell 1 k I'll be back in good time to get his supper.'

'Your wish is my command!' I muttered in my best imitation of a slave out of Chou Chin Chow. She chose to ignore it.

'And try not to leave the kitchen looking as though it's been hit by a bomb.'

'I hear, oh Master of the Blue Horizons.' I said this with a little more confidence, as she had by now started off on her errand of mercy, and I added, for good measure, 'She Who Must Be Obeyed'.

I had finished my breakfast and was already thinking how much easier life with the Old Bailey judge was than marriage.

* * *

Soon after I finished my breakfast with Hilda, and made plans to meet my son at the start of his holidays from school, Fred Timson, star of a dozen Court appearances, was seeing *his* son in the cells under the Old Bailey as the result of a specially arranged visit. I know he brought the boy his best jacket, which his mother had taken specially to the cleaners, and insisted on his putting on a tie. I imagine he told him that they had the best 'brief' in the business to defend him, Mr Rumpole having always done wonders for the Timson family. I know that Fred told young Jim to stand up straight in the witness box and remember to call the judge 'my Lord' and not show his ignorance by coming out with any gaffe such as 'Your Honour', or 'Sir'. The world, that day, was full of fathers showing appropriate and paternal concern.

The robbery with which Jim Timson was charged was an exceedingly simple one. At about 7 p.m. one Friday evening, the date being 16 September, the two elderly Brixton butchers, Mr Cadwallader and Mr Lewis Stein, closed their shop in Bombay Road and walked with their week's takings round the corner to a narrow alley-way known as Green's Passage, where their grey Austin van was parked. When they got to the van they found that the front tyres had been deflated. They stooped to inspect the wheels and, as they did so they were attacked by a number of boys, some armed with knives and one flourishing a cricket stump. Luckily, neither of the butchers was hurt, but the attaché case containing their money was snatched.

Chief Inspector 'Persil' White, the old darling in whose territory this outrage had been committed, arrested Jim Timson. All the other boys got clean away, but no doubt because he came from a family well known, indeed almost embarrassingly familiar, to the Chief Inspector, and because of certain rumours in the school playground, he was charged and put on an identity parade. The butchers totally failed to identify him; but, when he was in the Remand Centre, young Jim, according to the evidence, had boasted to another boy of having 'done the butchers'.

As I thought about this case on my way to the

Temple that morning, it occurred to me that Jim Timson was a year younger than my son, but that he had got a step further than Nick in following his father's profession. I had always hoped Nick would go into the law, and, as I say, he seemed to thoroughly enjoy my murders.

*   *   *

In the clerk's room in Chambers Albert was handing out the work for the day: rather as a trainer sends his string of horses out on the gallops. I looked round the familiar faces, my friend George Frobisher, who is an old sweetheart but an absolutely hopeless advocate (he can't ask for costs without writing down what he's going to say), was being fobbed off with a nuisance at Kingston County Court. Young Erskine-Brown, who wears striped shirts and what I believe are known as 'Chelsea Boots', was turning up his well-bred nose at an indecent assault at Lambeth (a job I'd have bought Albert a double claret in Pommeroy's for at his age) and saying he would prefer a little civil work, adding that he was sick to death of crime.

I have very little patience with Erskine-Brown.

'A person who is tired of crime,' I told him quite candidly, 'is tired of life.'

'Your Dangerous and Careless at Clerkenwell is on the mantelpiece, Mr Hoskins,' Albert said.

Hoskins is a gloomy fellow with four daughters; he's always lurking about our clerk's room looking for cheques. As I've told him often enough crime doesn't pay, or at any rate not for a very long time.

When a young man called MacLay had asked in vain for a brief I invited him to take a note for me down at the Old Bailey. At least he'd get a wig on and not spend a miserable day unemployed in Chambers. Our oldest member, Uncle Tom (very few of us remember that his name is T. C. Rowley) also asked Albert if there were any briefs for him, not in the least expecting to find one. To my certain knowledge, Uncle Tom hasn't appeared in Court for fifteen years, when he managed to lose an undefended divorce case, but, as he lives with a widowed sister, a lady of such reputed ferocity that she makes She Who Must Be Obeyed sound like Mrs Tiggywinkle, he spends most of his time in Chambers. He looks remarkably well for 78.

'You aren't actually *expecting* a brief, Uncle Tom, are you?' Erskine-Brown asked. I can't like Erskine-Brown.

'Time was,' Uncle Tom started one of his reminiscences of life in Chambers. 'Time was when I had more briefs in my corner of the mantelpiece, Erskine-Brown, than you've seen in the whole of your short career at the Bar. Now,' he was opening a brown envelope, 'I only get invitations to insure my life. It's a little late for that.'

Albert told me that the robbery was not before 11.30 before Mr Justice Everglade in Number 1 Court. He also told me who was prosecuting, none other than the tall, elegant figure with the silk handkerchief and gold wristwatch, leaning against the mantelpiece and negligently reading a large cheque from the Director of Public Prosecutions, Guthrie Featherstone, M.P. He removed the silk handkerchief, dabbed the end of his nose and his small moustache and asked in that voice which comes over so charmingly, saying nothing much about any important topic of the day in 'World at One',

'Agin me Rumpole? Are you agin me?' He covered a slight yawn with the handkerchief before returning it to his breast pocket. 'Just come from an all-night sitting down at the House. I don't suppose your robbery'll be much of a worry.'

'Only, possibly, to young Jim Timson,' I told him, and then gave Albert his orders for the day. 'Mrs Rumpole's gone down to see her father in Horsham.'

'How is Wystan? No better, is he?' Uncle Tom sounded as gently pleased as all old men do when they hear news of illness in others.

'Much the same, Uncle Tom, thank you. And Young Nick. My son...'

'Master Nick?' Albert had always been fond of Nick, and looked forward to putting him through his paces when the time came for him to join our stable in Chambers.

'He's breaking up today. So he'll need meeting at Liverpool Street. Then he can watch a bit of the robbery.'

'We're going to have your son in the audience? I'd better be brilliant.' Guthrie Featherstone now moved from the fireplace.

'You needn't bother, old darling. It's his Dad he comes to see.'

'Oh, *touché*, Rumpole! *Distinctement touché*!'

Featherstone talks like that. Then he invited me to walk down to the Bailey with him. Apparently

12

he was still capable of movement and didn't need a stretcher, even after a sleepless night with the Gas Mains Enabling Bill, or whatever it was.

We walked together down Fleet Street and into Ludgate Circus, Featherstone wearing his overcoat with the velvet collar and little round bowler hat, I puffing a small cigar and with my old mac flapping in the wind; I discovered that the gentleman beside me was quietly quizzing me about my career at the Bar.

'You've been at this game a long while, Rumpole,' Featherstone announced. I didn't disagree with him, and then he went on.

'You never thought of taking silk?'

'Rumpole, Q.C?' I almost burst out laughing. 'Not on your Nelly. Rumpole "Queer Customer". That's what they'd be bound to call me.'

'I'm sure you could, with your seniority.' I had no idea then, of exactly what this Featherstone was after. I gave him my view of Q.C.s in general.

'Perhaps, if I played golf with the right judges, or put up for Parliament, they might make me an artificial silk, or at any rate, a nylon.' It was at this point I realized I had put up a bit of a black. 'Sorry. I forgot. You *did* put up for Parliament.'

'Yes. You never thought of Rumpole, Q.C?' Featherstone had apparently taken no offence.

'Never,' I told him. 'I have the honour to be an Old Bailey Hack! That's quite enough for me.'

At which point we turned up into Newgate Street and there it was in all its glory, touched by a hint of early spring sunshine, the Old Bailey, a stately Law Court, decreed by the City Fathers, an Edwardian palace, with an extensive modern extension to deal with the increase in human fallibility. There was the Dome and the Blindfold Lady. Well, it's much better she doesn't see *all* that's going on. That, in fact, was our English version of the Palais de Justice, complete with murals, marble statues and underground accommodation for some of the choicest villains in London.

Terrible things go on down the Bailey—horrifying things. Why is it I never go in the revolving door without a thrill of pleasure, a slight tremble of excitement? Why does it seem a much *jollier* place than my flat in Gloucester Road under the strict rule of She Who Must Be Obeyed? These are questions which may only be partly answered in the course of these memoirs.

$\star$ $\qquad$ $\star$ $\qquad$ $\star$

At the time when I was waving a cheerful umbrella at Harry, the policeman in the revolving door of the Old Bailey extension, my wife Hilda was at her Daddy's bedside at the Horsham General arranging her dozen early daffs and gently probing, so she told me that evening, on the subject of his future, and mine.

'I'll have to give up, you know. I can't go on forever. Crocked up, I'm afraid,' said Wystan.

'Nonsense, Daddy. You'll go on for years.'

I imagine Hilda did her best to sound bracing, whilst putting the daffs firmly in their place.

'No, Hilda. No. They'll have to start looking for another Head of Chambers.'

This gave Hilda her opportunity. 'Rumpole's the senior man. Apart from Uncle Tom and he doesn't really practise nowadays.'

14

'Your husband the senior man.' Wystan looked back on a singularly uneventful life. 'How time flies! I recall when he was the junior man. My pupil.'

'You said he was the best youngster on bloodstains you'd ever known.' Hilda was doing her best for me.

'Rumpole! Yes, your husband was pretty good on bloodstains. Shaky, though, on the law of landlord and tenant. What sort of practice has Rumpole now?'

'I believe ... Today it's the Old Bailey.' Hilda was plumping pillows, doing her best to sound casual. And her father showed no particular enthusiasm for my place of work.

'It's always the Old Bailey, isn't it?'

'Most of the time. Yes. I suppose so.'

'Not a frightfully good *address*, the Old Bailey. Not exactly the S.W.I. of the legal profession.'

Sensing that Daddy would have thought better of me if I'd been in the Court of Appeal or the Chancery Division, Hilda told me she thought of a master stroke.

'Oh, Rumpole only went down to the Bailey because it's a family he knows. It seems they've got a young boy in trouble.'

This appealed to Daddy, he gave one of his bleak smiles which amount to no more than a brief withdrawal of lips from the dentures.

'Son gone wrong?' he said. 'Very sad that. Especially if he comes of a really good family.'

★   ★   ★

That really good family, the Timsons, was out in

15

force and waiting outside Number 1 Court by the time I had got on the fancy dress, yellowing horse-hair wig, gown become more than a trifle tattered over the years, and bands round the neck that Albert ought to have sent to the laundry after last week's death by dangerous driving. As I looked at the Timson clan assembled, I thought the best thing about them was the amount of work of a criminal nature they had brought into Chambers. They were all dressed for the occasion, the men in dark blazers, suede shoes and grey flannels; the ladies in tight-fitting suits, high heels and elaborately piled hairdos. I had never seen so many ex-clients together at one time.

'Mr Rumpole.'

'Ah, Bernard! You're instructing me.'

Mr Bernard, the solicitor, was a thirtyish, perpetually smiling man in a pinstriped suit. He regarded criminals with something of the naïve fervour with which young girls think of popular entertainers. Had I known the expression at the time, I would have called him a grafters' 'groupie'.

'I'm always your instructing solicitor in a Timson case, Mr Rumpole.' Mr Bernard beamed and Fred Timson, a kindly man and most innocent robber, stepped out of the ranks to do the honours.

'Nothing but the best for the Timsons, best solicitor and best barrister going. You know my wife Vi?'

Young Jim's mother seemed full of confidence. As I took her hand, I remembered I had got Vi off on a handling charge after the Croydon bank raid.

16

Well, there was really no evidence.

'Uncle Cyril.' Fred introduced the plumpish uncle with the small moustache whom I was sure I remembered. What was *his* last outing exactly? Carrying house-breaking instruments by night?

'Uncle Dennis. You remember Den, surely, Mr Rumpole?'

I did. Den's last little matter was an alleged conspiracy to forge log books.

'And Den's Doris.'

Aunty Doris came at me in a blur of henna-ed hair and darkish perfume. What was Doris's last indiscretion? Could it have been receiving a vast quantity of stolen scampi? Acquitted by a majority, at least I was sure of that.

'And yours truly. Frederick Timson. The boy's father.'

Regrettable, but we had a slip-up with Fred's last spot of bother. I was away with flu, George Frobisher took it over and he got three years. He must've only just got out.

'So, Mr Rumpole. You know the whole family.'

A family to breed from, the Timsons. Must almost keep the Old Bailey going single-handed.

'You're going to do your best for our young Jim, I'm sure, Mr Rumpole.'

I didn't find the simple faith of the Timsons that I could secure acquittals in the most unlikely circumstances especially encouraging. But then Jim's mother said something which I was to long remember.

'He's a good boy. He was ever so good to me while Dad was away.'

So that was Jimbo's life. Head of the family at fourteen, when Dad was off on one of his regular

17

visits to Her Majesty.

'It's young Jim's first appearance, like. At the Old Bailey.' Fred couldn't conceal a note of pride. It was Jim boy's Bar Mitzvah, his first Communion.

So we chatted a little about how all the other boys got clean away, which I told them was a bit of luck as none of them would go into the witness box and implicate Jim, and Bernard pointed out that the identification by the butchers was pretty hopeless. Well, what did he expect? Would you have a photographic impression of the young hopeful who struck you a smart blow on the back of the head with a cricket stump? We talked with that curious suppressed excitement there always is before a trial, however disastrous the outcome may be, and I told them the only thing we had to worry about, as if that were not enough, was Jim's confession to the boy in the Remand Centre, a youth who rejoiced in the name of Peanuts Molloy.

'Peanuts Molloy! Little grass.' Fred Timson spoke with a deep contempt.

'Old "Persil" White fitted him up with that one, didn't he?' Uncle Cyril said it as if it were the most natural thing in the world, and only to be expected.

'Chief Detective Inspector White,' Bernard explained.

'Why should the Chief Inspector want to fit up your Jimbo?' It was a question to which I should have known what their answer would be.

'Because he's a Timson, that's why!' said Fred.

'Because he's the apple of our eye, like,' Uncle Den told me, and the boy's mother added:

18

'Being as he's the baby of the family.'

'Old Persil'd fit up his mother if it'd get him a smile from his Super.' As Fred said this the Chief Inspector himself, grey-haired and avuncular, walked by in plain clothes, with a plain-clothes sergeant.

'Morning, Chief Inspector,' Fred carried on without drawing breath.

'Morning, Fred. Morning, Mrs Timson.' The Chief Inspector greeted the family with casual politeness, after all they were part of his daily work, and Vi sniffed back a 'Good morning, Chief Inspector.'

'Mr Timson. We'll shift our ground. Remove good friends.'

Like Hamlet, after seeing the ghost, I thought it was better to continue our conference in private. So we went and sat round a table in the canteen, and, when we had sorted out who took how many lumps, and which of them could do with a choc roll or a cheese sandwich, the family gave me the lowdown on the chief prosecution witness.

'The Chief Inspector put that little grass Peanuts Molloy into Jim's painting class at the Remand Centre.' Fred had no doubt about it.

'Jim apparently poured out his soul to Peanuts.' The evidence sounded, to my old ears, completely convincing, and Bernard read us a snatch from his file.

'We planned to do the old blokes from the butcher's and grab the wages...'

'That,' I reminded the assembled company, 'is what Peanuts will say Jim told him.'

'You think I'd bring Jim up to talk in the Nick like that? The Timsons ain't stupid!' Fred was

19

outraged, and Vi, pursing her lips in a sour gesture of wounded respectability added, 'His Dad's always told him. Never say a word to anyone you're banged up with—bound to be a grass.'

One by one, Aunty Doris, Uncle Den and Uncle Cyril added their support.

'That's right. Fred's always brought the boy up proper. Like the way he should be. He'd never speak about the crime, not to anyone he was banged up with.'

'Specially not to one of the Molloys!'

'The Molloys!' Vi spoke for the Timsons, and with deep hatred. 'Noted grasses. That family always has been.'

'The Molloys is beyond the pale. Well known for it.' Aunty Doris nodded her henna-ed topknot wisely.

'Peanuts's Grandad shopped my old father in the "Streatham Co-op Robbery". Pre-war, that was.'

I had a vague memory then of what Fred Timson was talking about. The Streatham Co-op case, one of my better briefs—a long case with not much honour shown among thieves, as far as I could remember.

'Then you can understand, Mr Rumpole. No Timson would ever speak to a Molloy.'

'So you're sure Jimbo never said anything to Peanuts?' I was wondering exactly how I could explain the deep, but not particularly creditable, origins of this family hostility to the jury.

'I give you my word, Mr Rumpole. Ain't that enough for you? No Timson would ever speak to a Molloy. Not under any circumstances.'

There were not many matters on which I would take Fred Timson's word, but the history of the Streatham Co-op case came back to me, and this was one of them.

＊　　＊　　＊

It's part of the life of an Old Bailey Hack to spend a good deal of his time down in the cells, in the basement area, where they keep the old door of Newgate, kicked and scarred, through which generations of villains were sent to the treadmill, the gallows or the whip. You pass this venerable door and ring a bell, you're let in and your name's taken by one of the warders who bring the prisoners from Brixton. There's a perpetual smell of cooking and the warders are snatching odd snacks of six inches of cheese butties and a gallon of tea. Lunch is being got ready, and the cells under the Bailey have a high reputation as one of the best caffs in London. By the door the screws have their pinups and comic cartoons of judges. You are taken to a waiting-room, three steel chairs and a table, and you meet the client. Perhaps he is a novice, making his first appearance, like Jim Timson. Perhaps he's an old hand asking anxiously which judge he's got, knowing their form as accurately as a betting-shop proprietor. Whoever he is, the client will be nervously excited, keyed up for his great day, full of absurd hope.

The worst part of a barrister's life at the Old Bailey is going back to the cells after a guilty verdict to say 'good-bye'. There's no purpose in it, but, as a point of honour, it has to be done.

21

Even then the barrister probably gets the best reaction, and almost never any blame. The client is stunned, knocked out by his sentence. Only in a couple of weeks' time, when the reality of being banged up with the sour smell of stone walls and his own chamber pot for company becomes apparent, does the convict start to weep. He is then drugged with sedatives, and Agatha Christies from the prison library.

When I saw the youngest Timson before his trial that morning, I couldn't help noticing how much smaller, and how much more experienced, he looked than my Nick. In his clean sports jacket and carefully knotted tie he was well dressed for the dock, and he showed all the carefully suppressed excitement of a young lad about to step into the limelight of Number 1 with an old judge, twelve jurors and a mixed bag of lawyers waiting to give him their undivided attention.

'Me speak to Peanuts? No Timson don't ever speak to a Molloy. It's a point of honour, like,' Jim added his voice to the family chorus.

'Since the raid on the Streatham Co-op. Your grandfather?'

'Dad told you about that, did he?'

'Yes. Dad told me.'

'Well, Dad wouldn't let me speak to no Molloy. He wouldn't put up with it, like.'

I stood up, grinding out the stub end of my small cigar in the old Oxo tin thoughtfully provided by H.M.'s government. It was, I thought, about time I called the meeting to order.

'So Jim,' I asked him, 'what's the defence?'

Little Jim knitted his brows and came out with his contribution. 'Well. I didn't do it.'

22

'That's an interesting defence. Somewhat novel—so far as the Timsons are concerned.'

'I've got my alibi, ain't I?'

Jim looked at me accusingly, as at an insensitive visitor to a garden who has failed to notice the remarkable display of gladioli.

'Oh, yes. Your alibi.' I'm afraid I didn't sound overwhelmed with enthusiasm.

'Dad reckoned it was pretty good.'

Mr Bernard had his invaluable file open and was reading from that less-than-inspiring document, our Notice of Alibi.

'Straight from school on that Friday September 2nd, I went up to tea at my Aunty Doris's and arrived there at exactly 5.30. At 6 p.m. my Uncle Den came home from work accompanied by my Uncle Cyril. At 7 p.m, when this alleged crime was taking place I was sat round the television with my Aunty and two Uncles. I well remember we was watching "The Newcomers".'

All very neat and workmanlike. Well, that was it. The family gave young Jim an alibi, clubbed together for it, like a new bicycle. However, I had to disappoint Mr Bernard about the bright shining alibi and we went through the swing doors on our way into Court.

'We can't use that alibi.'

'We can't?' Mr Bernard looked wounded, as if I'd just insulted his favourite child.

'Think about it Bernard. Don't be blinded by the glamour of the criminal classes. Call the Uncles and the Aunties? Let them all be cross-examined about their records? The jury'll realize our Jimbo comes from a family of villains who keep a cupboard full of alibis for all

23

occasions.'

Mr Bernard was forced to agree, but I went into my old place in Court (nearest to the jury, furthest from the witness box) thinking that the devilish thing about that impossible alibi was that it might even be true.

So there I was, sitting in my favourite seat in Court, down in the firing line, and there was Jim boy, undersized for a prisoner, just peeping over the edge of the dock, guarded in case he ran amok and started attacking the judge, by a huge Dock Officer. There was the jury, solid and grey, listening impassionately as Guthrie Featherstone spread out his glittering mass of incriminating facts before them. I don't know why it is that juries all look the same; take twelve good men and women off the street and they all look middle-aged, anonymous, slightly stunned, an average jury, of average people trying an average case. Perhaps being a jury has become a special profession for specially average people. 'What do you want to do when you grow up my boy?' 'Be a jury man, Daddy.' 'Well done my boy. You can work a five-hour day for reasonable expenses and occasionally send people to chokey.'

So, as the carefully chosen words of Guthrie Featherstone passed over our heads like expensive hair oil, and as the enthusiastic young MacLay noted it all down, and the Rumpole Supporters Club, the Timsons, sat and pursed their lips and now and then whispered, 'Lies. All lies' to each other, I sat watching the judge rather as a noted toreador watches the bull from the barrier during the preliminary stages of the corrida, and remembered what I knew of Mr Justice Everglade,

24

known to his few friends as 'Florrie'. Everglade's father was Lord Chancellor about the time when Jim's grandfather was doing over the Streatham Co-op. Educated at Winchester and Balliol, he always cracked *The Times* crossword in the opening of an egg. He was most happy with International Trust companies suing each other on nice points of law, and was only there for a fortnight's slumming down the Old Bailey. I wondered exactly what he was going to make of Peanuts Molloy.

'Members of the jury, it's right that you should know that it is alleged that Timson took part in this attack with a number of other youths, none of whom have been arrested,' Featherstone was purring to a halt.

'*The boy stood on the burning deck whence all but he had fled,*' I muttered, but the judge was busy congratulating learned counsel for Her Majesty the Queen who was engaged that morning in prosecuting the pride of the Timsons.

'It is quite right you should tell the jury that, Mr Featherstone. Perfectly right and proper.'

'If your Lordship pleases.' Featherstone was now bowing slightly, and my hackles began to rise. What was this? The old chums' league? Fellow members of the Athenaeum?

'I am most grateful to your Lordship for that indication.' Featherstone did his well-known butler passing the sherry act again. I wondered why the old darling didn't crawl up on the bench with Mr Justice Everglade and black his boots for him.

'So I imagine this young man's defence is—he wasn't *ejusdem generis* with the other lads?' The

25

judge was now holding a private conversation, a mutual admiration society with my learned friend. I decided to break it up, and levered myself to my feet.

'I'm sorry. Your Lordship was asking about the defence?'

The judge turned an unfriendly eye on me and fumbled for my name. I told you he was a stranger to the Old Bailey, where the name of Rumpole is, I think, tolerably well known.

'Yes, Mr ... er ...' The clerk of the Court handed him up a note on which the defender's name was inscribed. 'Rumpole.'

'I am reluctant to intrude on your Lordship's confidential conversation with my learned friend. But your Lordship was asking about the defence.'

'You are appearing for the young man ... Timson?'

'I have that honour.'

At which point the doors of the Court swung open and Albert came in with Nick, a boy in a blazer and a school-tie who passed the boy in the dock with only a glance of curiosity. I always thank God, when I consider the remote politeness with which I was treated by the Reverend Wilfred Rumpole, that I get on extremely well with Nick. We understand each other, my boy and I, and have, when he's at home, formed a strong but silent alliance against the almost invincible rule of She Who Must Be Obeyed. He is as fond as I am of the Sherlock Holmes tales, and when we walked together in Hyde Park and Kensington Gardens, young Nick often played the part of Holmes whilst I trudged beside him as Watson, trying to deduce the secret lives of those we

26

passed by the way they shined their shoes, or kept their handkerchiefs in their sleeves. So I gave a particularly welcoming smile to Nick before I gave my attention back to Florrie.

'And, as Jim Timson's counsel,' I told his Lordship, 'I might know a little more about his case than counsel for the prosecution.'

To which Mr Justice Everglade trotted out his favourite bit of Latin. 'I imagine,' he said loftily, 'your client says he was not *ejusdem generis* with the other lads.'

'*Ejusdem generis*? Oh yes, my Lord. He's always saying that. *Ejusdem generis* is a phrase in constant use in his particular part of Brixton.'

I had hit a minor jackpot, and was rewarded with a tinkle of laughter from the Timsons, and a smile of genuine congratulation from Nick.

*   *   *

Mr Justice Everglade was inexperienced down the Bailey, he gave us a bare hour for lunch and Nick and I had it in the canteen. There is one thing you can say against crime, the catering facilities aren't up to much. Nick told me about school, and freely confessed, as I'm sure he wouldn't have done to his mother, that he'd been in some sort of trouble that term. There was an old deserted vicarage opposite Schoolhouse (my old House and Nick's) and he and his friends had apparently broken in the scullery window and assembled there for poker parties and the consumption of Cherry Brandy. I was horrified as I drew up the indictment which seemed to me to contain charges of burglary at common law, house

27

breaking under the Forcible Entries Act, contravening the Betting, Gaming, Lotteries Act and Serving Alcohol on Unlicensed Premises.

'Crabtree actually invited a couple of girls from the village,' Nick continued his confession. 'But Bagnold never got to hear of that.'

Bagnold was Nick's headmaster, the school equivalent of 'Persil' White. I cheered up a little at the last piece of information.

'Then there's no evidence of girls. As far as your case goes there's no reason to suppose the girls ever existed. As for the other charges, which are serious...'

'Yes, yes, I suppose they are rather.'

'I imagine you were walking past the house on Sunday evening and, attracted by the noise ... You went to investigate?'

'Dad. Bagnold came in and found us—playing poker.'

Nick wasn't exactly being helpful. I tried another line.

'I know, "My Lord. My client was only playing poker in order not to look too pious whilst he lectured his fellow sixth formers on the evils of gambling and Cherry Brandy".'

'Dad. Be serious.'

'I am serious. Don't you want me to defend you?'

'No. Bagnold's not going to tell the police or anything like that.'

I was amazed. 'He isn't? What's he going to do?'

'Well ... I'll miss next term's exeat. Do extra work. I thought I should tell you before you got a letter.'

28

'Thank you, Nick. Thank you. I'm glad you told me. So there's no question of ... the police?'

'The police?' Nick was laughing. 'Of course not. Bagnold doesn't want any trouble. After all, we're still at school.'

I watched Nick as he finished his fish and chips, and then turned my thoughts to Jim Timson, who had also been at school; but with no kindly Bagnold to protect him.

*   *   *

Back in Court I was cross-examining that notable grass, Peanuts Molloy, a skinnier, more furtive edition of Jim Timson. The cross-examination was being greatly enjoyed by the Timsons and Nick, but not much by Featherstone or Chief Detective Inspector 'Persil' White who sat at the table in front of me. I also thought that Mr Justice 'Florrie' Everglade was thinking that he would have been happier snoozing in the Athenaeum, or working on his grosse-point in Egerton Terrace, than listening to me bowling fast in-swingers at the juvenile chief witness for the prosecution.

'You don't speak. The Molloys and the Timsons are like the Montagues and the Capulets,' I put it to Peanuts.

'What did you say they were?' The judge had, of course, given me my opportunity. I smacked him through the slips for a crafty single. 'Not *ejusdem generis*, my Lord,' I said.

Nick joined in the laughter and even the ranks of Featherstone had to stifle a smile. The usher called 'Silence'. We were back to the business in hand.

29

'Tell me, Peanuts ... How would you describe yourself?'

'Is that a proper question?' Featherstone uncoiled himself gracefully. I ignored the interruption.

'I mean artistically. Are you a latter-day Impressionist? Do all your oils in little dots, do you? Abstract painter? White squares on a white background? Do you indulge in watches melting in the desert like dear old Salvador Dali?'

'I don't know what you're talking about.' Peanuts played a blocking shot and Featherstone tried a weary smile to the judge.

'My Lord, neither, I must confess, do I.'

'Sit quietly, Featherstone,' I muttered to him. 'All will be revealed to you.' I turned my attention back to Peanuts. 'Are you a dedicated artist? The Rembrandt of the Remand centre?'

'I hadn't done no art before.' Peanuts confirmed my suspicions.

'So we are to understand that this occasion, when Jim poured out his heart to you, was the first painting lesson you'd ever been to?'

Peanuts admitted it.

'You'd been at the Remand Centre how long?'

'Couple of months. I was done for a bit of an affray.'

'I didn't ask you that. And I'm sure the reason you were on remand was entirely creditable. What I want to know is, what inspired you with this sudden fascination for the arts?'

'Well, the chief screw. He suggested it.'

Now we were beginning to get to the truth of the matter. Like his old grandfather in the Streatham Co-op days, Jim had been banged up

30

with a notable grass.

'You were suddenly told to join the painting class, weren't you ... and put yourself next to Jim?'

'Something like that, yeah.'

'What did he say?' Florrie frowned. It was all very strange to him and yet he was starting to get the hint of something that wasn't quite cricket.

'Something like that, my Lord,' I repeated slowly, giving the judge a chance to make a note. 'And you were sent there, not in the pursuit of art, Peanuts, but in the pursuit of evidence! You knew that and you supplied your masters with just what they wanted to hear—even though Jim Timson didn't say a word to you!'

Everyone in Court, including Nick, looked impressed. D.I. White bit hard on a polo mint and Featherstone oozed to his feet in a rescue bid.

'That's great, Dad!'

'Thanks, Nick. Sorry it's not a murder.'

'I don't know quite what my learned friend is saying. Is he suggesting that the police...'

'Oh, it's an old trick,' I said, staring hard at the Chief Inspector. 'Bang the suspect up with a notable grass when you're really pushed for evidence. They do it with grown-ups often enough. Now they're trying it with children!'

'Mr Rumpole,' the judge sighed, 'you are speaking a language which is totally foreign to me.'

'Let me try and make myself clear, my Lord. I was suggesting that Peanuts was put there as a deliberate trap.'

By now, even the judge had the point. 'You are suggesting that Mr Molloy was not a genuine

31

"amateur painter"?'

'No, my Lord. Merely an amateur witness.'

'Yes.' I actually got a faint smile. 'I see. Please go on, Mr Rumpole.'

Another day or so of this, I felt, and I'd get invited to tea at the Athenaeum.

'What did you say first to Jim? As you drew your easel alongside?'

'Don't remember.'

'Don't you?'

'I think we was speaking about the Stones.'

'What "stones" are these?' The judge's ignorance of the life around him seemed to be causing him some sort of wild panic. Remember this was 1965, and I was in a similar state of confusion until Nick, whispering from behind me, gave me the clue.

'The Rolling Stones, my Lord.' The information meant nothing to him.

'I'm afraid a great deal of this case seems to be taking place in a foreign tongue, Mr Rumpole.'

'Jazz musicians, as I understand it, my Lord, of some notoriety.' By courtesy of Nick, I filled his Lordship in on 'the scene'.

'Well, the notoriety hasn't reached me!' said the judge, providing the obedient Featherstone with the laugh of the year, if not the century. When the learned prosecuting counsel had recovered his solemnity, Peanuts went rambling on.

'We was talking about the Stones concert at the Hammersmith Odeon. We'd both been to it, like. And, well ... we talked about that. And then he said ... Jim said ... Well, he said as how he and the other blokes had done the butchers.'

The conversation had now taken a nasty turn. I

saw that the judge was writing industriously. 'Jim said ... that he and the other blokes ... had done the butchers.' Florrie was plying his pencil. Then he looked up at me, 'Well, Mr Rumpole, is that a convenient moment to adjourn?'

It was a very convenient moment for the prosecution, as the evidence against us would be the last thing the jury heard before sloping off to their homes and loved ones. It was also a convenient moment for Peanuts. He would have his second wind by the morning. So there was nothing for it but to take Nick for a cup of tea and a pile of crumpets in the ABC, and so home to She Who Must Be Obeyed.

★   ★   ★

So picture us three that evening, finishing dinner and a bottle of claret, celebrating the return of the Young Master at Hack Hall, Counsel's Castle, Rumpole Manor, or 25B Froxbury Court, Gloucester Road. Hilda had told Nick that his grandpa had sent his love and expected a letter, and also dropped me the encouraging news that old C.H. Wystan was retiring and quite appreciated that I was the senior man. Nick asked me if I was really going to be Head of Chambers, seeming to look at me with a new respect, and we drank a glass of claret to the future, whatever it might be. Then Nick asked me if I really thought Peanuts Molloy was lying.

'If he's not, he's giving a damn good imitation.' Then I told Hilda as she started to clear away, 'Nick enjoyed the case. Even though it was only a robbery. Oh, Nick ... I wish you'd been there to hear me cross-examine about the bloodstains in the "Penge Bungalow Murder".'

'Nick wasn't born, when you did the "Penge Bungalow Murder".'

My wife is always something of a wet blanket. I commiserated with my son. 'Bad luck, old boy.'

'You were great with that judge!'

I think Nick had really enjoyed himself.

'There was this extraordinary judge who was always talking Latin and Dad was teasing him.'

'You want to be careful,' Hilda was imposing her will on the pudding plates. 'How you tease judges. If you're to be Head of Chambers.' On which line she departed, leaving Nick and I to our claret and conversation. I began to discuss with Nick the horrifying adventure of *The Speckled Band*.

'You're still reading those tales, are you?' I asked Nick.

'Well ... not lately.'

'But you remember. I used to read them to you, didn't I? After She had ordered you to bed.'

'When you weren't too busy. Noting up your murders.'

'And remember we were Holmes and Watson? When we went for walks in Hyde Park.'

'I remember *one* walk.'

That was odd, as I recall it had been our custom ever at a weekend, before Nick went away to boarding school. I lit a small cigar and looked at the Great Detective through the smoke.

'Tell me, Holmes. What did you think was the most remarkable piece of evidence given by the witness Peanuts Molloy?'

'When he said they talked about the Rolling

Stones.'

'Holmes, you astonish me.'

'You see, Watson. We were led to believe they were such enemies I mean, the families were. They'd never spoken.'

'I see what you're driving at. Have another glass of claret—stimulates the detective ability.' I opened another bottle, a clatter from the kitchen telling me that the lady was not about to join us.

'And there they were chatting about a pop concert. Didn't that strike you as strange, my dear Watson?'

'It struck me as bloody rum, if you want to know the truth, Holmes.' I was delighted to see Nick taking over the case.

'They'd both been to the concert ... Well, that doesn't mean anything. Not necessarily ... I mean, *I* was at that concert.'

'Were you indeed?'

'It was at the end of the summer holidays.'

'I don't remember you mentioning it.'

'I said I was going to the Festival Hall.'

I found this confidence pleasing, knowing that it wasn't to be shared with Hilda.

'Very wise. Your mother no doubt feels that at the Hammersmith Odeon they re-enact some of the worst excesses of the Roman Empire. You didn't catch sight of Peanuts and young Jimbo did you?'

'There were about two thousand fans—all screaming.'

'I don't know if it helps...'

'No.'

'If they were old mates, I mean. Jim might really have confided in him. All the same, Peanuts

35

is lying. And *you* noticed it! You've got the instinct, Nick. You've got a nose for the evidence! Your career at the Bar is bound to be brilliant.' I raised my glass to Nick. 'When are you taking silk?'

Shortly after this She entered with news that Nick had a dentist's appointment the next day, which would prevent his re-appearance down the Bailey. All the same, he had given me a great deal of help and before I went to bed I telephoned Bernard the solicitor, tore him away from his fireside and instructed him to undertake some pretty immediate research.

*　　*　　*

Next morning, Albert told me that he'd had a letter from old C.H. Wystan, Hilda's Daddy, mentioning his decision to retire.

'I think we'll manage pretty well, with you, Mr Rumpole, as Head of Chambers,' Albert told me. 'There's not much you and I won't be able to sort out, sir, over a glass or two in Pommeroy's Wine Bar ... And soon we'll be welcoming Master Nick in Chambers?'

'Nick? Well, yes.' I had to admit it. 'He is showing a certain legal aptitude.'

'It'll be a real family affair, Mr Rumpole ... Like father, like son, if you want my opinion.'

I remembered Albert's words when I saw Fred Timson waiting for me outside the Court. But before I had time to brood on family tradition, Bernard came up with the rolled-up poster for a pop concert. I grabbed it from him and carried it as unobtrusively as possible into Court.

'When Jim told you he'd done up the butchers ...
He didn't tell you the date that that had
happened?' Peanuts was back, facing the bowling,
and Featherstone was up to his usual tricks, rising
to interrupt.

'My Lord, the date is set out quite clearly in the
indictment.'

The time had come, quite obviously, for a burst
of righteous indignation.

'My Lord, I am cross-examining on behalf of a
16-year-old boy on an extremely serious charge.
I'd be grateful if my learned friend didn't supply
information which all of us in Court
know—except for the witness.'

'Very well. Do carry on, Mr Rumpole.' I was
almost beginning to like Mr Justice Everglade.

'No. He never told me when, like. I thought it
was sometime in the summer.' Peanuts tried to
sound co-operative.

'Sometime in the summer? Are you a fan of the
Rolling Stones, Peanuts?'

'Yes.'

'Remind me ... they were ...' Still vaguely
puzzled the judge was hunting back through his
notes.

Sleek as a butler with a dish of peas,
Featherstone supplied the information. 'The
musicians, my Lord.'

'And so was Jim a fan?' I ploughed on, ignoring
the gentleman's gentleman.

'He was. Yes.'

'You had discussed music, before you met in

37

the Remand Centre?'

'Before the Nick. Oh yes.' Peanuts was following me obediently down the garden path.

'You used to talk about it at school?'

'Yes.'

'In quite a friendly way?' I was conscious of a startled Fred Timson looking at his son, and of Jim in the dock looking, for the first time, ashamed.

'We was all right. Yes.'

'Did you ever go to a concert with Jimbo? Please think carefully.'

'We went to one or two concerts together.' Peanuts conceded.

'In the evening?'

'Yes.'

'What would you do? ... Call at his home and collect him?'

'You're joking!'

'Oh no, Peanuts. In this case I'm not joking at all!' No harm, I thought, at that stage, in underlining the seriousness of the occasion.

'Course I wouldn't call at his home!'

'Your families don't speak. You wouldn't be welcomed in each other's houses?'

'The Montagues and the Capulets, Mr Rumpole?' The old sweetheart on the bench had finally got the message. I gave him a bow, to show my true love and affection.

'If your Lordship pleases ... Your Lordship puts it extremely aptly.' I turned back to Peanuts. 'So what would you do, if you were going to a concert?'

'We'd leave school together, like—and then hang around the caffs.'

'Hang around the caffs?'

'Caf*ays*, Mr Rumpole?' Mr Justice Everglade was enjoying himself, translating the answer.

'Yes, of course, the caf*ays*. Until it was time to go up West? If my Lord would allow me, up to the "West End of London" together?'

'Yes.'

'So you wouldn't be separated on these evenings you went to concerts together?' It was one of those questions after which you hold your breath. There can be so many wrong answers.

'No. We hung around together.'

Rumpole breathed a little more easily, but he still had the final question, the great gamble, with all Jim Timson's chips firmly piled on the red. *Faites vos jeux, m'sieurs et mesdames* of the Old Bailey jury. I spun the wheel.

'And did that happen ... When you went to the Rolling Stones at the Hammersmith Odeon?'

A nasty silence. Then the ball rattled into the hole.

Peanuts said, 'Yes.'

'That was the summer, wasn't it?' We were into the straight now, cantering home.

'In the summer, yeah.'

'You left school together?'

'And hung around the caffs, like. Then we went up the Odeon.'

'Together ... All the time?'

'I told you—didn't I?' Peanuts looked bored, and then amazed as I unrolled the poster Bernard had brought, rushed by taxi from Hammersmith, with the date clearly printed across the bottom.

'My Lord. My learned friend might be interested to know the date of the only Rolling

Stones concert at the Hammersmith Odeon this year.' I gave Featherstone an unwelcome eyeful of the poster.

'He might like to compare it with the date so conveniently set out in the indictment.'

*　　*　　*

When the subsequent formalities were over, I went down to the cells. This was not a visit of commiseration, no time for a 'sorry old sweetheart, but ...' and a deep consciousness of having asked one too many questions. All the same, I was in no gentle mood, in fact, it would be fair to say that I was bloody angry with Jimbo.

'You had an alibi! You had a proper, reasonable, truthful alibi, and, joy of joys, it came from the prosecution! Why the hell didn't you tell me?'

Jim, who seemed to have little notion of the peril he had passed, answered me quite calmly, 'Dad wouldn't've liked it.'

'Dad! What's Dad got to do with it?' I was astonished.

'He wouldn't've liked it, Mr Rumpole. Not me going out with Peanuts.'

'So you were quite ready to be found guilty, to be convicted of robbery, just because your Dad wouldn't like you going out with Peanuts Molloy?'

'Dad got the family to alibi me.' Jim clearly felt that the Timsons had done their best for him.

'Keep it in the family!' Though it was heavily laid on, the irony was lost on Jim. He smiled politely and stood up, eager to join the clan
40

upstairs.

'Well, anyway. Thanks a lot, Mr Rumpole. Dad said I could rely on you. To win the day, like. I'd better collect me things.'

If Jim thought I was going to let him get away as easily as that, he was mistaken. Rumpole rose in his crumpled gown, doing his best to represent the majesty of the law. 'No! Wait a minute. I didn't win the day. It was luck. The purest fluke. It won't happen again!'

'You're joking, Mr Rumpole.' Jim thought I was being modest. 'Dad told me about you . . . He says you never let the Timsons down.'

I had a sudden vision of my role in life, from young Jim's point of view and I gave him the voice of outrage which I use frequently in Court. I had a message of importance for Jim Timson.

'Do you think that's what I'm here for? To help you along in a career like your Dad's?' Jim was still smiling, maddeningly. 'My God! I shouldn't have asked those questions! I shouldn't have found out the date of the concert! Then you'd really be happy, wouldn't you? You could follow in Dad's footsteps all your life! Sharp spell of Borstal training to teach you the mysteries of housebreaking, and then a steady life in the Nick. You might really do well! You might end up in Parkhurst, Maximum Security Wing, doing a glamorous twenty years and a hero to the screws.'

At which the door opened and a happy screw entered, for the purpose of springing young Jim—until the inevitable next time.

'We've got his things at the gate, Mr Rumpole. Come on Jim. You can't stay here all night.'

'I've got to go,' Jim agreed. 'I don't know how

41

to face Dad, really. Me being so friendly with Peanuts.'

'Jim,' I tried a last appeal. 'If you're at all grateful for what I did...'

'Oh I am, Mr Rumpole, I'm quite satisfied.' Generous of him.

'Then you can perhaps repay me.'

'Why—aren't you on Legal Aid?'

'It's not that! Leave him! Leave your Dad.'

Jim frowned, for a moment he seemed to think it over. Then he said, 'I don't know as how I can.'

'You don't know?'

'Mum depends on me, you see. Like when Dad goes away. She depends on me then, as head of the family.'

So he left me, and went up to temporary freedom and his new responsibilities.

*   *   *

My mouth was dry and I felt about 90 years old, so I took the lift up to that luxurious eatery, the Old Bailey canteen, for a cup of tea and a Penguin biscuit. And, pushing his tray along past the urns, I met a philosophic Chief Inspector 'Persil' White. He noticed my somewhat lugubrious expression and tried a cheering 'Don't look so miserable, Mr Rumpole. You won didn't you?'

'Nobody won, the truth emerges sometimes, Inspector, even down the Old Bailey.' I must have sounded less than gracious. The wiley old copper smiled tolerantly.

'He's a Timson. It runs in the family. We'll get him sooner or later!'

42

'Yes. Yes. I suppose you will.'

At a table in a corner, I found certain members of my Chambers, George Frobisher, Percy Hoskins, and young Tony MacLay, now resting from their labours, their wigs lying among cups of Old Bailey tea, buns and choccy bics. I joined them. Wordsworth entered my head, and I gave him an airing ... *'Trailing clouds of glory do we come.'*

'Marvellous win, that. I was telling them.' Young MacLay thought I was announcing my triumph.

'Yes, Rumpole. I hear you've had a splendid win.' Old George, ever generous, smiled, genuinely pleased.

'It'll be *years* before you get the cheque,' Hoskins grumbled.

'Not in entire forgetfulness and not in utter nakedness, But trailing clouds of glory do we come From God who is our home ...' I was thinking of Jim, trying to sort out his situation with the help of Wordsworth.

'You don't get paid for years at the Old Bailey. I try to tell my grocer that. If you had to wait as long to be paid for a pound of sugar, I tell him, as we do for an armed robbery ...' Hoskins was warming to a well-loved theme, but George, dear old George was smiling at me.

'Albert tells me he's had a letter from Wystan. I just wanted to say, I'm sure we'd all like to say, you'll make a splendid Head of Chambers, Rumpole.'

'Heaven lies about us in our infancy, Shades of the prison house begin to close Upon the growing boy ... But he beholds the light, and whence it

43

flows, He sees it in his joy.' I gave them another brief glimpse of immortality. George looked quite proud of me and told MacLay, 'Rumpole quotes poetry. He does it quite often.'

'But does the growing boy behold the light?' I wondered. 'Or was the old sheep of the Lake District being unduly optimistic?'

'It'll be refreshing for us all, to have a Head of Chambers who quotes poetry,' George went on, at which point Percy Hoskins produced a newspaper which turned out to contain an item of news for us all.

'Have you seen *The Times*, Rumpole?'

'No, I haven't had time for the crossword.'

'Guthrie Featherstone. He's taken silk.'

*   *   *

It was the apotheosis, the great day for the Labour-Conservative Member for wherever it was, one time unsuccessful prosecutor of Jim Timson and now one of Her Majesty's counsel, called within the Bar, and he went down to the House of Lords tailored out in his new silk gown, a lace jabot, knee breeches with diamanté buckles, patent shoes, black silk stockings, lace cuffs and a full-bottomed wig that made him look like a pedigree, but not over-bright, spaniel. However, Guthrie Featherstone was a tall man, with a good calf in a silk stocking, and he took with him Marigold, his lady wife, who was young enough, and I suppose pretty enough, for Henry our junior clerk to eye wistfully, although she had the sort of voice that puts me instantly in mind of headscarves and gymkhanas, that high pitched

44

nasal whining which a girl learns from too much contact with the saddle when young, and too little with the Timsons of this world in later life. The couple were escorted by Albert, who'd raided Moss Bros for a top hat and morning coat for the occasion and when the Lord Chancellor had welcomed Guthrie to that special club of Queen's Counsel (on whose advice the Queen, luckily for her, never has to rely for a moment) they came back to Chambers where champagne (the N.V. cooking variety, bulk bought from Pommeroy's Wine Bar) was served by Henry and old Miss Patterson, our typist, in Wystan's big room looking out over Temple Gardens. C.H. Wystan, our retiring Head, was not among those present as the party began, and I took an early opportunity to get stuck into the beaded bubbles.

After the fourth glass I felt able to relax a bit and wandered to where Featherstone, in all his finery, was holding forth to Erskine-Brown about the problems of appearing *en travestie*. I arrived just as he was saying, 'It's the stockings that're the problem.'

'Oh yes. They would be.' I did my best to sound interested.

'Keeping them up.'

'I do understand.'

'Well, Marigold. My wife Marigold ...' I looked across to where Mrs Q.C. was tinkling with laughter at some old legal anecdote of Uncle Tom's. It was a laugh that seemed in some slight danger of breaking the wine glasses.

'*That* Marigold?'

'Her sister's a nurse, you know ... and she put me in touch with this shop which supplies suspender belts to nurses ... among other things.'

'Really?' This conversation seemed to arouse some dormant sexual interest in Erskine-Brown.

'Yards of elastic, for the larger ward sister. But it works miraculously.'

'You're wearing a suspender belt?' Erskine-Brown was frankly fascinated. 'You sexy devil!'

'I hadn't realized the full implications,' I told the Q.C., 'of rising to the heights of the legal profession.'

I wandered off to where Uncle Tom was giving Marigold a brief history of life in our Chambers over the last half-century. Percy Hoskins was in attendance, and George.

'It's some time since we had champagne in Chambers.' Uncle Tom accepted a refill from Albert.

'It's some time since we had a silk in Chambers,' Hoskins smiled at Marigold who flashed a row of well-groomed teeth back at him.

'I recall we had a man in Chambers once called Drinkwater—oh, before you were born, Hoskins. And some fellow came and paid Drinkwater a hundred guineas—for six months' pupillage. And you know what this Drinkwater fellow did? Bought us all champagne—and the next day he ran off to Calais with his junior clerk. We never saw hide nor hair of either of them again.' He paused. Marigold looked puzzled, not quite sure if this was the punch line.

'Of course, you could get a lot further in those days—on a hundred guineas,' Uncle Tom ended on a sad note, and Marigold laughed heartily.

'Your husband's star has risen so quickly, Mrs Featherstone. Only ten years call and he's an

46

M.P. *and* leading counsel.' Hoskins was clearly so excited by the whole business he had stopped worrying about his cheques for half an hour.

'Oh, it's the P.R. you know. Guthrie's frightfully good at the P.R.'

I felt like Everglade. Marigold was speaking a strange and incomprehensible language.

'Guthrie always says the most important thing at the Bar is to be polite to your instructing solicitor. Don't you find that, Mr Rumpole?'

'Polite to solicitors? It's never occurred to me.'

'Guthrie admires you so, Mr Rumpole. He admires your style of advocacy.'

I had just sunk another glass of the beaded bubbles as passed by Albert, and I felt a joyous release from my usual strong sense of tact and discretion.

'I suppose it makes a change from bowing three times and offering to black the judge's boots for him.'

Marigold's smile didn't waver. 'He says you're most amusing out of Court, too. Don't you quote poetry?'

'Only in moments of great sadness, Madam. Or extreme elation.'

'Guthrie's so looking forward to leading you. In his next big case.'

This was an eventuality which I should have taken into account as soon as I saw Guthrie in silk stockings; as a matter of fact it had never occurred to me.

'Leading *me*? Did you say, *leading* me?'

'Well, he has to have a junior now ... doesn't he? Naturally he wants the best junior available.'

'Now he's a leader?'

47

'Now he's left the Junior Bar.'

I raised my glass and gave Marigold a version of Browning. 'Just for a pair of knee breeches he left us ... Just for an elastic suspender belt, as supplied to the Nursing profession ...' At which the Q.C. himself bore down on us in a rustle of silk and drew me into a corner.

'I just wanted to say, I don't see why recent events should make the slightest difference to the situation in Chambers. You *are* the senior man in practice, Rumpole.'

Henry was passing with the fizzing bottle. I held out my glass and the tide ran foaming in it.

'*You wrong me, Brutus,*' I told Featherstone. '*You said an older soldier, not a better.*'

'A quotation! *Touché,* very apt.'

'Is it?'

'I mean, all this will make absolutely no difference. I'll still support you Rumpole, as the right candidate for Head of Chambers.'

I didn't know about being a candidate, having thought of the matter as settled and not being much of a political animal. But before I had time to reflect on whatever the Honourable Member was up to, the door opened letting in a formidable draught and the Head of Chambers. C.H. Wystan, She's Daddy, wearing a tweed suit, extremely pale, supported by Albert on one side and a stick on the other, made the sort of formidable entrance that the ghost of Banquo stages at dinner with the Macbeths. Wystan was installed in an armchair, from which he gave us all the sort of wintry smile which seemed designed to indicate that all flesh is as the grass, or something to that effect.

'Albert wrote to me about this little celebration. I was determined to be with you. And the doctor has given permission, for no more than one glass of champagne.' Wystan held out a transparent hand into which Albert inserted a glass of non vintage. Wystan lifted this with some apparent effort, and gave us a toast.

'To the great change in Chambers! Now we have a silk. Guthrie Featherstone, Q.C., M.P.!'

I had a large refill to that. Wystan absorbed a few bubbles, wiped his mouth on a clean, folded handkerchief, and proceeded to the oration. Wystan was never a great speech maker, but I claimed another refill and gave him my ears.

'You, Featherstone, have brought a great distinction to Chambers.'

'Isn't that nice, Guthrie?' Marigold proprietorially squeezed her master's fingers.

'You know, when I was a young man. You remember when we were young men, Uncle Tom? We used to hang around in Chambers for weeks on end.' Wystan had gone on about these distant hard times at every Chambers meeting. 'I well recall we used to occupy ourselves with an old golf ball and mashie-niblick, trying to get chip shots into the waste-paper baskets. Albert was a boy then.'

'A mere child, Mr Wystan,' Albert looked suitably demure.

'And we used to pray for work. *Any* sort of work, didn't we, Uncle Tom?'

'We were tempted to crime. Only way we could get into Court,' Uncle Tom took the feed line like a professional. Moderate laughter, except for Rumpole who was busy drinking. And then I

49

heard Wystan rambling on.

'But as you grow older at the Bar you discover it's not having any work that matters. It's the *quality* that counts!'

'Here, here! I'm always saying we ought to do more civil.' This was the dutiful Erskine-Brown, inserting his oar.

'Now Guthrie Featherstone, Q.C., M.P. will, of course, command briefs in all divisions—planning, contract,' Wystan's voice sank to a note of awe, 'even Chancery! I was so afraid, after I've gone, that this Chambers might become known as merely a criminal set.' Wystan's voice now sank in a sort of horror. 'And, of course, there's no doubt about it, too much criminal work does rather lower the standing of a Chambers.'

'Couldn't you install pithead baths?' I hadn't actually meant to say it aloud, but it came out very loud indeed.

'Ah, Horace.' Wystan turned his pale eyes on me for the first time.

'So we could have a good scrub down after we get back from the Old Bailey?'

'Now, Horace Rumpole. And I mean no disrespect whatever to my son-in-law.' Wystan returned to the oration. From far away I heard myself say, 'Daddy!' as I raised the hard-working glass. 'Horace does practise almost exclusively in the Criminal Courts!'

'One doesn't get the really fascinating points of *law*. Not in criminal work,' Erskine-Brown was adding unwanted support to the motion. 'I've often thought we should try and attract some really lucrative tax cases into Chambers.'

That, I'm afraid, did it. Just as if I were in

Court I moved slightly to the centre and began my speech.

'Tax cases?' I saw them all smiling encouragement at me. 'Marvellous! Tax cases make the world go round. Compared to the wonderful world of tax, crime is totally trivial. What does it matter? If some boy loses a year, a couple of years, of his life? It's totally unimportant! Anyway, he'll grow up to be banged up for a good five, shut up with his own chamber pot in some convenient hole we all prefer not to think about.' There was a deafening silence, which came loudest from Marigold Featherstone. Then Wystan tried to reach a settlement.

'Now then, Horace. Your practice no doubt requires a good deal of skill.'

'Skill? Who said "skill"?' I glared round at the learned friends. 'Any fool could do it! It's only a matter of life and death. That's all it is. Crime? It's a sort of a game. How can you compare it to the real world of Off Shore Securities. And Deductible Expenses?'

'All you young men in Chambers can learn an enormous amount from Horace Rumpole, when it comes to crime.' Wystan now seemed to be the only one who was still smiling. I turned on him.

'You make me sound just like Fred Timson!'

'Really? Whoever's Fred Timson?' I told you Wystan never had much of a practice at the Bar, consequently he had never met the Timsons. Erskine-Brown supplied the information.

'The Timsons are Rumpole's favourite family.'

'An industrious clan of South London criminals, aren't they, Rumpole,' Hoskins added.

Wystan looked particularly pained. 'South

51

London criminals?'

'I mean, do we want people like the Timsons forever hanging about in our waiting room? I merely ask the question.' He was not bad, this Erskine-Brown, with a big future in the nastier sort of Breach of Trust cases.

'Do you? Do you merely ask it?' I heard the pained bellow of a distant Rumpole.

'The Timsons ... and their like, are no doubt grist to Rumpole's mill,' Wystan was starting on the summing up. 'But it's the balance that *counts*. Now, you'll be looking for a new Head of Chambers.'

'Are we still looking?' My friend George Frobisher had the decency to ask. And Wystan told him, 'I'd like you all to think it over carefully. And put your views to me in writing. We should all try and remember. It's the good of the Chambers that matters. Not the feelings, however deep they may be, of any particular person.'

He then called on Albert's assistance to raise him to his feet, lifted his glass with an effort of pure will and offered us a toast to the good of Chambers. I joined in, and drank deep, it having been a good thirty seconds since I had had a glass to my lips. As the bubbles exploded against the tongue I noticed that the Featherstones were holding hands, and the brand new artificial silk was looking particularly delighted. Something, and perhaps not only his suspender belt, seemed to be giving him special pleasure.

*   *   *

Some weeks later, when I gave Hilda the news,

she was deeply shocked.

'*Guthrie Featherstone*! Head of Chambers!' We were at breakfast. In fact Nick was due back at school that day. He was neglecting his cornflakes and reading a book.

'By general acclaim.'

'I'm sorry.' Hilda looked at me, as if she'd just discovered that I'd contracted an incurable disease.

'He can have the headaches—working out Albert's extraordinary book-keeping system.' I thought for a moment, yes, I'd like to have been Head of Chambers, and then put the thought from me.

'If only you could have become a Q.C.' She was now pouring me an unsolicited cup of coffee.

'Q.C.? C.T. That's enough to keep me busy.'

'C.T.? Whatever's C.T.?'

'Counsel for the Timsons!' I tried to say it as proudly as I could. Then I reminded Nick that I'd promised to see him off at Liverpool Street, finished my cooling coffee, stood up and took a glance at the book that was absorbing him, expecting it to be, perhaps, that spine-chilling adventure relating to the Footprints of an Enormous Hound. To my amazement the shocker in question was entitled simply *Studies in Sociology*.

'It's interesting,' Nick sounded apologetic.

'You astonish me.'

'Old Bagnold was talking about what I should read if I get into Oxford.'

'Of course you're going to read law, Nick. We're going to keep it in the family.' Hilda the barrister's daughter was clearing away

53

deafeningly.

'I thought perhaps P.P.E. and then go on to Sociology.' Nick sounded curiously confident. Before Hilda could get in another word I made my position clear.

'P.P.E., that's very good, Nick! That's very good indeed! For God's sake. Let's stop keeping things in the family!'

Later, as we walked across the barren stretches of Liverpool Street Station, with my son in his school uniform and me in my old striped trousers and black jacket, I tried to explain what I meant.

'That's what's wrong, Nick. That's the devil of it! They're being born around us all the time. Little Mr Justice Everglades ... Little Timsons ... Little Guthrie Featherstones. All being set off ... to follow in father's footsteps.' We were at the barrier, shaking hands awkwardly. 'Let's have no more of that! No more following in father's footsteps. No more.'

Nick smiled, although I have no idea if he understood what I was trying to say. I'm not totally sure that I understood it either. Then the train removed him from me. I waved for a little, but he didn't wave back. That sort of thing is embarrassing for a boy. I lit a small cigar and went by tube to the Bailey. I was doing a long firm fraud then; a particularly nasty business, out of which I got a certain amount of harmless fun.

54

RUMPOLE AND THE ALTERNATIVE SOCIETY

In some ways the coppers, the Fuzz, Old Bill, whatever you may care to call them, are a very conservative body. When they verbal up the criminal classes, and report their alleged confessions in the Nick, they still use the sort of Cockney argot that went out at the turn of the century, and perfectly well-educated bank robbers, who go to the ballet at Covent Garden and holidays in Corfu, are still reported as having cried, 'It's a fair cop, guv,' or 'You got me bang to rights,' at the moment they're apprehended. In the early 1970s however, when Flower Power flooded the country with a mass of long hair, long dresses and the sweet smell of the old quarter of Marrakesh, the Fuzz showed itself remarkably open to new ideas. Provincial drug squads were issued with beads, Afghan waistcoats, headbands and guitars along with their size eleven boots, and took lessons in a new language, learning to say, 'Cool it man,' or 'Make love not war,' instead of 'You got me bang to rights.'

It was also a time when the barrister figures of the establishment fell into disrepute and to be a barrister, however close to the criminal fraternity, was to be regarded by the young as a sort of undesirable cross between Judge Jeffries and Mr Nixon, as I knew from the sullen looks of the young ladies Nick, who was then at Oxford and reading P.P.E., brought home in the holidays. I have never felt so clearly the number of different

55

countries, all speaking private languages and with no diplomatic relations, into which England is divided. I cannot think for instance of a world more remote from the Temple or the Inns of Court than that tumble-down Victorian house in the west country (No. 34 Balaclava Road, Coldsands) which the community who inhabited it had christened 'Nirvana', and which contained a tortoise who looked to me heavily drugged, a number of babies, some surprisingly clean young men and women, a pain-in-the neck named Dave, and a girl called Kathy Trelawny whom I never met until she came to be indicted in the Coldsands Crown Court on a charge of handling a phenomenal amount of cannabis resin, valued at about ten thousand pounds.

Coldsands is a rather unpopular resort in the west of England with a high rainfall, a few Regency terraces, a large number of old people's homes, and a string quartet at tea-time in the Winter Gardens; on the face of it an unlikely place for crime to flourish. But a number of young people did form a community there at 'Nirvana', a place which the local inhabitants regarded as the scene of numerous orgies. To this house came a dealer named Jack, resplendent in his hippie attire, to place a large order for cannabis which Kathy Trelawny set about fulfilling, with the aid of a couple of Persian law students with whom she had made contact at Bristol University. Very soon after the deal was done, and a large quantity of money handed over, Jack the Hippie was revealed as Detective Sergeant Jack Smedley of the local force, the strong arm of the law descended on 'Nirvana', the

Persian law students decamped to an unknown address in Morocco, and Rumpole, who had had a few notable successes with dangerous drugs, was dug out of Old Bailey and placed upon the 12.15 from Paddington to Coldsands, enjoying the rare luxury of a quiet corner seat in the first-class luncheon car, by courtesy of the Legal Aid Fund of Great Britain.

I could afford the first-class luncheon, and spread myself the more readily, as I was staying in a little pub on the coast not five miles from Coldsands kept by my old mates and companions in arms (if my three years in the R.A.F. ground staff can be dignified by so military a title), ex-Pilot Officer 'Three-Fingers' Dogherty and his wife Bobby, ex-WAAF, unchallenged beauty queen of the station at Dungeness, who was well known to look like Betty Grable from behind and Phyllis Dixey from the front and to have a charm, a refreshing impertinence and a contempt for danger unrivalled, I am sure, by either of those famous pinups from *Reveille*. I have spoken of Bobby already in these reminiscences and I am not ashamed to say that, although I was already married to Hilda when we met, she captured my heart, and continued to hold it fast long after the handsome Pilot Officer captured hers. I was therefore keenly looking forward to renewing my acquaintance with Bobby; we had had a desultory correspondence but we hadn't met for many years. I was also looking forward to a holiday at the seaside, for which Miss Trelawny's little trouble seemed merely to provide the excuse and the financial assistance.

So I was, as you can imagine, in a good mood

57

as we rattled past Reading and cows began to be visible, standing in fields, chewing the cud, as though there were no law courts or judges in the world. You very rarely see a cow down the Bailey, which is one of the reasons I enjoy an occasional case on circuit. Circuit takes you away from Chambers, away from the benevolent despotism of Albert the clerk, above all, away from the constant surveillance of She Who Must Be Obeyed (Mrs Hilda Rumpole). I began to look forward to a good, old-fashioned railway lunch. I thought of a touch of Brown Windsor soup, rapidly followed by steamed cod, castle pudding, mouse-trap, cream crackers and celery, all to be washed down with a vintage bottle of Chateau Great Western as we charged past Didcot.

A furtive-looking man, in a short off-white jacket which showed his braces and a mournful expression, looked down at me.

'Ah waiter. Brown Windsor soup, I fancy, to start with.'

'We're just doing the Grilled Platter, sir.' I detected, in the man's voice, a certain gloomy satisfaction.

'Grilled—what?'

'Fried egg and brunch-burger, served with chips and a nice tomato.'

'A nice tomato! Oh, very well.' Perhaps with a suitable anaesthetic the brunch-burger could be taken. 'And to drink. A reasonable railway claret?'

'No wines on this journey, sir. We got gin in miniatures.'

'I don't care for gin, at lunchtime, especially in miniatures.' Regretfully I came to the conclusion that circuit life had deteriorated and wondered

58

what the devil they had done with all the Brown Windsor soup.

*   *   *

At Coldsands Station a middle-aged man in a neat suit and rimless glasses was there to meet me. He spoke with a distinct and reassuring west-country accent.

'Mr Horace Rumpole? I'm Friendly.'

'Thank God someone is!'

'I was warned you liked your little joke, Mr Rumpole, by London agents. They recommended you as a learned counsel who has had some success with drugs.'

'Oh, I have had considerable success with drugs. And a bit of luck with murder, rape and other offences against the person.'

'I'm afraid we don't do much crime at Friendly, Sanderson and Friendly. We're mainly conveyancing. By the way, I think there's a couple of typing errors in the instructions to counsel.' Mr Friendly looked deeply apologetic.

I hastened to reassure him. 'Fear not, Friendly. I never read the instructions to counsel. I find they blur the judgement and confuse the mind.'

We were outside the Station now, and a battered taxi rattled into view.

'You'll want to see the client?' Friendly sounded resigned.

'She might expect it.'

'You're going to "Nirvana"?'

'Eventually. Aren't we all? No, Friendly. I shall steer clear of the lotus eaters of No. 34 Balaclava Road. A land, I rather imagine, in which it seems

59

always afternoon. Bring the client for a con at my hotel. After dinner. Nine o'clock suit you?'

'You'll be at the George? That's where the Bar put up.'

'Then if it's where the Bar put up, I shall avoid it. I'm staying with old mates, from my days in the R.A.F. They run a stately pleasure-dome known as the Crooked Billet.'

'The little pub place out on the bay?' I noticed Friendly smiled when he spoke of the Doghertys delight, a place, I had no doubt, of a high reputation. The taxi had stopped now, and I was wrestling with the door. When I had it open, I was in a high and holiday mood.

'Out on the bay indeed! With no sound but the sea sighing and the muted love call of the lobster. Know what I say, Friendly? When you get a bit of decent crime at the seaside ... Relax and enjoy it!'

Friendly was staring after me, perhaps understandably bewildered, as I drove away.

★　　★　　★

The taxi took me out to the Crooked Billet and back about twenty-five years. The pub was on the top of some cliffs, above a sandy beach and a leaden sea. From the outside it seemed an ordinary enough building, off-white, battered, with a neglected patch of garden; but inside it was almost a museum to the great days of World War Two. Behind the bar were Sam's trophies, a Nazi helmet, a plaster Mr Churchill which could actually puff a cigar, a model Spitfire dangled from the ceiling, there were framed photographs of ex-Pilot Officer Dogherty in his flying jacket,

60

standing by his beloved Lancaster and a signed portrait of Vera Lynn at the height of her career. Even the pin-table appeared to be an antique, looted from some NAAFI. There was also an old piano, a string of fairy lights round the bottles and a comforting smell of stale booze. Someone was clanking bottles behind the bar, but I could see no more than a comfortable bottom in old blue slacks. I put out a red alert.

'Calling all air crew! Calling all air crew! Parade immediately!'

At which Bobby Dogherty turned, straightened up and smiled.

Age had not withered her, but it had added to the generosity of her curves. Her blonde hair looked more metallic than of old, and the lines of laughter round her mouth and eyes had settled into permanent scars. She had a tipped cigarette in her mouth and her head was tilted to keep the smoke out of her eyes. She looked, as always, irrepressibly cheerful, as if middle age, like the War, was a sort of joke, and there to be enjoyed.

'Rumpole. You old devil!'

'You look beautiful,' I said, as I had often done in the past, and meant it just as much.

'Liar! Drop of rum?' I didn't see why not and perched myself on a bar stool while she milked the rum bottle. Soon Rumpole was in reminiscent mood.

'Takes me right back to the NAAFI hop. New Year's Eve, 1943. Sam was out bombing something and I had you entirely to myself—for a couple of hours of the Boomps-a-Daisy ... Not to mention the Lambeth Walk.' I raised my glass and gave our old salutation, 'Here's to the good old duke!'

'The good old duke.' Bobby was on her second gin and tonic, and she remembered. 'You never took advantage.'

I lit a small cigar. It caught me in the back of the throat. 'Something I shall regret till the day I cough myself into extinction. How's old Sam? How's ex-Pilot Officer "Three-Fingers" Dogherty?'

'Bloody doctor!' For the first time, Bobby looked less than contented.

'Doctor?'

'Doctor Mackay. Came here with a face like an undertaker.' She gave a passable imitation of a gloomy Scottish medico. '"Mrs Dogherty, your husband's got to get out of the licensing trade or I'll not give him more than another year. Get him into a small bungalow and on to soft drinks." Can you imagine Sam in a bungalow?'

'Or on soft drinks! The mind boggles!'

'He'll find lime juice and soda has a pleasant little kick to it. That's what the doctor told me.'

'The kick of a mouse, I should imagine. In carpet slippers.'

'I told the quack, Sam's not scared. Sam used to go out every night to kill himself. He misses the war dreadfully.'

'I expect he does.'

'Saturday night in the Crooked Billet and a bloody good piss-up. It's the nearest he gets to the old days in the R.A.F.'

'You want to be careful ... he doesn't rush out and bomb Torquay,' I warned her, and was delighted to see her laugh.

'You're not joking! The point is ... should I tell

62

Sam?'

'Won't your Doctor Mackay tell him?'

'You know how Sam is. He won't see hide nor hair of the doctor. So what should I do?'

'Why ask me?' I looked at her, having no advice to give.

'You're the bloody lawyer, darling. You're meant to know everything!'

At which point I was aware that, behind us, a man had come into the bar. I turned and saw him scowling at us. He was wearing a blazer, an R.A.F. scarf in an open shirt and scuffed suede shoes. I saw a good-looking face, grey hair and a grey moustache, all gone slightly to seed. It was none other than ex-Pilot Officer Sam 'Three-Fingers' Dogherty.

'We're not open yet!' He seemed to have not yet completely awakened from a deep afternoon kip, as he advanced on us, blinking at the lights round the bar.

'Sam! Can't you see who it is?' Bobby said, and her husband, who had at last identified the invasion, roared at me.

'My God, it's old grounded Rumpole! Rumpole of the ops room!' He moved rapidly to behind the bar and treated himself to a large Teachers which he downed rapidly. 'What the hell brings you to this neck of the woods?'

'He wrote us a letter.'

'Never read letters. Here's to the good old duke!' He was on his second whisky, and considerably more relaxed.

'What brings me? A lady ... you might say, a damsel in bloody great distress.'

'You're not still after Bobby, are you?' Sam was

63

only pretending to be suspicious.

'Of course. Till the day I die. But your wife's not in distress exactly.'

'Aren't I?' Bobby looked down into the depths of her gin and tonic, and I filled them in on the nature of my mission.

'The lady in question is a certain Miss Kathy Trelawny. One of the lotus eaters of "Nirvana", 34 Balaclava Road. Done for the possession of a suitcase full of cannabis resin.'

I had put up, as we used to say in the old days, a Black. If I had asked the Reverend Ian Paisley to pray for the Pope, I couldn't have invited an icier gaze of disapproval than Sam gave me as he said, 'You're *defending* her?'

'Against your crafty constabulary. Come in here, does she?'

'Not bloody likely! That crowd from Balaclava Road wouldn't get past the door. Anyway, they don't drink.' The glass of Teachers was recharged to banish the vision of the lotus eaters invading the Crooked Billet.

'Dear me. Is there no end to their decadence? But you know my client?'

'Never clapped eyes on her, thank God! No doubt she's about as glamorous as an unmade bed.'

'Oh, no doubt at all.' Gloomily, I thought he was almost certainly right, something peering through glasses, I thought, out of a mop of unwashed hair. Sam came out from behind the bar and started to bang about, straightening chairs and tables, switching on more lights.

'How can you defend that creature?'

'Easy! Prop myself to my feet in Court and do

64

my best.'

'But you know damn well she's guilty!'

It's the one great error everyone makes about my learned profession; they think we defend people who have told us they did the deed. This legend doesn't add to the esteem in which barristers are held, and I sighed a little as I exploded the myth for the thousandth time.

'Ah, there you're wrong. I don't know that at all.'

'Pull the other one!' Sam shared the usual public view of legal eagles.

'I don't know. And if she ever admitted it to me, I'd have to make her surrender and plead "Guilty". We've got a few rules, old sweetheart. We don't deceive Courts, not on purpose.'

'You mean, you think she's innocent?' Sam made it clear that no one who lived in a commune called 'Nirvana' could possibly be innocent of anything.

'He told you, Sam! He's got rules about it.' Bobby was polishing glasses and coming to the rescue of an old friend.

'At the moment I think she's the victim of a trick by the police. That's what I'll have to go on thinking, until she tells me otherwise.'

'That's ridiculous! The police don't trick people. Not in England.' Sam clearly felt he'd not delivered us from the Nazi hordes for nothing.

'Never had a plain clothes copper come in here and order a large Scotch after closing time?' I asked him.

'The bastards! But that's entirely different.'

'Yes, of course.'

'Anyway, who's paying you to defend Miss

Slag-Heap? That's what I'd like to know.' Sam was triumphant. It hurt me, but I had to tell him.

'Fasten your seat belt, old darling. You are! Miss Kathy Trelawny is on legal aid. And I am here by courtesy of the ratepayers of Coldsands.' I lifted my rum in Sam's direction. 'Thank you, "Three-Fingers". Thank you for your hospitality.'

'Bloody hell.' Sam sounded more sorrowful than angry, and it gave him an excuse to turn the handle once more on the Teachers.

'We don't mind, do we, Sam?' As always Bobby's was the voice of tolerance. 'We don't mind buying Horace the odd drink occasionally.'

*   *   *

Later I sat in the residents' lounge, a small room which opened off the bar, and tried to shut out the considerable noise made by Sam's regular customers, middle-aged men mostly, in a sort of uniform of cavalry twill trousers and hacking jackets. I was working on my brief and already I had a plan of campaign. When the Detective Sergeant went to buy Miss Trelawny's cannabis he was disguised as a hippie and acting, I was quite prepared to argue, as an *agent provocateur*. If I could establish that my client would never have committed any sort of crime unless the police had invited her to I might, given a fair wind and a sympathetic judge, have the whole of the police evidence excluded which would lead to the collapse of the prosecution, a Zen service of thanksgiving at 'Nirvana', and Rumpole triumphant. I had brought a number of law reports on the question of *agent provocateur* and

66

was interested to discover that it was the old hanging judges who regarded these beasts with particular disfavour; it's odd how gentler days have somehow dimmed our passion for liberty.

I had worked out an argument that might appeal to a judge who still had some of the old spark left in him when the door from the bar opened to admit Mr Friendly and my client.

I had, I felt, known Miss Kathy Trelawny for a long time. She had floated before my eyes from my early days with the old *Oxford Book of English Verse*, as Herrick's Julia, or Lovelace's Lucasta, or 'La Belle Dame Sans Merci', or the 'Lady of Shallot'. As she smiled, she reminded me strongly of Rosalind in the forest of Arden, or Viola comforting the love-sick Duke. She had a long, slender neck, a mass of copper-coloured hair, friendly blue eyes and she was exceedingly clean. As soon as I saw her I decided that my one ambition in life was to keep her out of Holloway. I had to take a quick gulp from my glass beside me before I could steady my nerve to read out a passage from the depositions. Miss Trelawny was sitting quietly looking at me as if I was the one man in the world she had always wanted to meet, and she hoped we would soon be finished with the boring case so we could talk about something interesting, and deeply personal.

'"Real cool house, man,"' I was reading out the Detective Sergeant's evidence with disgust. '"You can't score nothing in this hick town. You don't get no trouble from the Fuzz". Just from the way the old darling talked, didn't you twig he was a Sergeant from the local Drug Squad?'

Miss Trelawny showed no particular reaction,

and Friendly quickly filled the silence. 'My client has never come up against the police before.'

'We'll have a bit of fun with this case,' I told them.

'What sort of fun exactly?' Friendly sounded doubtful, as if he didn't exactly look on the coming trial as the annual dinner dance of the Coldsands Rotary.

'A preliminary point! In the absence of the jury we will ask the judge to rule the whole of Detective Sergeant Jack Smedley, alias Jack the Hippie's evidence inadmissible. On the sole ground...'

'On what sole ground?'

'That it was obtained contrary to natural justice, in that it constituted a trick. That it is the testimony of an *agent provocateur*.'

'We don't get many of those in conveyancing.' Friendly looked distinctly out of his depth.

'A nasty foreign expression, for a nasty foreign thing. Spies and infiltrators! Policemen in disguise who worm their way into an Englishman's home and trap him into crime!'

'Why should they do that, Mr Rumpole?' I stood up and directed my answer at my client. Her warm and all-embracing smile, and her total silence, were beginning to unnerve me. 'So they can clap innocent citizens into chokey and notch up another conviction on their collective braces! Bloody unBritish—like bidets and eating your pud after the cheese! Now, I mean your average circuit judge ... Circus judges ... we call them down the Bailey.'

Friendly consulted a note. 'It's his Honour James Crispin-Rice tomorrow.'

We were in luck. I knew old Rice Crispies well at the Bar. He was a thoroughly decent chap, who had once stood as a Liberal candidate. He was the product of the Navy and a minor public school. No doubt he'd had it firmly implanted in him in the fourth form—never trust a sneak.

They had left the door slightly open, and through it I could hear the old familiar sound of Bobby thumping the piano.

'You think he might rule out the evidence?'

I got up and shut the door, blotting out some remarkable tuneless rendering of the Golden Oldies which had started up *à côté de* Chez Dogherty.

'If we can implant a strong dislike of Sergeant Smedley in the old darling,' I told them. 'Disgusting behaviour, your Honour. The police are there to detect crime, not manufacture it. What's the country coming to? Constables tricked out in beads and singing to a small guitar conning an innocent girl into making huge collections of cannabis resin from some Persian pushers she met at Bristol University. She'd never have done it if the policeman hadn't asked her!'

'Wouldn't you, Miss Trelawny?' Friendly gave her the cue to speak. She ignored it, so on I went showing her my quality.

'Withdraw the evidence from the jury, your Honour! It's un-English, unethical and clearly shows that this crime was deliberately created by the police. The whole business is a vile outrage to our age-old liberties.' Wordsworth crept into my mind and I didn't send him about his business. *'It is not to be thought of that the Flood Of British freedom, which to the open sea ...'* I paused,

69

insecure on the words and then, very quietly and for the first time, Miss Kathy Trelawny spoke, with words appropriately supplied by the old sheep of the Lake District.

'*Of the world's praise, from dark antiquity Hath flowed, "with pomp of waters unwithstood,"* ... *Should perish.*'

She looked at me, I took over.

'*We must be free or die, who speak the tongue That Shakespeare spake* ...' I decided I'd had enough of Wordsworth, and asked her, surprised, 'You know it?'

'Wordsworth? A little.'

'I thought no one did nowadays. Whenever I come out with him in the Bar Mess they look amazed. Unusual, for a client to know Wordsworth.'

'I teach kids English.'

'Oh yes. Of course you do.' I had learned from the brief that all the inhabitants of 'Nirvana' were in work.

'There's one thing I wanted to ask you.' Now she had broken the ice, there seemed to be no holding her, but Friendly stood up, as if anxious to bring the conference to an end.

'Well, we shouldn't keep Mr Rumpole any longer.'

'Ask me, Miss Trelawny?'

'Yes.' Her smile was unwavering. 'What do you want *me* to say exactly?'

'Say? Say nothing! Look ... rely on me, with a little help from Wordsworth. And keep your mouth firmly closed.'

I opened the door. Great gusts of singing blew in on us from the bar. Bobby's voice was leading,

70

'*We'll meet again   Don't know where   Don't know when, But we're bound to meet again Some Sunny day.*'

I remembered my craven cowardice in not speaking to Bobby on the occasion of the NAAFI hop, and I asked Miss Trelawny to join me for a drink. Fortunately, Friendly remembered that his wife would be waiting up for him, and I took my client alone into the bar.

As we sat at the counter, Sam came up to us swaying only slightly, like a captain on the deck of his well-loved ship. He looked at Kathy Trelawny with amazed approval.

'Where did you get this popsy, Rumpole?' He leant across the bar to chat to my client intimately. 'You shouldn't be with the ground staff, my dear. You're definitely officer material. What's it to be?'

'I'll have a coke. I don't drink really.' She was smiling at him, the smile I thought, uncomfortably, of universal love bestowed on everyone, regardless of age or sex.

'Oh, don't you? You don't drink!' Sam took offence. 'There's nothing else you don't do, is there?'

'Quite a lot of things.' Sam ignored this and recalled the Good Old Days as he passed me a rum.

'Remember, Rumpole? We used to divide the popsies into beer WAAFS and gin WAAFS.' He winked at Kathy Trelawny. 'In my opinion you're a large pink gin.'

'She told you, Sam. She doesn't drink,' I reminded Sam. He was getting impatient.

'Did you pick up this beautiful bit of crackling

71

in a bloody Baptist Chapel?' He poured Miss Trelawny a Coca-Cola.

'Take no notice of him, my dear. You can be teetotal with Rumpole. But let's launch *our* friendship on a sea of sparkling shampoo!'

'I'd probably sink,' Kathy Trelawny smiled at him.

'Not with me you wouldn't. Let me introduce myself. Pilot Officer "Three-Fingers" Dogherty. "Three-Fingers" refers to the measures of my whisky. My hands are in perfect order.' To demonstrate this he put a hand on hers across the bar.

'I haven't met many pilot officers.'

Kathy, I feel I know her well enough to call her Kathy for the rest of this narrative, withdrew her hand. She was still smiling.

'Well, you've met *me*, my dear!' Sam rambled on undiscouraged. 'One of the glamour boys. One of the Brylcreem brigade. One of the very, very few.' He stood himself another Teachers. 'And if I had a crate available, I'd bloody well smuggle you up in the sky for a couple of victory rolls. You see him ... You see "Groundstaff Rumpole?" Well, we'd leave him far below us! Grounded!'

'I don't think we should do that,' Kathy protested. The only time she stopped smiling was when Sam made a joke.

'Why ever not?' Sam frowned.

'I think I'm going to need him.' As she said this I felt ridiculously honoured.

'Rumpole? Why ever should you *need* Rumpole? What did you say your name was?'

'I didn't.'

Now my time had come. I had great pleasure in

72

performing the introduction.

'This is Miss Kathy Trelawny. Of "Nirvana", 34 Balaclava Road.' And I added, in a whisper to Sam, 'the well-known unmade bed.'

Sam looked like a man who has just lifted what he imagined was a glass of vintage champagne and discovered it contained nothing but Seven Up. He looked at Kathy with pronounced distaste and said, 'No bloody wonder you don't drink.'

'It's just something I don't like doing.' She smiled back at him.

'Naturally. Naturally you won't have a pink gin like a normal girl. Excuse me.' He moved away from us, shouting, 'Drink up please. Haven't any of you lot got homes?'

The piano stopped, people started to drift out into the night.

'Was that meant to be a joke ... All that "pilot officer" business?' Kathy asked me.

'No joke at all. Sam was a great man on bombers. He could find any target you'd care to mention, in the pitch dark, on three fingers of whisky ... He was good, Sam. Extremely good.'

'You mean good at killing people?' When she put it like that, I supposed that was what I did mean. Kathy turned to look at Bobby, who was sitting on the piano stool, lighting a cigarette. She asked me and I told her that was Sam's wife and I used to think she was gorgeous.

'Gorgeous for the war time, anyway. Things were a bit utility then.'

'And now?'

I looked at her. 'Children seem to grow up more beautiful. It must be the orange juice.'

'Or the peace?'

73

Sam gave us a crescendo version of 'Time Please' and I walked my client to the bus shelter. It was a still, rather warm September night. The sea murmured perpetually, and the moonlight lit up the headland and whitened the strip of beach. There were only very few words for it, and I recited them to Kathy as we moved away from the cars starting up round the Crooked Billet.

'*It is a beauteous evening, calm and free, The holy time is quiet as a Nun Breathless with adoration ...*'

'We read poetry. At the house,' Kathy told me. 'It's a good way to end the day. Someone reads a poem. Anything.' And then she shivered on that warm night, and said, 'They won't lock me up will they?'

'I told you. We'll knock out the evidence! Put your trust in Rumpole!' I tried to sound as cheerful as possible, but she stood still, trembling slightly, her hand on my arm.

'My brother Pete's locked up in Turkey ... twelve years. He was always such a scared kid. He couldn't sleep with the door shut. Neither of us could.'

'What on earth did your brother do in Turkey?'

'Drugs,' she said, and I wondered what sort of an idiot her brother must be. Then she asked me, 'Will it be over soon?'

'It'll be over.'

There were lights coming up the hill, to take her away from me.

'That's my bus ... why don't you come and see me in "Nirvana"?'

Then the most strange thing happened, she leant forward and kissed me, quite carefully on

74

the cheek. Then she was gone, and I was saying to myself, '"Nirvana"? Why ever not?' I walked back to the Crooked Billet in a state of ridiculous happiness. Flower power that year was exceedingly potent.

★ ★ ★

I was up early the next morning, sinking a boiled egg in the residents' lounge as the sun sparkled on the sea and Bobby fussed around me, pouring tea. Sam was still asleep, God was in his heaven and with old Rice Crispies on the bench I could find nothing particularly wrong with the world. After breakfast I put a drop of eau-de-cologne on the handkerchief, ran a comb through the remaining hair and set off for the Coldsands seat of justice.

When I got down to the Shire Hall, and into the wig and gown, I had my first view of the inhabitants of 'Nirvana', the lotus eaters of 34 Balaclava Road. They were out in force, clean jeans, Mexican-looking shawls, the statutory baby. One tall coloured boy whom I later discovered to be called 'Oswald' was carrying a small flute. I just hoped they weren't going to mistake the whole business for a bit of harmless fun round the South African Embassy.

'Morning. You must be Rumpole. Welcome to the Western Circuit.' I was being addressed by a tall fellow with a rustic tan beneath his wig, a gentleman farmer and gentleman barrister. I looked down to discover if he had jodhpur boots on under the pinstripes.

'Tooke. Vernon Tooke's my name. I'm prosecuting you.'

'Awfully decent of you.' I smiled at him.

Tooke glanced disapprovingly at my supporters club.

'I say, Rumpole. Where did you get that shower from? Rent-a-hippie. What a life, eh ... Gang-bangs on the National Assistance?'

Did I detect in Farmer Tooke's voice—a note of envy?

'Used to be a decent area,' he continued, 'Balaclava Road. Until that lot got their foot in the door. Squatters, are they?'

'They've got a nine-year lease. And they've all got jobs. The only fellows scrounging off the State, Tooke, are you and I!'

'Really Rumpole?' Tooke looked pained.

'Well, they're paying you on the rates, aren't they?'

'Most amusing!' He looked as if I'd pointed out a bad case of foot and mouth in the herd, but he offered me a cigarette from a gold case. I refused and produced the remains of a small cigar from the waistcoat pocket. Tooke ignited it with a gold lighter.

'Is this going to take long?' he asked anxiously. 'Coldsands gymkhana tomorrow. We tend to make it rather a day out.'

'Take long? I don't suppose so. It's quite a simple point of law.'

'Law, Rumpole ... Did you say law?' The casually dropped word seemed to fill Tooke with a certain amount of dread.

'That's right. You do have law, I suppose, down on the Western Circuit?'

I left Tooke and moved towards the commune. A young man with dark hair and a permanent

76

frown who seemed to be their leader greeted me, as I thought, in an unfriendly fashion.

'You her lawyer?'

I admitted it. Kathy, smiling as ever, introduced him to me as a friend of hers, named Dave Hawkins. I speculated, with a ridiculous stab of regret, that the friendship was a close one.

'This is Dave.'

'Oh yes?'

'Will she be going in today?' Dave wanted to be put in the picture.

'In?'

'Into the witness box. I mean, there's something I want her to say. It's pretty important.'

I was accustomed to being the sole person in charge of my case. I put Dave right patiently. 'Dave. May I call you Mr Hawkins? If I were a doctor taking out your appendix, old darling, you wouldn't want Kathy, would you, telling me where to put the knife?' At this point the usher came out of court and called,

'Katherine Trelawny.'

'You'd better answer your bail.' As I said this Kathy gave a little shiver and asked me. 'Will they lock me up now?'

'Of course not. Trust me.'

The usher called her again. I dropped the remnants of the small cigar on the marble floor of the Shire Hall and ground it underfoot. The lance was in the rest, Sir Galahad Rumpole was about to do battle for the damsel in distress, or words to that effect.

* * *

77

Half-way through the afternoon things were going pretty well. Rice Crispies, doing his job in a very decent fashion, was decidedly interested in the point of *agent provocateur*. Kathy was smiling in the dock, the commune were gripped by the spectacle, and outside the Court room the baby, unaware of the solemnity of the occasion, was yelling lustily. In the witness box, Detective Sergeant Jack Smedley was looking extremely square, clean shaven and in his natty Old Bill uniform.

'I see Detective Sergeant,' I had the pleasure to put to him, 'you are no longer wearing your beads.'

'Beads? What beads are those?' The judge was puzzled.

'I was wearing beads, your Honour—on the occasion of my visits to 34 Balaclava Road.'

'*Beads!* With the uniform?' His Honour couldn't believe his ears. No one had sported beads in the Navy.

'Not with the uniform! With the embroidered jeans, and the waistcoat of Afghan goat, and the purple silk drapery knotted round your neck.' I pursued my advantage.

'I was in plain clothes, your Honour.'

'Plain clothes, Sergeant? You were in fancy dress!' I rode over a titter from the commune. 'Now perhaps you'll tell the Court. What's happened to your gaucho moustache?'

'I . . . I shaved it off.'

'Why?'

'In view of certain comments, your Honour, passed in the Station. It wasn't a gaucho. More a

78

Viva Zapata, actually.'

'A Viva, *what* was that, Mr Rumpole?' The judge seemed to feel the world slipping away from him.

'The officer was affecting the moustache, your Honour, of a well-known South American revolutionary.' This news worried the old darling on the bench deeply.

'A South American! Can you tell me, officer, what was the purpose of this elaborate disguise?' The witness paused. I filled the gap with my humble submission.

'May I suggest an answer, Sergeant? You took it into your head to pose as a drug dealer in order to trap this quite innocent young woman ...' I had the pleasure of pointing out Kathy in the dock ... 'into taking part in a filthy trade she wouldn't otherwise have dreamed of.'

'Well yes, but ...'

'What did he say?' Rice Crispies pounced on the grudging admission.

'Your Honour.' The witness tried to start again.

'Shorthand writer, just read me that answer.'

There was a long pause while the elderly lady shuffled through her notes, but at last the passage was reproduced.

'... in order to trap this quite innocent young woman into taking part in a filthy trade.' 'Well yes, but ...'

The judge made a note of that. I could have kissed the old darling. However, I pressed on.

'But what, Sergeant?'

'She wasn't so innocent.'

'What reason had you to suppose that?'

'Her way of life, your Honour.'

79

'What I want you to tell me, officer, is this.' The judge weighed in in support of Rumpole. 'Did you have any reason to believe that this young woman was dealing in drugs before you went there in your Viva ... What?'

'Zapata, your Honour,' I helped him along.

'Thank you, Mr Rumpole. I'm much obliged.'

'We had received certain information.' The sergeant did his best to make it sound sinister.

'And will you let us into the secret, officer. What was this information?'

'That Miss Trelawny was the type to get involved.'

'Involved by you?'

'Involved already.'

Tooke, who seemed to feel the case was eluding his grasp, rose to his feet. 'I shall be calling the evidence, your Honour, of the neighbour, Miss Tigwell.'

'Very well, Mr Tooke.'

'But if the evidence shows no previous attempt to deal in drugs, then you would agree the whole of this crime was a result of your fertile imagination.' I fired a final salvo at the witness but the judge interrupted me, perfectly fairly.

'Doesn't that rather depend, Mr Rumpole, on the effect of Miss Tigwell's evidence? When we hear it?'

'If your Honour pleases. Of course, as always, your Honour is perfectly right!' I rewarded that upright fellow Rice Crispies with a low bow and sat down in a mood of quiet self-congratulation. I hadn't been sitting long before the man, Dave, was at my side, whispering furiously, 'Is that *all* you're going to ask?'

80

'You want to have a go?' I whispered back. 'Do borrow the wig, old darling.'

*   *   *

The evidence of Kathy's previous malpractices was offered to us in the person of Miss Tigwell who lived opposite at No. 33 Balaclava Road, and whose idea of entertainment appeared to be gazing into the windows of 'Nirvana' in the daily hope of moral indignation.

'I could tell exactly what they were.'

'What were they, Miss Tigwell?'

'Perverted. All living higgledy-piggledy. Men and women, black and white.'

'Did your supervision include the bedrooms?'

'Well ... No. But they all sat together in the front room.'

'Sat together? What did they talk about?'

'I couldn't hear that.'

'They were a community, that's what it comes to. They might well have been Trappist monks for all you knew.'

'I don't know if Mr Rumpole is suggesting his client is a Trappist monk.' Tooke made a mistake, he should have left the jokes to me. Rice Crispies didn't smile.

'Now, Miss Tigwell, apart from the fact that persons of different sex, *sat* together ... Did you ever observe anything suspicious from your post in the crow's nest?'

'I saw a man giving her money.' Miss Tigwell was playing her King. 'Quite a lot of money. It was in ten pound notes.'

'Was this the first time you had ever seen

81

money passing or any sort of dealing going on in "Nirvana"?'

'The first time, yes.'

The judge was making a note. I decided to play my Ace and prayed that I wouldn't be trumped by the prosecution.

'Can you describe to his Honour the man you saw passing the money?'

'Dreadful-looking person. A clear criminal type. Looked as if he'd been dragged through a hedge backwards.'

'Long hair?'

'And a horrible sort of moustache.'

'Beads? Embroidered jeans? Afghan goat's hair and purple silk fancy for the neck?' I saw Detective Sergeant ex-hippie Smedley bow his head in shame, and I knew I was home and dry.

'Disgusting! I saw it all quite distinctly!' Miss Tigwell ended in triumph.

'Congratulations, madam. You have now given us a perfectly accurate description of Detective Smedley of the local force.'

As I took off the wig in the robing room, Farmer Tooke was looking distinctly worried. I did my best to cheer him up. 'Ah, Tooke ... I have good news for you. Hope to get you all off in time for the gymkhana tomorrow. Got a daughter, have you, in the potato race?'

'Do you think the judge is agin me?' Tooke felt all was not well with the prosecution.

'Not you, personally. But I know what he's thinking.'

'Do you?'

'Encourage that sort of police officer and he'll be out in a frock on the Prom tomorrow—soliciting the chairman of the bench.'

Tooke saw the point. 'I say. I suppose that sort of thing is worrying.'

'Not English, if you want my opinion.'

At which Tooke, climbing into his Burberry, put the law behind him and extended an invitation.

'What are you doing tonight, Rumpole? I mean, there'll be a few of us dining at the Bar hotel ... With the leader of the Circuit.'

'Roast lamb, sea shanties and old jokes from Quarter Sessions? No. Not tonight, Tooke.'

'Oh well. I'm sorry. We like to give our visitors a little hospitality.'

'Tonight, I am dropping out.'

*   *   *

Dinner at 'Nirvana' was a distinct surprise. I'd expected nut cutlets and carrot juice. I got an excellent steak and kidney pud and a very drinkable claret. Oswald had told me he was something of a 'wine freak'. The house was clean and the big cushions and old sofas remarkably comfortable. The babies were good enough to withdraw from the company, the record-player gave us unobtrusive flute music from the Andes and Kathy tended to all my needs, filling my glass and lighting my cigar, and remained a perpetual pleasure to the eye. I began to think that I'd rather live at 34 Balaclava Road than at the Gloucester Road mansion flat with She Who Must Be Obeyed; I'd rather sit back on the scatter cushions at 'Nirvana' and let my mind go a complete blank than drag myself down to the

Bailey on a wet Monday morning to defend some over-excited Pakistani accused of raping his social worker. In fact I thought that for tuppence, for a packet of small cigars, I'd give up the law and spend the rest of my life in a pair of old plimsolls and grey flannel bags, shrimping on the beach at Coldsands.

The only fly in this soothing ointment was the fellow Dave. When I told Kathy she wouldn't even have to go into the witness box if we won our *agent provocateur* argument, Dave said, 'I'm not sure I agree with that.' I told him firmly that I wasn't sure he had to.

'When we brought you here I thought you'd understand ... It's not just another case,' Dave protested. Protesting seemed to be his main occupation.

'Every case is just another case,' I told him.

'To you, all right! To us it's a chance to say what we have to. Can't we put the law straight—on the drug scene?'

'I mean, this isn't a den of thieves, is it? You've seen "Nirvana"!' Oswald put the point more gently. He was right, of course, I had seen 'Nirvana'.

'Now's our only chance to get *through* to the law,' Dave told me. I decided to instruct him on the facts of life.

'The law? You know where the law is now? Down in the George Hotel drinking the Circuit port and singing "What Shall We Do with the Drunken Sailor". The law is talking about the comical way the old Lord Chief passed a death sentence. The law is in another world; but it thinks it's the *whole* world. Just as you lot think

84

the world's nothing but poetry, and perhaps the occasional puff of a dangerous cigarette.'

'That's what we've got you for. To put our point of view across.' Dave had mistaken my function.

'You've got me to get you out of trouble. That's what you've got me for. I'm not going to get up tomorrow and teach old Rice Crispies to sing protest songs ... to a small guitar.'

'You're just not taking this case seriously!' Dave was totally wrong, and I told him so.

'Oh yes I am. I am seriously determined to keep Kathy out of prison.'

At which Miss Trelawny said it was time for their nightly poem. She found a book and gave it to me open.

'Me?'

'You like this. Read it to us...'

So I read to the lotus eaters, quietly at first and then with more emphasis, enjoying the sound of my own voice. '*It is a beauteous evening, calm and free, The holy time is quiet as a Nun Breathless with adoration; the broad sun Is sinking down in its tranquillity.*'

They were all listening as though they actually enjoyed it, except for Dave who was whispering to Kathy.

'*Dear Child! dear Girl! that walkest with me here, If thou appear untouched by solemn thought...*'

Kathy was shushing Dave, making him listen to the old sheep. I looked at her as I read the last lines.

'*Thy nature is not therefore less divine: Thou liest in Abraham's bosom all the year; And worshipp'st at the Temple's inner shrine, God being with thee*

85

when we know it not.'

I slammed the book shut. I needed to sleep before Court in the morning.

*   *   *

'The Officer was only doing his duty. Active, your Honour, in the pursuit of crime!' Tooke was making his final speech on the point of evidence, to an unenthusiastic audience.

'Or in the manufacture of a crime? That's what troubles me.' The judge was really troubled, bless him. He went on. 'If I thought this young woman only collected drugs ... only got in touch with any sort of supplier because of the trap set for her—then would you concede, Mr Tooke, I would have to reject the evidence?'

'I think your Honour would.'

Tooke was a lovely prosecutor. Everything was going extremely well when Rice Crispies adjourned for lunch. So I was in festive mood when I set off for a crab sandwich and a nourishing stout in the pub opposite the Shire Hall, looking forward to whetting my whistle and putting the final touch on my clinching argument. But I was stopped by Friendly who said the client wanted to see me as a matter of urgency. He led me into a small room, decorated with old framed leases and eighteenth-century maps of Coldsands, and there, clearly bursting with news to impart, were Miss Kathy Trelawny and her friend Dave.

*   *   *

'We want to tell the truth.' I closed the door

carefully and looked at her Dave without encouragement.

'What truth?'

'It's the only way I can get Peter's case across,' Kathy said. She was smiling no longer.

'Peter?'

'My brother. I told you. He was busted.'

'In Turkey. I remember. Well, this isn't Turkey. And it's not Peter's case or anyone else's.' I looked at Kathy. 'It's yours.'

'Kathy wants you to know why she did it.'

She was about to speak, and I almost shouted at her, hoping it still wasn't too late.

'Shut up!'

'You see I had...'

'The conference is over! Got to get a bite of lunch. Come on, Friendly.' I moved to the door.

'It appears we have new instructions, Mr Rumpole.' Friendly looked concerned, not half so concerned as I was.

'The old instructions are doing very nicely, thank you. Don't say a word until this evening. When it's all over tell me what you like.'

'She wants everyone to know. How else can we get Pete's case into the papers?'

Dave, like an idiot, had moved between me and the door. I had no way of escaping the fusillade of truth which Kathy then let fly.

'I got the stuff last year after Pete got busted in Istanbul. I was going to sell it anyway. It was going to cost ten thousand pounds to get him out in lawyers' fees and ...' she looked at me almost accusingly, 'bribes, I suppose ... He got twelve years. We've got to get people to care about Peter!'

87

So it was quite clear, she was telling me that she hadn't committed her crime as the result of a request from an *agent provocateur*. She had the stuff before Detective Sergeant Smedley of the west country Drug Squad first came to 'Nirvana'. That was the truth, the last thing in the world I wanted to know. I looked at my watch, and turned to Friendly.

'What is there—a 2.25 back to London? Friendly, run outside, for God's sake, and see if you can't whistle me up a taxi. I'm retiring from this case.'

Friendly, totally puzzled by the turn of events, left us.

'Running out on us?' Dave never made an unexpected remark.

'Why, for God's sake?' Kathy asked me, and I had to tell her. 'Let me try and explain. My existence is bound by a small blue volume handed down like the Tablets on the day of my Call to the Bar by a Master of my Inn in a haze of port and general excitement.'

'What the hell's he talking about!' Dave couldn't resist interrupting, but Kathy told him to listen. I went on with such calm as I could muster.

'Barristers down the ages have killed. They have certainly committed adultery. Although that sort of thing doesn't appeal to me some may well have coveted their neighbours' camels and no doubt worshipped graven images. But I don't believe there's one of us who has ever gone on to fight a case after our client has told us, in clear crystal ringing tones, that they actually did the deed.'

88

'You mean—you won't help me?' Kathy looked as if it had never occurred to her.

'I can't now.'

'But Kathy wants to tell the judge the pot law's ridiculous. And about Pete.'

'It's my duty to preside over your acquittal, not your martyrdom to the dubious cause of intoxication,' I told her. 'I'll see the judge and tell him I can't act for you any longer ... personal reasons.'

'The old fool'll think you fancy her.' I can't imagine where Dave got that far-fetched idea, and I went on ignoring him.

'You'll get another barrister. What you tell him is your business. I'll ask the judge to adjourn for a week or two ... You'll still be on bail.'

'What's the matter? Afraid to stick your neck out? Or would you starve to death if they made pot legal?' Dave was about to start on another of his political speeches, but Kathy silenced him. She asked him to leave us alone, and I told him to go and find Friendly and my taxi. He went. He had smashed my defence and I was alone with Kathy, looking at the pieces.

'I thought ... We got along together.' Kathy was smiling again. I couldn't help admiring her courage. 'I mean, you keep talking about clients. I didn't think I was a client. I thought I was more of a friend, actually.'

'Never have friends for clients. That really ought to be one of the Ten Commandments.'

'I don't suppose you could forget what I told you?'

'Of course I could. I'd like nothing more than to forget it. I'd forget it at once if I wasn't a bloody barrister!'

'And there's nothing more important than that in your life? Being a barrister.'

I thought about this very carefully. Unfortunately, there was only one answer.

'No.'

'Poetry doesn't mean a damn thing to you! Friendship doesn't mean anything. You're just an old man with a heart full of a book about legal etiquette!' Kathy was angry now, she'd stopped smiling.

'You're saying just what I have long suspected,' I had to agree with her.

'Why don't you do something about it?'

'What do you suggest?' She moved away from me, and went and looked out of the window, at the sunshine and the municipal begonias. At last she said, 'I might leave Coldsands and come up to London. Do a language course.'

'And Dave? Would Dave be coming with you?'

'Dave's stuck here organizing the house. I want to get away. Have a bit of a rest from home-made muesli and debates about the geyser. I thought. Well. I'd get a flat in London. I could come and have lunch with you sometimes. When you're in the Old Bailey.'

'Every man has his price. Is that mine? A lunch down the Old Bailey?'

'Not enough?'

'More than enough. Probably, much more. Something to think about, in the long cold nights with She Who Must Be Obeyed.'

She suddenly turned on me, she was holding on to my arm, as if afraid of falling.

'I'm not going to prison! You won't let them

90

send me to prison!'

There was only one way, now Dave had done his damnedest.

'I can go and see the judge. He might agree to a suspended sentence. I don't know. I can go and see him.'

'That's right! He likes you. I could see you get along. Go and see him. Please go and see him.' She was smiling again, eager. I had to tell her the facts of life.

'You know what it means. If I go and see the judge for you?'

'I ... I plead guilty.' She knew. I left her then and went to the door. We still had our trump card. Dear old Rice Crispies was simply aching to get away to the gymkhana.

*   *   *

His Honour Judge Crispin-Rice was delighted to see Rumpole and the prosecuting Tooke. He made us Nescafé with the electric kettle in his room. He looked younger with his wig off, and, when we had settled such vital matters as how much milk and no sugar thank you, he and Tooke tried to make me envious of their previous night's revelry in the Bar Mess.

'We had a good evening. You should have been with us, Rumpole. Didn't we have a splendid evening, Vernon?'

'The leader gave us "The Floral Dance".' Tooke relived the great moment.

'Old Pascoe is wonderful for 75. He entertained us in song.' The judge offered us a Senior Service. 'You'd have enjoyed it.'

91

'A splendid evening! We fined little Moreton a dozen bottles of claret for talking shop at dinner.' Tooke was bubbling at the memory.

'We then started hacking away at the penalty! How many bottles were left?'

'None, Judge. As far as I remember.'

I thought the time had come to return their thoughts to the business in hand.

'Look here, Judge,' I said. 'At the risk of being fined for talking shop. If ... If it so happened I could persuade my client to plead guilty ...' His Honour was stirring his cup, giving me no great assistance. 'You might be grateful for a short afternoon.' Even this didn't hook him. I went on, a little desperately. 'She's a remarkable girl.'

'So I can see.' Old Rice Crispies smiled then. Perhaps, I thought, I could rope him into 'Nirvana'.

'Knows a good deal about Wordsworth.' I didn't know if this would sway the judicial mind.

'Wordsworth? Is he a mitigating factor?'

'Poor old sheep of the Lake District. He can't afford to lose admirers.'

'No. Well. She'd get the full benefit of pleading guilty.' He was using his judge's voice. I stood up, like a barrister.

'Can't you tell me any more than that?'

'There *are* rules.'

'I thought you might indicate...'

'The tariff? You know the tariff. How much was it? Twenty pounds weight. A fair wallop!'

'It was only cannabis.' I tried to make it sound like broken biscuits. 'They use the stuff just like whisky. It doesn't occur to them...'

'But it isn't whisky, is it?' The Judge's voice

again. 'It's a Class B drug as defined by the Dangerous Drugs Act.'

'But what do we *know* about it?'

'That it's illegal. Isn't that all we need to know?' He looked at me then, and gave me a charming smile. 'My God, Rumpole. Are we going to see *you* turning up in Court in beads?'

'She's got a good character.' I played my last card.

The judge drained his Nescafé. 'Well, you know about a "good character". Everyone had a "good character" once ... I mean, if we let everyone out because of their "good character" no one would ever go inside.'

'That'd be a scandal. All those empty prisons.' I said it with too much feeling. Rice Crispies looked at me as if I were coming out in a rash.

'I say, Rumpole. You're not getting *involved* in this case, are you?'

'Involved? Of course not. No, naturally. But I was thinking possibly a suspended sentence?' At which his Honour Judge Crispin-Rice put his wig back on and said something which was no help at all.

'You've got your job to do, Rumpole, and I've got mine.'

*   *   *

I sweated my guts out in my speech in mitigation, and the judge listened to me with perfect courtesy. He then gave Kathy Trelawny three years in the nicest possible way, and she was taken down to the cells. Vernon Tooke came up to me in the robing room. He was on his way to

93

the gymkhana.

'Well. Ended nice and quick.'

'Yes, Tooke, very quickly.'

'Going back to London?'

'Tomorrow. I'll be going back tomorrow.'

'Quite an attractive sort of person, your client.'

'Yes, Tooke.'

'All the same. To prison she had to go.'

When I came out into the main hall the commune was standing in a little group. Oswald was playing a lament on his flute and the baby was silent. None of them spoke to me, but I heard a voice at my elbow say, 'It seems a shame, sir. A girl like that.' It was Detective Sergeant Jack the Hippie Smedley. And he added what we both knew, 'It's an evil place, Holloway.'

Out in the street I was nearly run over by a police car. Miss Kathy Trelawny was sitting in the back and saw me. She was still smiling.

*   *   *

Joviality was at its height in the Crooked Billet that night. Sam told all his old stories, and Bobby played the piano. I stood beside her, my glass of rum on the piano top, and in a pause she looked across at her husband.

'Look at Sam,' she said. 'He's happy as a tick! What's he want with a slow death on lime juice in a bungalow? I made up my mind. I'm not going to tell him. Are you in favour of that?'

'People not telling people things? People not scattering information like bombs? Oh yes,' I told her. 'I'm all in favour of that.'

Then she played 'Roll out the Barrel' and we all

94

joined in, our voices floating out over the sea until Sam called 'Time Please'. I never saw the people from 'Nirvana' again.

RUMPOLE AND THE HONOURABLE MEMBER

'You're giving me a rape?'

My clerk, Albert, had just handed me a brief. He then returned to the complicated business of working out the petty cash account; his desk was covered with slips of paper, a cash box and odd bits of currency. I never inquired into Albert's system of book-keeping, nor did anyone else in Chambers.

'Don't you want it, Mr Rumpole?' I turned to look at Henry, our second clerk. Henry had joined as an office boy, a small tousled figure who scarcely seemed able to read or write. Albert used him mainly to run errands and make instant coffee, and told him he would only be allowed to take a barrister into Court when he'd learnt to shine his shoes and clean his fingernails. Henry had changed over the years. His shoes were now gleaming, he wore a neat pinstriped suit with a waistcoat, and was particularly assiduous in his attentions to Guthrie Featherstone, Q.C., M.P., our Head of Chambers. Albert, as head clerk, got ten per cent of our earnings, but Henry was on a salary. I had thought for a long time that Henry thought Albert past it, and had his eye on a head clerk's position. I should add, so you can get the complete picture of life in our clerk's room, that our old lady typist had left us and we had a new girl called Dianne who read quite extraordinarily lurid novels when she wasn't typing, spent a great deal of the day titivating in the loo, and joined

96

Henry in looking pityingly at Albert as he struggled to adjust the petty cash.

'You don't ask whether you want a rape,' I told Henry sharply. 'Rape comes uninvited.' I was gathering my post from the mantelpiece and looked at it with disgust. 'Like little brown envelopes from the Inland Revenue.'

'Morning Rumpole.' I became aware of the presence of young Erskine-Brown who was standing by the mantelpiece, also watching Albert in his struggle to balance the budget. He was holding some sort of legal document and wearing a shirt with broad stripes, elastic-sided boots and an expression of amused contempt at Albert's business methods. As I have made clear earlier in these reminiscences, I don't like Erskine-Brown. I greeted him civilly, however, and asked him if he'd ever done a rape.

'As you know, Rumpole, I prefer the civil side. I really find crime moderately distasteful.'

At this point Erskine-Brown started to complain to Albert about the typing of the distasteful document, some mortgage or other act of oppression, he was carrying, and Albert said if he was interrupted he'd have to start again on his column of figures. I happened to glance down at the pound notes on Albert's desk and noticed one marked with a small red cross in the corner; but I thought no more of it at the time. I then turned my attention to my brief, which I immediately noticed was a paying one and not Legal Aided. I carried it into my room with increased respect.

* * *

97

The first thing I discovered was that my client was a Labour M.P. named Ken Aspen. The next was that he was accused of no less a crime than the rape of one of his loyal party workers, a girl called Bridget Evans, in his committee room late on the night before the election. I couldn't help feeling pleased, and slightly flattered, that such a case had come my way; the press box at the Bailey was bound to be full and the words of the Rumpole might once again decorate the *News of the World*. Then I unfolded an election poster and saw the face of Aspen, the workers' friend, a reasonably good-looking man in his early forties, frowning slightly with the concentrated effort of bringing us all a new heaven and a new earth which would still be acceptable to the Gnomes of Zurich. The poster I had was scrawled over and defaced, apparently by the hand of the complainant, Miss Bridget Evans, at the time of the alleged crime.

I lit a small cigar and read on in my instructions, and, as I read, the wonder grew that an Honourable Member, with a wife and family and a house in Hampstead Garden Suburb, should put it all at risk for a moment of unwelcomed pleasure on the floor of his committee room by night. I had heard of political suicide, but this was ridiculous, and I believed that any jury would find it incredible too. Of course at that time I hadn't had the pleasure of meeting Mrs Kenneth Aspen.

*   *   *

'So Bumble Whitelock, when they made him Chief Justice of the Seaward Isles, I don't know, some God-forsaken hole, had this man in the dock before him, found guilty of living on immoral earnings, and he was puzzled about the sentence. So he sent a runner down to the Docks where the old Chief Justice was boarding a P. & O. steamer home with the urgent message, "How much do you give a ponce?" Look, I'll do this...'

It was my practice to retire with my old clerk Albert to Pommeroy's Wine Bar in Fleet Street at the end of a day's work to strengthen myself with a glass or two of claret before braving the tube and She Who Must Be Obeyed. During such sessions I seek to divert Albert with a joke or two, usually of a legal nature. I was in full swing when one of the girls who works at Pommeroy's interrupted us with the full glasses of Chateau Fleet Street. Albert had his wallet out and was paying for the treat.

'No, sir. Quite honestly.' I happened to see the note as Albert handed it over. It was marked with a small red cross in the corner.

'All right. My turn next. "So the message was," I returned to my story, "How much do you give a ponce?" and the answer came back immediately from the old Chief Justice by very fast rickshaw—"Never more than two and six!" Cheers.'

I don't know why but that story always makes me laugh. Albert was laughing politely also.

'Never more than two and six! You like that one, do you Albert?'

'I've always liked it, sir.'

'It's like a bloody marriage, Albert. We've got to know each other's anecdotes.'

'Perhaps you'd like a divorce, sir. Let young

Henry do your clerking for you?'

I looked over to the bar. Erskine-Brown was having a drink with Henry and Dianne, they were drinking Vermouth and Henry seemed to be showing some photographs.

'Henry? We'd sit in here over a Cinzano Bianco, and he'd show me the colour snaps of his holiday in Majorca ... No, Albert. We'll rub along for a few more years. Who got me this brief, for instance?'

'The solicitors, sir. They like the cut of your jib.'

I ventured to contradict my old clerk. 'Privately paid rapes don't fall from the sky, like apples in a high wind—however my jib is cut.'

Then Albert told me how the job had been done, proving once again his true value as a clerk. 'I have the odd drink in here, with Mr Myers of your instructing solicitors. Their managing clerk. Remember old Myersy, he grows prize tomatoes? Likes to be asked about them, sir. If I may suggest it.'

'Fellow with glasses. Overcoat pockets stuffed with writs. Smokes a mixture of old bed socks?' I remember Myersy.

'That's him, Mr Rumpole. He thinks our only chance is to crucify the girl.'

'Seems a bit extreme.'

Now Albert started to reminisce, recalling my old triumphs.

'I remember you, sir. When you cross-examined the complainant in that indecent assault in the old Kilburn Alhambra. You brought out as he'd touched her up during the Movietone News.'

'And she admitted she'd sat through the whole

of *Rosemarie* and a half-hour documentary about wild life on the River Dee before she complained to the manager!'

'As I recollect, she fainted during your questioning.'

'Got her on the wing around the tenth question.' It was true. The witness had plummeted like a partridge. Right out of the witness box!

'I told old Myersy that,' said Albert proudly. '"Will Rumpole be afraid of attacking her?" he said. I told him, "There's not a woman in the world my Mr Rumpole's afraid of."'

I was, I suppose, a little late in returning to the mansion flat in Gloucester Road. As I hung up the coat and hat I was greeted by a great cry from the kitchen of 'Rumpole!' It was my wife Hilda, She Who Must Be Obeyed, and I moved towards the source of the shout, muttering, *'Being your slave, what should I do but tend, Upon the hours and times of your desire?'*

In the kitchen, Mrs Rumpole was to be seen dimly as through a mist of feathers. She was plucking a bird.

'I have no precious time at all to spend, Nor services to do till you require...'

'I was watching the clock,' Hilda told me, ignoring Shakespeare. 'I've been watching it since half past six!'

'Something blew up. A rape. I bought a bottle of plonk.' I put my peace-offering down on the table. Hilda told me that wouldn't be enough for the feast planned for the morrow, for which she was denuding a guinea-fowl. Our son Nick, back from his year at an American university, was

101

bringing his intended, a Miss Erica Freyburg, to dinner with the family.

'If he's bringing Erica,' I said, 'I'll slip down to the health food centre and get a magnum of carrot juice.' I had already met my potential daughter-in-law, a young lady with strong views on dietary matters, and indeed on every other subject under the sun, whom Nick had met in Baltimore.

'Sometimes I think you're just jealous of Erica.'

'Jealous? About Nicky?' I had got the bottle of plonk open and was sitting at the kitchen table, the snow of feathers settling gently.

'You want your son to be happy, don't you?'

'Of course. Of course I want him to be happy.' Then I put my problem to Hilda. 'Can you understand why an M.P., an Honourable Member, with a wife and a couple of kids should suddenly take it into his head to rape anyone?'

'An M.P.? What side's he on?'

'Labour.'

'Oh well then.' Hilda had no doubt about it. 'It doesn't surprise me in the least.'

*   *   *

The next day the Honourable Member, Ken Aspen, was sitting in my Chambers, flanked by his solicitor's clerk Myers and a calm, competent, handsome woman who was introduced to me as his wife, Anna. I suggested that she might find it less embarrassing to slip out while we discussed the intimate details, perhaps to buy a hat. Well, some judges still like hats on women in Court, but Mrs Aspen, Anna, told me that she intended to stay with her husband every moment that she could. A dutiful wife, you see, and the loyalty shone out of her.

Aspen spoke in a slightly modified public-school accent, and I thought the 'Ken' and the just flattened vowels were a concession to the workers, like a cloth cap on a Labour Member. Being a politician, he started off by looking for a compromise, couldn't I perhaps have a word with Miss Bridget Evans? No, I couldn't, nor could i form a coalition with the judge to defeat her on a vote of no confidence. I received 'Ken's' permission to call him 'Mr Aspen' and then I asked him to tell his story.

It seemed that it was late at night in the committee room and both Janice Crowshott, the secretary, and Paul Etherington, the agent, had gone home. Bridget Evans asked Aspen into her office, saying the duplicating machine was stuck. When he got in she closed the door, and started to talk about politics.

'You're going to tell me that the door of the duplicating room was locked so you could have a good old chat about Home Rule for Wales?'

'Of course not.'

'Or that it was during a few strong words about the export figures that her clothes got torn?'

'She started to accuse me of being unfaithful.'

'To her?' I was puzzled.

'To my principles.'

'Oh. Those.' I wanted to hear his defence, not his platitudes.

'She said I'd betrayed her, and all the Party workers. I'd betrayed Socialism.'

'Well, you were used to hearing that,' I

103

supposed. 'That must be part of the wear and tear of life in the dear old Labour Party.'

'Then she started talking about Anna.'

'She wanted Ken to leave me.' Mrs Aspen was leaning forward, half smiling at me.

'It was the whole set-up she objected to. The house in Hampstead Garden Suburb. The kids' schools.'

'Where do they go exactly?

'Sarah's at the convent and Edward's down for Westminster.'

'And the loyal voters are down for the Comprehensive.' I couldn't resist it, but it earned me a distinctly unfriendly look from Mrs Aspen.

'I think after that, she started screaming at me. All sorts of abuse. Obscenities. I can't remember. Righteous indignation! And then she started clawing at me. Telling me I didn't even have the courage to...'

'The courage. To what?'

'To make love to her. That's what Ken believed,' Mrs Aspen supplied the answer. She'd have made an excellent witness, and I began to regret she wasn't on trial.

'Thank you. Is that true?'

'Of course it's true. Ken made love to her. As she wanted. On the floor.' Again Mrs Aspen provided the answer.

'You believed that was what she wanted?'

At last my client spoke up for himself. 'Yes. Yes. That's what I believed.'

I lit a small cigar, and began to get a sniff of a defence. The House of Lords has decided it's a man's belief that matters in a rape case; there are very few women among the judges of the House

104

of Lords. Meanwhile the Honourable Member carried on with the good work.

'She was goading me. Shouting and screaming. And then, when I saw what she'd done to my face on the poster!'

I found the election poster, scored over with a pen and torn.

'You saw that *then*?'

'Yes. Yes. I think so.'

'You'd better be sure about this. You saw this poster scrawled on before anything happened?'

'Yes. I'm almost sure.'

'Not *almost* sure, Mr Aspen. *Quite*, quite sure?'

'Well. Yes.'

'She didn't do it when you were there?'

'No.'

'So she must have done it before she called you into the room?'

'That would seem to follow,' Mr Myers took his pipe out of his mouth for the first time.

'Oh yes, Mr Myers. You see the point?' I congratulated him.

'Is it important?' the Member asked innocently.

'Oh, no. A triviality. It only means she hated your guts before anyone suggests you might have raped her. You know, Mr Aspen, if you're applying the same degree of thought to the economy as you are to this case, no wonder the pound's dickie.' I have been politer to clients, but Aspen took it very well. He stood up, smiling, and said,

'You're right. The case is yours, Mr Rumpole. I'll go back to worrying about the pound.'

Mrs Aspen also stood and looked at me as though I was a regrettable necessity in their important lives, like drains.

I said nothing cheering. 'Case?' I told them. 'We haven't got a case. Yet. Because at the moment, Mr Myers doesn't know a damn thing about Miss Bridget Evans.'

*   *   *

That evening the fatted guinea-fowl was consumed. I brought home three very decent bottles of claret from Pommeroy's and we entertained Nick and his intended. It was always a treat to have Nick at home with us, even though he'd given up reading Sherlock Holmes and taken to sociology, a subject which might, for me, be entirely written in the hieroglyphics of some remote civilization. I can think of no social theory which could possibly account for such sports as Rumpole and She Who Must Be Obeyed, and I honestly don't believe we're exceptions, being surrounded by a sea of most peculiar, and unclassifiable individuals.

Dinner was over, but we still sat round the table and I was giving the company one of my blue-chip legal anecdotes, guaranteed to raise a laugh. It was the one about the retiring Chief Justice of the Seaward Isles.

'How much do you give a ponce!' I was laughing myself now, in joyful anticipation of the punch line, 'And the answer came back by very fast rickshaw, "Never more than two and six."' Nick joined me in a burst of hilarity.

Hilda said, 'Well! Thank goodness that's over,' and Erica looked totally mystified. Then she told us that Nick had been offered a vacancy in the department of social studies in the University of Baltimore, which came as something of a surprise to us as we both thought Nick had settled on the job he'd been offered at Warwick.

'So it's not decided,' Hilda said, voicing the general anxiety.

'From our point of view I suppose Warwick would have certain advantages over Baltimore,' I told Nick.

'I doubt the academic standards are any higher,' Erica was defensive.

'No. But it is a great deal nearer Gloucester Road. Another glass of water?' I rose and poured for Erica. She was a good-looking girl and seemed healthy enough, although I regretted her habit of drinking water, as I told her. 'Scientific research has conclusively proved that water causes the hair to drop out, fallen arches and ingrowing toe nails. They should pass a law against it.' At this point Erica did her best to raise the level of the conversation, by saying, 'Nicky's told me all about your work. I think it's just great the way you stand up in Court for the underprivileged!'

'I will stand up in Court for absolutely any underprivileged person in the world. Provided they've got Legal Aid!'

'What's your motivation—in taking on these sort of cases?' Erica asked me seriously, and I told her, 'My motivation is the money.'

'I think you're just rationalizing.'

'He does it because he can't resist the sound of his own voice,' Nick, who knows most about me, told her; but I would allow no illusions.

'Money! If it wasn't for the Legal Aid cheque, I tell you, Rumpole would be silent as the tomb!

107

The Old Bailey would no longer echo with my pleas for acquittal and the voice of the Rumpole would not be heard in the Strand. But, as it is, the poor and the underprivileged can rely on me.'

'I'm sure they can,' Erica sounded consoling.

'And the Legal Aid brings us a quite drinkable claret.' I refilled my glass. 'From Jack Pommeroy's Wine Bar. As a matter of fact I get privately paid sometimes. Sometimes I get a plum!'

'Erica wants to come and hear you in Court,' Nick told me and she smiled.

'How could I miss it?'

'Well, I'm not exactly a tourist attraction.'

'If I'm going to live in England I want to know all I can about your mores,' Erica explained. Well, if she wanted to see the natives at their primitive crafts who was I to stop her?

'Come next week. Down the Bailey. Nick'll bring you for lunch. We'll have steak and kidney pud. Like the old days. Nick used to drop in at the Bailey when he came back from school. He enjoyed the occasional murder, didn't you Nick? That's settled then. We'll have a bit of fun!'

'Fun? What sort of fun?' Erica sounded doubtful, and I told her, 'Rape.'

★   ★   ★

Mr Myers, of my instructing solicitors, went to the Honourable Member's constituency and discovered gold. Miss Bridget Evans was not greatly liked in the local party, being held to be a left-wing activist, and a bloody nuisance. More important than her adherence to the late Leon

Trotsky was her affair with Paul Etherington, the Labour Party agent. I was gloating over this, and other and more glorious goodies provided by the industrious Myers, when there was a knock on my door in Chambers and in filtered Erskine-Brown, glowing with some mysterious triumph.

'Rumpole. One doesn't want to bother the Head of Chambers...'

'Why not bother him? He's got very little on his mind, except settling a nice fat planning case and losing at golf to the Lord Chancellor. Guthrie Featherstone, Q.C., old sweetheart, is ripe for bothering!' I turned my attention back to the past of Miss Bridget Evans.

'It's our head clerk,' Erskine-Brown went on mysteriously.

'Albert? You want to go and bother him?'

Erskine-Brown could restrain himself no longer. 'He's a criminal! Our head clerk is a criminal, Rumpole.'

I looked at the man with considerable disapproval. 'As an ornament of the civil side, don't you find that sort of word a little distasteful?'

'I have proof.' And Erskine-Brown fished a pound note out of his pocket. I examined it curiously.

'Looks like a fairly conventional portrait of Her Majesty.'

'There's a red cross in the corner,' he announced proudly. 'I put it there. I marked the money in the petty cash!'

I looked at my fellow barrister in astonishment.

'I've suspected Albert for a long time. Well, I saw him in Pommeroy's Wine Bar and I got the note he'd paid with off one of the girls. Perhaps it's difficult for you to believe.'

'Extremely!' I stood up and fixed him with an unfriendly gaze. 'A private eye. Taking up the Bar as a profession!'

'What do you mean, Rumpole?'

'I mean, in my day they used to be nasty little men in macs, sniffing round the registers in cheap hotels. They used to spy into bedrooms with field-glasses, in the ever-present hope of seeing male and female clothing scattered around. It's the first time I ever heard of a private Dick being called to the Bar, and becoming an expert on the law of contract.'

I handed the marked pound back to Erskine-Brown, the well-known Dick. He looked displeased.

'It's obvious that I will have to go straight to the Head of Chambers.' As he made for the door I stopped him.

'Why not?' I said. 'Oh just one thing that may have escaped your attention, my dear Watson.'

'What's that?'

'Yesterday afternoon, I borrowed five pound notes from petty cash—no doubt notes decorated by you. And I paid for all of Albert's drinks in Pommeroy's.'

'Rumpole. Are you sure?' I could see he felt his case crumbling.

'I would really advise you, Erskine-Brown, as a learned friend, not to go round Chambers making these sort of wild allegations against our clerk. A man who's been here, old darling, since you were in nappies!'

'Very well, Rumpole. I'm sorry I interrupted

110

your rape.' Erskine-Brown had the door open, he was about to slink away.

'Say no more, old sweetheart. Not one word more. Oh, convey my condolences to the unfortunate Henry. The position of second clerk must be continually frustrating.'

When I was alone I was well pleased. Albert and I had been together now for forty years and I was anxious not to cross my old Dutch. And the evidence little Myersy had uncovered put me in mind of Lewis Carroll.

'Oh, hast thou slain the Jabberwock? Come to my arms! Thou beamish boy ...' 'Not yet father', I said to myself. 'But I will. Oh yes. I certainly will...'

* * *

'Tomatoes doing well, Mr Myers, are they?'

'I apply a great deal of artificial, you see, Mr Rumpole. And they're just coming up to the fourth truss.'

'Fourth truss, are they? Lively little blighters, then!'

We were waiting outside Court. Mr and Mrs Aspen were sitting on a bench, he looking curiously relaxed, she glaring across at Miss Bridget Evans who was looking young and demure on a bench some distance away. Meanwhile I was going through the old legal gambit of chatting up the instructing solicitor. I showed concern for his tomatoes, he asked after my son whom he remembered as a visitor to the Courts of Law.

'Nick? Oh, he's the brains of the family.

111

Sociology. They've offered him a lectureship at Warwick University! And he's engaged to be married. Met her in America and now he's bringing the lady to live in England.'

'I never had a family,' Mr Myers told me, and added, 'I do find having young kids about plays merry hell with your tomatoes.'

At which point Mrs Anna Aspen drew me aside for a conference. The first thing she said surprised me a little.

'I just hope you're not going to let me down.'

'Let *you* down, Mrs Aspen? So far as I can see you're in no danger of the Nick.'

'I'm in danger of losing everything I ever worked for.'

'I understand.'

'No. You don't understand, Mr Rumpole. It's been hard work, but I made Ken fight. I made him go for the nomination. I made him fight for the Seat. When he got in he wanted ... I don't know, to relax on the back benches. He said he'd throw in ideas. But I told him to fight for the P.P.S.'s job and he's got it!' She looked across to where her husband was actually trying the ghost of a smile in Bridget's direction. 'He can't see it's either him or her now. Ken can't see that! You're right about him looking for compromises. Sometimes it makes me so angry!'

'Angrier than the idea of your husband and Miss Bridget Evans. On the floor of the office?'

'Oh that! Why should I worry about that?'

Before I could answer her question, an usher came out to invite the Honourable Member to step into the dock, and we were away.

112

* * *

When you go into Court in a rape case it's like stepping into a refrigerator with the light off. All the men on the jury are thinking of their daughters, and all the women are sitting with their knees jammed together. I found a sympathetic-looking, moderately tarty, middle-aged juror, the sort that might have smiled at the Honourable Member and thought, 'Why didn't you ring me, dearie. I'd have saved you all this trouble.' But her lips snapped shut during the opening by Mr Twentyman, Q.C. for the prosecution, and I despaired of her.

Even the judge, old Sam Parkin, an amiable old darling, perfectly capable of giving a conditional discharge for manslaughter or putting an old lag on probation, even old Sam looked, when the case opened, as if he'd just heard the clerk say, 'Put up Jack the Ripper.' Now he seemed to be warming to Miss Bridget Evans who was telling her hair-raising story with effective modesty. As I tottered to my feet old Sam gave me an icy look. When you start to cross-examine in a rape case you open the flap of the tent, and you're out in the blizzard.

'Miss Bridget Evans. This ... this incident involving Mr Aspen occurred at 11.30 on Wednesday night?'

'I don't know. I wasn't watching the clock.'

The door of the Court opened, to admit the Rumpole fan club, my son Nick and Erica his intended. She was wearing an ethnic skirt and gave me a warm smile, as though to encourage my efforts on behalf of the underprivileged and the

113

oppressed.

'After all the witnesses had conveniently departed. When there was no one there, to establish my client's innocence. After it was all over, what did you do?'

'I went home.'

'A serious and terrible crime had been committed and you went home, tucked yourself up in bed and went to sleep! And you said not one word to the police about it until 6.30 the following day?'

Albert, also of the fan club, was sitting in front of me next to Mr Myers. I heard his penetrating whisper, 'He's doing the old Alhambra cinema technique.' It was nice to feel that dear old Albert was proud of me.

'When you went to bed. Did you go alone?'

'I don't see what that's got to do with it.' Her answer had a hint of sharpness and, for the first time, there was a centimetre up in some of the juror's eyebrows.

'Did you go alone?'

'I told you. I went to bed.'

'Miss Evans. I shall ask my question again and I shall go on asking it all night if it's necessary in the interests of my client. Did you go to bed alone?'

'Do I have to answer that sort of question, my Lord?'

'Yes you do. And my Lord will so direct.' I got in before Sam could draw breath.

'Perhaps if you answer Mr Rumpole's questions shortly you will be out of the box quite quickly, and your painful experience will be over.' Sam Parkin meant well, but I intended to keep her

114

there a little longer.

'Yes. I went to bed alone.'

'How long had that been going on?'

'How long had what been going on, Mr Rumpole?' Sam asked.

'That the witness had taken to sleeping alone, my Lord. You were no longer friendly with Mr Etherington?'

'Paul and I? We split about two years ago. If you're interested in the truth.' I began to hear what a barrister longs for when he's cross-examining, the note of anger.

'Yes, Miss Evans. I am interested in the truth, and I expect the ladies and gentlemen of the jury are also.'

The tarty lady nodded perceptibly. She and I were beginning to reach an understanding.

'Mr Rumpole. Is it going to help us to know about this young lady and Paul ...' Sam was doing his best.

'Paul Etherington, my Lord. He was the Parliamentary agent.'

'I'm anxious not to keep this witness longer than is necessary.'

'I understand, my Lord. It must be most unpleasant.' Almost as unpleasant I thought, as five years in the Nick, which was what the Honourable Member might expect if I didn't demolish Miss Evans. 'But I have my duty to do.'

'And a couple of refreshers to earn,' Mr Twentyman, Q.C., whispered, I thought bitchily, to his junior.

'You had been living with Paul Etherington for two years before you parted?'

'Yes.'

115

'So you were eighteen when you started living together.'

'Just ... nearly eighteen.'

'And before that?'

'I was at school.'

'You had lovers before Paul?'

'Yes.'

'How many?'

'One or two.'

'Or three or four? How many? or didn't they stay long enough to be counted?'

My dear friend the lady juror gave a little disapproving sigh. I had misjudged her. The old darling was less a *fille de joie* than a member of the festival of light, but I saw Erica whisper to Nick, and he held her hand, shushing her.

'Mr Rumpole!' Sam had flushed beneath his wig. I took a swift move to lower his blood pressure.

'I apologize my Lord. Pure, unnecessary comment. I withdraw it at once.'

'Your Mr Rumpole is doing us proud,' I heard Mr Myers whisper to Albert who replied complacently, 'His old hand has lost none of its cunning, Myersy.'

After a dramatic pause, I played the ace. 'How old were you when you had the abortion?'

I looked round the Court and met Erica's look; not exactly a gaze of enraptured congratulation.

'I was nineteen ... It was perfectly legal.' Miss Evans was now on the defensive. 'I got a certificate. From the psychiatrist.'

'Saying you were unfit for childbirth?'

'I suppose so.'

'And the psychiatrist certified ... you were

116

emotionally unstable?' It was a shot in the bloody dark, but I imagine that's what trick cyclists always say, to prevent any unwanted increase in the population.

'Something like that ... yes.' I gave Ken Aspen a cheering glance. He was busy writing a note, containing, I hoped, more ammunition for Rumpole in the firing line.

'So the jury have to rely, in this case, on the evidence of a young woman who has been certified emotionally unstable.'

The jury were looking delightfully doubtful as the usher brought me the note from the dock. No ammunition, not even any congratulation, but just one line scrawled, 'Leave her alone now, please! K.A.' I crumpled the note with visible irritation; in such a mood, no doubt, did Nelson put the glass to his blind eye when reading the signal to retreat.

'Just three months ago, you were rushed into hospital. You'd taken a number of sleeping tablets. By accident?' I continued to attack.

'No.'

'Why?'

'Well, it was ... I told you. I'd just parted from Paul.'

'Come now, Miss Evans. Just think. You'd parted from Paul over a year ago.'

'I was ... I was confused.'

'Was it then you first met Mr Aspen?'

'Just ... Just about that time.'

'And fell in love with him?'

'No!'

She was really angry now, but she managed to smile at the jury who didn't smile back. If I could

117

have dropped dead of a coronary at that moment, I thought, Miss Bridget Evans might be dancing for joy.

'Became so obsessed with him that you were determined to pursue him at any cost to him, or to his family?'

'Shall I tell you the truth? I didn't even like him!'

'And that night after you and Mr Aspen had made love...'

'Love! Is that what you call it?'

'He refused to leave his wife and children.'

'We never discussed his wife and children!'

'And it was in rage, because he wouldn't leave his family, that you made up this charge to ruin him. You hate him so much.'

'I don't hate him.'

'Oh. Can it be you are still in love with him?'

'I never hated him, I tell you. I was indifferent to him.'

It was the answer I wanted, and just the moment to hold up the poster of Ken's face, scrawled on by Miss Evans in her fury.

'So indifferent that you did that. To his face on the wall?'

'Perhaps. After.'

'Before! Because you had done that early in the evening, hadn't you? In one of your crazy fits of rage and jealousy?'

Now Bridget Evans was crying, her face in her hands, but whether in fury or grief, or simply to stop the questions, not I but the jury would have to judge.

'Will that poster be Exhibit 24, Mr Rumpole?' Sam spoke in his best matter-of-fact judge's voice,

118

and I gave him a bow of deep satisfaction and said, 'If your Lordship pleases.'

★   ★   ★

'Is *that* your work?' I was entertaining Nick and Erica to an *après*-Court drink in Pommeroy's Wine Bar. A group from Chambers, Guthrie Featherstone, Erskine-Brown, my friend George Frobisher and old Uncle Tom were at the bar. The Rumpole family occupied a table in that part of Pommeroy's where ladies are allowed to assemble. I felt as if I'd spent a day digging the roads, in a muck sweat and exhausted after the cross-examination. I was, of course, moderately well pleased with the way it had gone and I had asked Joan the waitress to bring us a bottle of Pommeroy's cooking champagne, and Erica's special, a Coca-Cola. When it came I took a quick glassful and answered her question.

'When it goes well. We made a bit of headway, this afternoon.'

'You sure did.'

'Erica was a bit upset,' Nick looked from one to the other of us, embarrassed.

'Is that the way you make your living?' Erica repeated.

'A humble living. With an occasional glass of cooking champagne, with paying briefs.'

'Attacking women?' I must confess I hadn't thought of Bridget Evans as a woman, but as a witness. I tried to explain.

'Not women in particular. I attack anyone, regardless of age or sex, who chooses to attack my client.'

'God knows which is the criminal. Him or her.'

'But, old darling. That's what we're rather trying to find out.'

'What worries Ricky is,' Nick was doing his best to explain, 'the girl has to go through all that. I mean, it's not only the rape.'

'Not *only* the rape?'

'Well, it's like *she's* getting punished, isn't it?'

'Aren't you rather rushing things? I mean, who's saying a rape took place?'

'Well, isn't she?'

'Oh, I see. You think it's enough if she *says* it? It's a different sort of crime, is it? I mean, not like murder or shoplifting, or forging cheques. They still have to be proved in the old-fashioned way. But rape ... Some dotty girl only has to *say* you did it and you trot off to chokey without asking embarrassing questions ... Look, you don't want to discuss a boring old case. What've you been doing Nick? Getting ready for Warwick?'

But Erica wasn't to be deterred.

'Of course we should discuss the case.' She'd have made an advocate, this Erica, she was dogged. 'I mean, it's the greatest act of aggression that any human being can inflict!'

'Ricky! Dad's just doing his job. I'm sorry we came.' Nicky looked at his watch, no doubt hoping they had an appointment.

'I'm glad! Oh sure I'm glad,' Erica was smiling, quite mirthlessly. 'He's a field study in archaic attitudes!'

'Look, old sweetheart. Is it archaic to believe in some sort of equality of the sexes?'

She looked taken aback at that. 'Equality! You're into equality?'

120

'For God's sake, yes! Give you equal pay, certainly. Let you be all-in wrestlers and Lord Chancellor. By all means! I'll even make the supreme sacrifice and give up giving my seat in the bus ... But you're asking for women witnesses to be more equal than any other witnesses!'

'But in that sort of case,' Erica wasn't to be won over by any sort of irony, 'a man forcing his masculinity...'

'Or a woman getting her revenge?' I suggested. 'I mean, I don't suppose I'll ever have to actually choose between being raped and being put in the cooler for five years, banged up with a bar of soap and a chamber pot, but if I ever had...'

'You're being defensive again!' Erica smiled at me, quite tolerantly.

'Am I?'

'The argument's kind of painful so you make a little joke.'

'Perhaps. But it's not exactly a joke. I mean, have you considered the possibility of my client being innocent?'

'Well, he'd better be. That's all I can say. After what you did to that girl this afternoon, he'd better be!'

Then Nick remembered they were due at the pictures and they left me, Erica with the warm feeling of having struck a blow for her sex, Nick perhaps a little torn between us, but holding Erica's arm he steered her out. I went over to the bar for a packet of small cigars and there were the learned friends poring over a pink slip of paper which Jack Pommeroy was showing them. As soon as I drew up beside the bar, Jack showed me the cheque; it was made out to me from a firm of

121

solicitors called Sprout and Pennyweather and had my name scrawled on the back. It was for the princely sum of nine pounds fifty, my remuneration for a conference. I looked at my purported signature and felt unaccountably depressed.

'No need to tell us, Rumpole,' said Guthrie Featherstone, q.c., m.p. 'It's Albert's signature.'

★   ★   ★

'It's peaceful down here. Extraordinarily peaceful.'

The Honourable Member was eating spaghetti rings and drinking hot, sweet tea down in the cells; Sam Parkin had declined bail in the lunch hour. He seemed extraordinarily contented, a fact which worried me not a little.

'I'm afraid it's hardly a three rosettes in the Michelin, as far as the grub's concerned,' I apologized to Aspen.

'It's tasteless stodge. Like nursery tea. Sort of comforting.'

'Really there are only two important things to remember. One. You saw the poster scribbled on as soon as you came into the room.' I tried to wrench his attention back to the case. 'And you believed she wanted it. That's all! You just believed it.'

'Did you *have* to ask her those questions?' Aspen looked at me, more in sorrow than in anger.

'Yes.'

'Dragging out her life, for the vultures in the press box.'

122

'I want you to win.' This bizarre ambition of mine made the Honourable Member smile.

'You sound like my wife. She wants me to win. Always. I'm so tired. It's peaceful down here, isn't it? Very peaceful.'

'Look out old darling. You're not falling in love with the Nick, are you?' I had seen it before, that terrible look of resignation.

'For years, oh, as long as I can remember, Anna's worked so hard. On me winning.' He seemed to be talking to himself; I felt strangely superfluous. 'Sitting on platforms. Chatting up ministers. Keeping in with the press. Trying to convince the faithful that it all still meant something. My wife ... Anna, you know. She wanted me in the cabinet. She'd like to have been—a minister's wife.'

'And what did you want?' It was a long time before he answered me, and then he said, 'I wanted it to stop!'

★   ★   ★

Calling your own client is the worst part of a trial. You can't attack him, or lead him, or do anything but stand with your palms sweating and hope to God the old nitwit tells the right story. Mrs Aspen was staring at her husband, as if to transfer to him a little of her indomitable will. He stood in the witness box, smiling gently, as though someone else was on trial and he was a not very interested spectator. I showed him the defaced poster and asked the five thousand dollar question, 'Did you see that had been done when you went into the room?'

123

He looked at me almost as if I was the one to be pitied, and said, after a pause, 'I can't remember.'

I smiled as if I'd got exactly the answer I wanted, a bit of a sickly smile. 'Did Miss Evans start talking about your wife?'

'About Anna. Yes.'

'Did she want you to leave your wife?'

'Did she?' Sam Parkin was helping me out in the silence.

'I can't ... I can't exactly remember. She went on and on, goading me.'

'What happened then?'

It was then the Honourable Member showed his first sign of passion. 'She'd been asking for it! All that clap-trap about betraying the Party. All those clichés about power corrupting. I suddenly got angry. It was then I...'

'Then you what?'

'Made...Made love to her.'

'In anger?' Sam Parkin was frowning.

'I suppose so. Yes.'

I saw Anna's look of fear, and then the judge leaned forward to ask, 'Just tell us this, Mr Aspen. Did you believe that was what she wanted?'

So the old darling on the bench had chucked Ken Aspen a lifebelt. I hoped to God the drowning man wasn't going to push it away. It seemed about a year before he answered. 'I don't know, what I believed then. Exactly.'

★   ★   ★

'It wasn't your fault, if I may say sir.' When I got back to the clerk's room, Albert was, as ever,

124

consoling. 'It was the client.'

'That's right, Albert. These things are always so much easier without clients.'

I saw that Henry, our second clerk, was smiling as he told me that there was a Chambers meeting and I was to go up to our learned leader's room. When Albert offered to take me up, Henry said that Featherstone had said that it was a meeting for members of Chambers only, and our head clerk wasn't invited. Albert looked at me and I could see he was worried.

'Cheer up Albert,' I told him. 'See you at Pommeroy's later.'

Featherstone was pouring us all Earl Grey out of his fine bone china tea service.

'It seems that Albert has been pursuing a long career of embezzlement,' he said as he handed round sugar.

'That seems a very long word for nine pounds fifty,' I told them. 'I'd say the correct legal expression was fiddling.'

'I don't see how we can excuse crime. Whatever you call it.' Erskine-Brown was clearly appearing for the prosecution.

'Anyway, it was my nine pounds fifty. It seems to me I can call it what I like. I can call it a Christmas present.'

At which Uncle Tom, who was dozing in the corner said, 'I suppose it will be Christmas again soon. How depressing.'

'Apparently, it's not just *your* money, Rumpole.' Featherstone sat judicially behind his desk.

'Isn't it? Is there the slightest evidence that anyone else suffered?' I asked the assembled

125

company.

'The petty cash!' Erskine-Brown was the only one to answer.

'I told you about the petty cash.' I was too tired to argue with Erskine-Brown.

'You told me *you'd* borrowed from Albert's float.'

'Yes. And paid for the drinks in Pommeroy's.'

'You were lying, weren't you, Rumpole?' Now even Featherstone realized Erskine-Brown had gone too far. 'Erskine-Brown,' he said. 'That's not the sort of language we use to another member of Chambers. If Rumpole says he borrowed the money then I for one am prepared to accept his word as a gentleman.'

Suddenly I grew impatient with the learned friends. I pushed myself to my feet. 'Then you're a fool, that's all I can say as a gentleman. Of course I was lying.'

'What does Rumpole say he was doing?' Uncle Tom asked George for information.

'Lying.'

'Dear me, how extraordinary.'

'I lied because I don't like people being condemned,' I explained. 'It goes against my natural instincts.'

'That's very true. He never prosecutes. You don't prosecute, do you, Rumpole?' George gave me a friendly smile. I liked old George.

'No. I don't prosecute.'

'All right. Now we'll hear Rumpole's defence of Albert.' Erskine-Brown leant back in Featherstone's big leather chair, trying to look like a juvenile judge.

'It doesn't seem to me that it's Albert that's in

126

trouble.'

'Not in trouble?'

'It's us! Legal gentlemen. Learned friends. So friendly and so gentlemanly that we never check his books, or ask to see his accounts. Of course he cheats us, little small bits of cheating, nine pounds fifty, to buy a solicitor a drink or two in Pommeroy's. He feels it's a mark of respect. Due to a gent. Like calling you "Sir" when you go wittering on about the typing errors in your statement of claim.'

'Rather an odd mark of respect, wouldn't you say, Rumpole?' Featherstone stopped me, and called the meeting to order. 'I move we vote on this.'

'It's a matter for the police,' Erskine-Brown said predictably.

'Rumpole. You wouldn't agree?' The learned leader was asking for my vote.

'You'd hardly expect him to.' Erskine-Brown could never let a sleeping Rumpole lie.

'Well ... Albert's part of my life ... He always has been.'

'I remember when Albert first came to us. As a boy. He was always whistling out of tune.' Uncle Tom was reminiscing. And I added my tuppence worth. 'He's like the worn-out lino in the Chambers loo and the cells under the Old Bailey. I feel comfortable with Albert. He's like home. And he goes out and grubs for briefs in a way we're too gentlemanly to consider.'

'He's cheated us. There's no getting away from that.' George interrupted me, quite gently.

'Well, we've got to be cheated occasionally. That's what it's all about, isn't it?' I looked round

127

at their blank faces. 'Otherwise you'd spend your whole life counting your change and adding up bills, and chucking grown men into chokey because they didn't live up to the high ideals of the Chambers, or the Party, or some bloody nonsense.'

'I don't know that I exactly follow.' George was doing his best.

'Neither do I. I've done a rather bloody case. I'm sorry.' I sat down beside our oldest member. 'How are you, Uncle Tom?'

'I never expected Christmas to come again so quickly!' This was Uncle Tom's contribution. Now Featherstone was summing up. 'Personally, speaking quite personally, and without in any way condoning the seriousness of Albert's conduct...'

'Rape's bloody tiring,' I told them. 'Specially when you lose.'

'I would be against calling the police.' This was Featherstone's judgement.

'Not very gentlemanly having Old Bill in Chambers. Stamping with his great feet all over the petty cash vouchers.' I lit my last small cigar.

'On the other hand, Albert, in my view, must be asked to leave immediately. All those in favour?' At Featherstone's request all the other hands went up.

'Well, Rumpole,' said Erskine-Brown, teller for the 'Ayes'. 'Have you anything to say?'

'Have you anything to say why sentence of death should not be passed against you?' I blew out smoke as I told them an old chestnut. 'They say Mr Justice Snaggs once asked a murderer that. "Bugger all", came a mutter from the dock. So Snaggs J. says to the murderer's counsel, "Did your client *say* something?" "Bugger all, my Lord," the counsel replied. "Funny thing," says Mr Justice Snaggs. "I thought I heard him *say* something."' My story ended in a hoot of silence. It was one that my old clerk Albert laughed at quite often, in Pommeroy's Wine Bar.

★   ★   ★

A couple of night later I was sitting alone in Pommeroy's, telling myself a few old legal anecdotes, when to my surprise and delight Nick walked in alone. He sat down and I ordered a bottle of the best Chateau Fleet Street.

'I dropped into Chambers. Albert wasn't there.'

'No. We have a new clerk. Henry.'

'I'm sorry about the case.'

'Yes. The Honourable Member got five years.' I took a mouthful of claret to wash away the taste of prisons, and saw Nick looking at me. 'He had a strong desire to be found guilty. I don't know why exactly.'

'So really you needn't have asked all those questions?'

'Well, yes, Nick. Yes. I had to ask them. Now, are we going to see you both on Sunday?'

There was a pause. Nick looked at me. He obviously had something far more difficult to communicate than the old confessions of poker games in the deserted vicarage during his schooldays.

'I wanted to tell you first. You see. Well, I've decided to take the job in Baltimore. Ricky wants to go back. I mean, we can get a house there ... and ... well, her family'd miss her if she were

129

stuck with me in England.'

'*Her* family?'

'They're very close.'

'Yes. Yes, I suppose they are.'

'Apparently her mother hates the idea of Ricky being in England.' He smiled 'She's the sort of woman that'd start sending us food parcels.'

I could think of nothing to say, except, 'It was good of you, Nick. Good of you to spare the time to drop into Chambers.'

'We'll be back quite often. Ricky and I. We'll be back for visits.'

'You and Ricky, of course. Well then, Cheers.'

We had one for our respective roads and I gave my son a bit of advice. 'There's one thing you'll have to be careful of, you know, living in America.'

'What's that?'

'The hygiene! It can be most awfully dangerous. The purity! The terrible determination not to adulterate anything! You will be very careful of it, won't you, Nick?'

*   *   *

Some weeks later, as I was packing the bulging briefcase after breakfast for a day down the Bailey with a rather objectionable fraud, She Who Must Be Obeyed came in with a postcard from our son and his intended, written in mid-air, with a handsome picture of a jet and a blue sky on the front and kisses from Nick and Ricky on the back. I handed it back to her and she gave it an attentive re-read as she sat down for another cup of tea. Then she said, 'You know why Erica went

130

back home, don't you?'

I confessed total ignorance.

'She didn't like it when she came to see you in Court. She didn't like the way you asked all those questions. She made that quite clear, when they were here for lunch last Sunday. When they came to say "Good-bye". She thought the questions you asked that girl were tasteless.'

'Distasteful.' I was on my way to the door. 'That's the word. Distasteful.'

'There's a picture of their jet on the front of this postcard.'

'I saw it. Very handsome.' I opened the kitchen door as dramatically as possible. *'Fare thee well! and if forever still forever, fare thee well.'* It takes a bad moment to make me fall back on Lord Byron.

'Don't be silly.' Hilda frowned. 'What're you going to do today, Rumpole?'

It was a day, like all the others, and I said, 'I suppose. Go on asking distasteful questions.'

RUMPOLE AND THE MARRIED LADY

Life at the Bar has its ups and downs, and there are times when there is an appalling decrease in crime, when all the decent villains seem to have gone on holiday to the Costa Brava, and lawfulness breaks out. At such times, Rumpole is unemployed, as I was one morning when I got up late and sat in the kitchen dawdling over breakfast in my dressing gown and slippers, much to the annoyance of She Who Must be Obeyed who was getting the coffee cups shipshape so that they could be piped on board to do duty as teacups later in the day. I was winning my daily battle with the tormented mind who writes *The Times* crossword, when Hilda, not for the first time in our joint lives, compared me unfavourably with her late father.

'Daddy got to Chambers dead at nine every day of his life!'

'Your old dad, old C. H. Wystan, got to Chambers dead on nine and spent the morning on *The Times* crossword. I do it at home, that's the difference between us. You should be grateful.'

'Grateful?' Hilda frowned.

'For the companionship,' I suggested.

'I want you out of the house, Rumpole. Don't you understand that? So I can clear up the kitchen!'

'*O woman! in our hours of ease Uncertain, coy and hard to please.*' Hilda doesn't like poetry, I could tell by her heavy sigh.

'Just a little peace. So I can be alone. To get on with things.'

'And when I come home a little late in the evenings. When I stop for a moment in Pommeroy's Wine Bar, to give myself strength to face the Inner Circle. You never seem particularly grateful to have been left alone in the house. To get on with things!'

'You've been wasting time. That's what I resent.'

'*I wasted Time—and now doth Time waste me.*' I switched from Scott to Shakespeare. The reaction of my life-mate was no better.

'Chattering to that idiot George Frobisher! I really don't know why you bother to come home at all. Now Nick's gone it seems quite unnecessary.'

'Nick?' It was a year since Nick had gone to America and we hadn't had a letter since Christmas.

'You know what I mean! We used to be a family. We had to try at least, for Nick's sake. Oh, why don't you go to work?'

'Nick'll be back.' I moved from the table and put an arm on her shoulder. She shook it off.

'Do you believe that? When he's got married? When he's got his job at the University of Baltimore? Why on earth should he want to come back to Gloucester Road?'

'He'll want to come back sometime. To see us. He'll want to hear all our news. What I've been doing in Court,' I said, giving Hilda her opening.

'What you've been doing in Court? You haven't been doing anything in Court apparently!'

At which moment the phone rang in our

133

living-room and Hilda, who loves activity, dashed to answer it. I heard her telling the most appalling lies through the open door.

'No, it's *Mrs* Rumpole. I'll see if I can catch him. He's just rushing out of the door on his way to work.'

I joined her in my dressing gown; it was my new clerk, the energetic Henry. He wanted me to come into Chambers for a conference, and I asked him if the world had come to its senses and crime was back in its proper place in society. No, he told me, as a matter of fact it wasn't crime at all.

'You haven't even shaved!' Hilda rebuked me. 'Daddy'd never have spoken to his clerk on the telephone before he'd had a shave!'

I put down the telephone and gave Mrs Rumpole a look which I hoped was enigmatic. 'It's a divorce,' I told her.

★   ★   ★

As I walked through the Temple, puffing a small cigar on the way to the factory, I considered the question of divorce. Well, you've got to take what you can nowadays, and I suppose divorce is in a fairly healthy state. Divorce figures are rising. What's harder to understand is the enormous popularity of marriage! I remembered the scene at breakfast that morning, and I really began to wonder how marriage ever became so popular. I mean, was it 'Home Life' with She Who Must Be Obeyed? Gloucester Road seemed to be my place of work, of hard, back-breaking toil. It was a relief to get down to the Temple, for relaxation. By that time I had reached my Chambers, No. 1 Equity Court, a place of peace and quiet. It felt like home.

When I got into the hallway I opened the door of the clerk's room, and was greeted by an extraordinary sight. A small boy, I judged him to be about ten years old, was seated on a chair beside Dianne our typist. He was holding a large, lit-up model of a jet aeroplane and zooming it through the air at a noise level which would have been quite unacceptable to the New York Port authority.

I shut the door and beat a hasty retreat to the privacy of my sanctum. But when I opened my own door I was astounded to see a youngish female seated in my chair, wearing horn-rimmed specs and apparently interviewing a respectable middle-aged lady and a man who gave every appearance of being an instructing solicitor. I shut that door also and turned to find the zealous Henry crossing the hall towards me, bearing the most welcome object in my small world, a brief.

'Henry,' I said in some panic. 'There's a woman, seated in my chair!'

'Miss Phyllida Trant, sir. She's been with us for the last few months. Ex-pupil of Mr Erskine-Brown. You haven't met her?'

I searched my memory. 'I've met the occasional whiff of French perfume on the stairs.'

'Miss Trant's anxious to widen her experience.'

'Hence the French perfume?'

'She wants to know if she could sit in on your divorce case. I've got the brief here. "Thripp v. Thripp." You're the wife, Mr Rumpole.'

'Am I? Jolly good.' I took the brief and life

135

improved considerably at the sight of the figure written on it. 'Marked a hundred and fifty guineas! These Thripps are the sort to breed from! Oh, and I don't know if you're aware of *this*, Henry. There seems to be a child in the clerk's room, with an aeroplane!'

'He's here for the conference.'

I didn't follow his drift. 'What's the child done? It doesn't want a divorce too?'

'It's the child of the family in "Thripp *v.* Thripp",' Henry explained patiently, 'and I rather gather the chief bone of contention. So long now, Mr Rumpole.' He moved away towards the clerk's room. 'Sorry to have interrupted your day at home.'

'You can interrupt my day at home any time you like, for a brief marked a hundred and fifty guineas! Miss Phyllida *Trant*, did you say?'

'Yes sir. You don't mind her sitting in, do you?'

'Couldn't you put her off, Henry? Tell her a divorce case is sacrosanct. It'd be like a priest inviting a few lady friends to join in the confessional.'

'I told her you'd have no objection. Miss Trant's very keen to practise.'

'Then couldn't she practise at home?'

'We're about the only Chambers without a woman, Mr Rumpole. It's not good for our image.' He seemed determined, so I gave him a final thought on my way into the conference. 'Our old clerk Albert never wanted a woman in Chambers. He said there wasn't the lavatory accommodation.'

*   *   *

136

So there I was at the desk having a conference in a divorce case with Miss Phyllida Trant 'sitting in', Mr Perfect the solicitor looking grave, and the client, Mrs Thripp, leaning forward and regarding me with gentle trusting eyes. As I say, she seemed an extremely nice and respectable woman, and I wasn't to know that she was to cause me more trouble than all the murderers I have ever defended.

'As soon as you came into the room I felt *safe* somehow, Mr Rumpole. I knew Norman and I would be safe with you.'

'Norman?'

'The child of the family.' Miss Trant supplied the information.

'Thank you, Miss Trant. The little aviator in the clerk's room. Quite. But if I'm to help you, you'll have to do your best to help me too.'

'Anything! What is it you want exactly?' Mrs Thripp seemed entirely co-operative.

'Well, dear lady, a couple of black eyes would come in extremely handy,' I said hopefully. Mrs Thripp looked at Miss Trant, puzzled.

'Mr Rumpole means, has your husband ever used physical violence?' Miss Trant explained.

'Well, no ... Not actual violence.'

'Pity.' I commiserated with her. 'Mr Thripp doesn't show a very helpful attitude. You see, if we're going to prove "cruelty"...'

'We don't have to, do we?' I noticed then that Miss Trant was sitting in front of a pile of legal text books. 'Intolerable conduct. Since the Divorce Law Reform Act 1969.'

I thought then that it's not the frivolity that

makes women intolerable, it's the ghastly enthusiasm, the mustard keeness to get into the lacrosse team, the relentless drive to learn the Divorce Law Reform Act by heart: that *and* the French perfume. I could have managed that conference quite nicely without Miss Trant. I said to her, however, as politely as possible, 'The Divorce Law Reform Act, which year did you say?'

'1969.'

'Yes,' I smiled at Mrs Thripp. 'Well, you know how it is. Go down the Old Bailey five minutes and you've found they've passed another Divorce Reform Act. Thank you, Miss Trant, for reminding me. Now then what's this intolerable conduct, exactly?'

'He doesn't speak,' Mrs Thripp told me.

'Well, a little silence can come as something of a relief. In the wear and tear of married life.'

'I don't think you understand,' Mrs Thripp smiled patiently. 'He hasn't spoken a word to me for three years.'

'*Three* years? Good God! How does he communicate?' The instructing solicitor laid a number of little bits of paper on my desk.

'By means of notes.'

I then discovered that the man Thripp, who I was not in the least surprised to learn was a chartered accountant, used his matrimonial home as a sort of Post Office. When he wished to communicate with his wife he typed out brusque and businesslike notes, documents which threw a blinding light, in my opinion, on the man's character.

'To my so-called wife,' one note read, 'if you

138

and your so-called son want to swim in hot water you can go to the Public Baths. From your so-called husband.' This was fixed, it seemed, to a padlocked geyser. Another billet doux was found in the biscuit tin in the larder. 'To my so-called wife. I have removed what you left of the assorted tea biscuits to the office for safe keeping. Are you determined to eat me into bankruptcy? Your so-called husband.' 'To my so-called wife. I'm going out to my Masonic Ladies' Night tomorrow (Wednesday). It's a pity I haven't got a lady to take with me. Don't bother to wait up for me. Your so-called husband, F. Thripp.'

I made two observations about this correspondence, one was that it revealed a depth of human misery which no reasonable woman would tolerate, and the other was that all the accountant Thripp's notes were written on an Italian portable, about ten years old.

'My husband's got an old Olivetti. He can't really type,' Mrs Thripp told me.

Many years ago I scored a notable victory in the 'Great Brighton Benefit Club Forgery' case, and it was during those proceedings I acquired my vast knowledge of typewriters. Having solved the question of the type, however, got me no nearer the heart of the mystery.

'Let me understand,' I said to Mrs Thripp. 'Are you interested in someone else?'

'Someone else?' Mrs Thripp looked pained.

'You're clearly an intelligent, obviously still a reasonably attractive woman.'

'Thank you, Mr Rumpole,' Mrs Thripp smiled modestly.

'Are there not other fish in your particular sea?'

'One man's quite enough for me, thank you.'

'I see. Apparently you're still *living* with your husband.'

'Living with him? Of course I'm living with him. The flat's in our joint names.' Mrs Thripp said this as though it explained everything. I was still bewildered.

'Wouldn't you, and the young hopeful outside, be better off somewhere else? *Anywhere* else?'

'There's your mother in Ruislip.' Mr Perfect supplied the information.

'Thank you Mr Perfect.' I turned back to Mrs Thripp. 'As your solicitor points out. Anyone's mother in Ruislip must surely be better than life with a chartered accountant who locks up the geyser! And removes the tea biscuits to his office.'

'I move out?' Apparently the thought had never occurred to her.

'Unless you're a glutton for punishment.'

'Move out? And let *him* get away with it?'

I rose to my feet, and tried to put the point more clearly. 'Your flat in Muswell Hill, scene of historic events though it may well be, is not the field of Waterloo, Mrs Thripp, if you withdraw to happier pastures there would be no defeat, no national disaster.'

'Mrs Thripp is anxious about the furniture,' Mr Perfect offered an explanation.

'The furniture?'

'She's afraid her husband would dispose of the lounge suite if she left the flat.'

'How much human suffering can be extracted by a *lounge suite*?' I asked the rhetorical question. 'I can't believe it's the furniture.'

There was a brief silence and then Mrs Thripp

140

asked quietly, 'Won't you take me on, Mr Rumpole?'

I thought of the rent and the enormous amounts of money She Who Must Be Obeyed spends on luxuries like Vim. I also remembered the fact that crime seemed remarkably thin on the ground and said I, 'Of course, dear lady. Of course I'll take you on! That's what I'm here for. Like an old taxi cab waiting in the rank. Been waiting quite a little time, if you want to know the truth. You snap your fingers and I'll drive you almost anywhere you want to go. Only it'd be a help if we knew exactly what destination you had in mind.'

'I've told Mr Perfect what I want.'

'You want a divorce. Those are my instructions,' Mr Perfect told me, but his client put it a little differently.

'I want my husband taken to Court. Those are *my* instructions, Mr Rumpole.'

*   *   *

I have spoken in these reminiscences of my old friend George Frobisher. George is a bachelor who has lived in an hotel in Kensington since his sister died. He is a gentle soul, unfitted by temperament for a knock-about career at the Bar, but he is a pleasant companion for a drink at Pommeroy's after the heat and labour of the day. That evening I bought the first round, two large clarets, flushed with the remunerative collapse of the Thripp marriage.

'Things are looking up, George,' I raised my glass to my old friend and he, in turn, toasted me.

141

'A little.'

'There's light at the end of the tunnel. Today I got a hundred and fifty pound brief. For a divorce.'

'That's funny. So did I.' George sounded puzzled.

'Sure to last at least six days. Six refreshers at fifty pounds a day. Think of that, George! Well, there's that much to be said. For the institution of marriage?'

'I never felt the need of marriage somehow,' George told me.

'*With one chained friend, perhaps a jealous deadly foe,   The longest and the dreariest journey go.*' I gave George a snatch of Shelley and a refill.

'I've had a bit of an insight into marriage. Since reading that divorce brief.' George was in a thoughtful mood.

'If we were married we couldn't sit pleasantly together,' I told him. 'You'd be worrying what time I got home. And when I did get home you wouldn't be pleased to see me!'

'I really can't see why a person puts up with marriage,' George went on. 'When a woman starts conversing with her husband by means of little notes!'

I looked at him curiously. 'Got one of those, have you?' There seemed to be an epidemic of matrimonial note-leaving.

'*And* she cut the ends off his trousers.' George seemed deeply shocked.

'Sounds a sordid sort of case. Cheers!' We refreshed ourselves with Pommeroy's claret and George went on to tell me about his divorce.

'He was going to an evening at his Lodge. You

142

know what this Jezebel did? Only snipped off the ends of his evening trousers. With nail scissors.'

'Intolerable conduct that, you know. Under the 1969 Act.' I kept George abreast of the law.

'Moss Bros was closed. The wretched fellow had to turn up at the Café Royal with bags that looked as if they'd been gnawed by rats. Well! That's marriage for you. Thank God I live by myself, in the Royal Borough Hotel.'

'Snug as a bug in there, are you George?'

'We have television in the Residents' Lounge now. Coloured television. Look here, you must dine with me there one night, Rumpole. Bring Hilda if you'd care to.'

'We'd like to George. Coloured television? Well, I say. That'll be a treat.'

'Quiet life, of course. But the point of it is. A man can keep his trousers more or less safe from destruction in the Royal Borough Hotel.'

*   *   *

I must admit that George Frobisher and I loitered a little in Pommeroy's that night and, when I got home, Hilda had apparently gone up to bed; she often had an early night with a glass of milk and a library book. I went into the kitchen and switched on the light. All was quiet on the Western front, but I saw it on the table—a note from my lady wife.

'If you condescend to come home, your dinner's in the oven.' I took the hint and was removing a red-hot plate of congealed stew from the bowels of our ancient cooker when the telephone rang in the living-room. I went to

143

answer it and heard a woman's voice.

'I just *had* to ring you. I feel so alone in the world, so terribly lonely.'

'Look it's not terribly convenient. Just now.' It was my client in the case of Thripp *v.* Thripp.

'Don't say that! It's my life. How can you say it's not convenient?'

'All right. A quick word.' I supposed the ancient stew could wait a little longer.

'He's going to say the most terrible things about me. I've got to see you.'

'Shall we say tomorrow, four o'clock. But not here!' I told her firmly.

'I don't know how I can wait.'

'You've waited for three years haven't you? Look forward to seeing you then. Goodnight now, beloved lady.' I said that, I suppose, to cheer up Mrs Thripp and to soften the blow as I put down the receiver. Just before I did so I heard a little click, and remembered that Hilda had insisted on an extension in our bedroom.

★   ★   ★

The next day our clerk's room was buzzing. Henry was on the telephone dispatching barristers to far-flung Magistrates Courts. That smooth young barrister, Erskine-Brown, was opening his post and collecting papers, and Uncle Tom, old T. C. Rowley, was starting his day of leisure in Chambers by standing by the mantelpiece and greeting the workers. The ops room was even graced by the presence of our Head of Chambers, Guthrie Featherstone, Q.C., M.P., who was taking time off from such vital affairs of state as the

Poultry Marketing Act to supervise Dianne who was beating out one of his learned opinions on our old standard Imperial.

Henry told me that my divorce conference was waiting in my room, and Erskine-Brown gave his most condescending smile. 'Divorcing now, Rumpole?' he asked me. I told him I was and asked him if he was still foreclosing on mortgages. 'I'm all for a bit of divorce in Chambers,' Featherstone smiled tolerantly. 'Widens our repertoire. You were getting into a bit of a rut with all that crime, Horace.'

'Crime! It seems a better world. A cleaner world. Down at the Old Bailey,' I told him.

'Don't you find criminal clients a little— depressing?'

'Criminal clients? They behave so well.'

'Really Rumpole?' Erskine-Brown sounded quite shocked.

'What do they do?' I asked him. 'Knock people on the head, rob banks, cause, at the worst, a temporary inconvenience. They don't converse by means of notes. They don't lock up the geyser. They don't indulge in three years silence to celebrate the passage of love.'

'Love? Have you become an expert on that, Rumpole?' Erskine-Brown seemed amused. '*Rumpole in Love*. Should sell a bomb at the Solicitors' Law Stationers.'

'And I'll tell you another great advantage of criminal customers,' I went on. 'They're locked up, mostly, pending trial! They can't ring you up at all hours of the day and night. Now you get involved in a divorce and your life's taken over!'

'We used to have all the facts of divorce cases

145

printed out in detail in *The Times*,' Uncle Tom remembered.

'Oh, hello, Uncle Tom.'

'It used to make amusing reading! Better than all this rubbish they print now, about the Common Market. Far more entertaining.'

Erskine-Brown left to go about his business, not before I had told him that divorce, for all its drawbacks, was a great deal less sordid than foreclosing on mortgages and then Henry presented me with another brief, a mere twenty-five guineas this time, to be heard by old Archie McFee, the Dock Street magistrate.

'You're an old girl called Mrs Wainscott, sir,' Henry told me. 'Charged with keeping a disorderly house.'

'An old Pro? Is this what I've sunk to now, Henry? Plodding the pavements! Flogging my aged charms round the Dock Street Magistrates Court!' I checked the figure on the front of the brief. 'Twenty-five smackers! Not bad, I suppose. For a short time in Dock Street. Makes you wonder what I could earn round the West End.'

I left Henry then; he seemed not to be amused.

★   ★   ★

The other side, that is to say Mr F. Thripp and his legal advisers, had supplied his wife, married in some far-off and rash moment in a haze of champagne and orange blossom, with the evidence to be used against her. I was somewhat dismayed when I discovered that this evidence included an equal number of notes, typed on the same old Olivetti as that used by the husband, but travelling in the opposite direction. I picked out at random, 'To my so-called husband. If you want your shirts washed, take them down to the office and let *her* do them. She does everything else for you doesn't she? Your so-called wife.'

'Oh dear, Mrs Thripp. I wish you hadn't written this.' I put down the note which I had been viewing through a magnifying glass to check the type. 'By the way, whom did you suspect of doing his washing for him?'

I looked at the client, so did Miss Trant who was 'sitting in' in pursuit of knowledge of Rumpole's methods, so did Mr Perfect. Master Norman Thripp, who had joined us, sat in a corner pointing a toy sub-machine gun at me in a way I did my best to ignore.

'Who?'

'We had him watched Mr Rumpole,' Mr Perfect told me.

'He has an elderly secretary. Apparently she's a grandmother. There doesn't seem to be anyone else.'

'There doesn't seem to be anyone else for either of you.' I picked up the husband's answer. 'He alleges you assaulted his trousers.'

'No. No I didn't do that, Mr Rumpole.'

'His evening trousers were damaged apparently.'

'Probably at the cleaners. You remember, he refused to take me to his Ladies Night—he went on his own, so his trousers can't have been all that bad can they?'

'Did you *mind* him going?' I was finding the Thripp marriage more and more mysterious.

'Mind? Of course I minded.'

147

'Why?'

'Because I wanted to go with him, of course.'

'You wanted to go with the man who hasn't spoken to you for three years, who communicates by wretched little notes, who locked up your bath water?'

At this point Mrs Thripp brought out a small lace handkerchief and started to sob.

'I don't know. I don't *know* why I wanted to go with him.'

The sobs increased in volume. I looked at Mrs Thripp with deep approval.

'All right, Mrs Thripp. I'm simply asking the questions your husband's barrister will ask unless we're extremely lucky.'

'You think my case is hopeless?' Mrs Thripp was mopping up noisily.

'Mr Rumpole's afraid you may not make a good witness.' It was Miss Phyllida Trant, giving her learned opinion uninvited.

'Miss Trant!' I'm afraid I was somewhat sharp with her. 'You may know all about Divorce Law Reform Acts. But I know all about witnesses. Mrs Thripp will be excellent in the box.' I patted the still slightly heaving Thripp shoulder. 'Well done, Mrs Thripp! You broke down at exactly the right stage of the cross-examination.'

I picked up the first of the wretched chartered accountant's notes; I was by now looking forward to blasting him out of the witness box, and saw, 'I am going to my Masonic Ladies Night. It's a pity I haven't got a lady to take with me.' 'There's not a man sitting as a judge in the Family Division,' I promised her, 'who won't find that note from your husband absolutely intolerable.'

148

When the Thripps, *mère et fils*, had been shepherded out by their solicitor, Perfect, Miss Trant loitered and said she wanted my advice. I expressed some surprise that she didn't know it all; but I lit a small cigar and, in the best tradition of the Bar, prepared to have my brains picked. It seemed that Miss Trant had been entrusted with a brief for the prosecution, before that great tribunal, old Archibald McFee at the Dock Street Magistrates Court.

'It's a disorderly house. I mean it's an open and shut case. I can't think why Mrs Wainscott's defending.'

'The old trout's probably got a weird taste for keeping out of Holloway.' I blew out smoke, savouring a bit of fun in the offing. Fate had decreed that I should be prosecuted by Miss Phyllida Trant. I kept cunningly quiet about my interest in the case of the Police *v.* Wainscott and Erskine-Brown's former pupil proceeded to deliver herself into my hands.

'What I wanted to ask you was how much law should I...'

'Yes?'

'Take? I mean, how many books will this magistrate want, on the prosecution case?'

Miss Trant had asked for it. I stood and gave her my learned opinion.

'My dear Miss Trant. Old Archie McFee is a legal beaver. Double First in Jurisprudence. Reads Russel on Crime in bed and the Appeal Cases on holiday. You want to pot the old bawdy-house keeper? Quote every case you can think of. Archie'll love you for it. How many books do you need? My advice to you is, fill the taxi!'

149

*   *   *

So we all gathered at Dock Street Magistrates Court. There was old Mother Wainscott, sitting beneath a pile of henna-ed hair in the dock, and there was old Archie McFee, looking desperately bored and gazing yearningly at the clock as Miss Trant with a huge pile of dusty law books in front of her and her glasses on the end of her nose, lectured him endlessly on the law relating to disorderly houses.

'Section 8 of the 1751 Statute, sir. "Any person who acts or behaves him- or herself as Master or Mistress or as the person having the care, government, or managements of any bawdy house or other disorderly house shall be deemed to be the keeper thereof." Now, if I might refer you to Singleton and Ellison, 1895, I, Q.B. page 607...'

'Do you *have* to refer me to it, Miss Trant?' the learned magistrate sighed heavily.

'Oh yes, sir. I'm sure you'll find it most helpful.'

I sat smiling quietly, like a happy spider as Miss Trant walked into the web. She had looked shocked when she discovered that I was defending. Now she would discover that I had deceived her. Archie McFee couldn't *stand* law: his sole interests were rose growing, amateur dramatics and catching the 3.45 back to Esher. I was amazed she couldn't see the fury rising to the level of his stiff collar as he watched the clock and longed for Victoria.

'It is interesting to observe that in R *v.* Jones it was held that all women under 21 years of age are

150

'girls' although females may be 'women' at the age of eighteen.' Miss Trant was unstoppable.

'I suppose it interests you, Miss Trant.'

'Oh yes, indeed, sir. Turning now, if you please, sir, to the Sexual Offences Act, 1896...'

A very long time later, when it came to my turn, and the prosecution had sunk under the dead weight of the law, I made a speech guaranteed to get old Archie off to the station in three minutes flat.

'Sir. My learned friend has referred you to many books. I would only remind you of one: a well-known book in which it is written "Thou shalt not bear false witness."' I glared at the young officer in charge of the case. 'And I would apply that remark to the alleged observations of the police officer.'

'Yes. I'm not satisfied this charge is made out. Summons dismissed.' As Archie went, he fired his parting shot. 'With costs, Miss Trant.'

        *   *   *

Mrs Thripp rang me at home again that evening and told me that her solicitor, Perfect, had fixed up a hearing in ten days' time. She wondered how she could live until then and told me I was her only friend in the world. I was comforting her as best I could and stemming the threatened flow of tears over the wire by saying, 'You'll be free in a couple of weeks. Think of that old darling,' when I noticed that Hilda had come into the room and was viewing me with a look of disapproval. I put down the phone: I suppose to a hostile observer the movement may have looked guilty. However,

151

She Who Must Be Obeyed affected to ignore it and said casually, 'I'm having tea with Dodo tomorrow.'

'Dodo?'

'Dodo Perkins and I were tremendously close at Wycombe Abbey,' said Hilda coldly.

'Oh, Dodo! Yes, of course. The live one.'

'She's living in Devon nowadays. She's running her own tea shop.'

'Well. Nice part, Devon. You won't have seen her for some years.'

'We correspond. I sent her a postcard and said, let's meet when you're next up in London.' She gave me a look I can only describe as meaningful. 'I want to ask her advice about something. We may do some shopping—and have tea at Harrods.'

'Well, go easy on the chocolate gateaux.'

'What?'

'I know how much these teas at Harrods cost. I don't want to see all my profit on the disorderly house vanishing down Dodo's little red lane.'

Hilda ignored this and merely gave me some quite gratuitous information. 'Dodo never liked you. You know that, Rumpole?'

She went, leaving me only vaguely disconcerned. When I went to the gin bottle, however, to prepare an evening Booths and tonic, I was astonished to notice a pencil mark on the label, apparently intended to record the drinking habits of Rumpole. I sloshed out the spirit, well past the plimsoll line. Our existence in Froxbury Court, I thought, was beginning to bear an uncomfortable resemblance to the way life was lived in Maison Thripp.

My life in those days seemed inseparable from women and their troubles. When I got to Chambers the next morning I found Miss Phyllida Trant in my room, her glasses off, her eyes red and her voice exceedingly doleful. She announced that, after careful thought, she had decided, in view of her disastrous appearance at the Dock Street Magistrates Court, to give up the Bar and take up some less demanding profession.

'And after you'd been so helpful!' Miss Trant's undeserved gratitude gave me an unusual twinge of guilt.

'Please! Don't mention it.' I wanted to get her off the subject of my unhelpful advice.

'I know I'll never make it! I mean, I know the law. I was top student of my year and...'

I interrupted her and said, 'Being a lawyer's got almost nothing to do with knowing the law.'

'An open and shut case! I had all the police observations! And I went and lost it.'

'That wasn't because you didn't know all about the law. It was because you didn't know enough about Archie McFee.'

'You just made rings round me!'

'Never underestimate the craftiness of Rumpole.' Now I was giving her genuinely helpful advice.

'It seems ungrateful. After you'd been so kind to me.'

'I wish you wouldn't go on saying that, Miss Trant.'

'But I'll have to give it up!'

'You can't! Once you're a lawyer you're addicted. It's like smoking, or any other habit-forming drug. You get hooked on cross-examination, you get a taste for great gulps of fresh air from the cells. You'll find out.'

'No! No, I won't ever.'

I lit a small cigar and sat down at the desk opposite her. She looked surprisingly young and confused and I found myself warming to Miss Trant. For some reason I wanted her to continue her struggle against magistrates and judges and cunning opponents: even her appearance at Dock Street had shown some misguided courage.

'You know, we all have our disappointments. I do.'

'*You?*' She looked incredulous.

'One year I did the "Penge Bungalow Murder". Without a leader. *And* the "Great Brighton Benefit Club Forgery" case, which is where I got my vast knowledge of typewriters. And what am I doing now? Playing around with disorderly houses. I have even sunk to a divorce!' I looked at her, and saw a solution. 'You know what your mistake is, in Court, I mean?'

Miss Trant shook her head, she still had no idea of where she'd gone wrong.

'I would suggest a little more of the feminine qualities. Ask anyone in the Temple. How does Rumpole carry on in Court? Answer. Rumpole woos, Rumpole insinuates, Rumpole winds his loving fingers round the jury box, or lies on his back purring, "If your Lordship pleases," like old mother Wainscott from Dock Street.'

I was rewarded with a small smile as she said, 'That's ridiculous!'

154

'Lawyers and tarts,' I told her, and I meant it, 'are the two oldest professions in the world. And we always aim to please.'

* * *

If I had managed to cheer up Miss Trant, and even return her small nose to the legal grindstone, I had no luck with She Who Must Be Obeyed. Relations, as they say, deteriorated and I got up one morning to find her suitcase packed and standing in the hall. Hilda was in the living-room, hatted, coated and ready for travel.

'You can come home as late as you like now, Rumpole. And you can spend all the time you like with *her*.'

'Her?' Whoever could she be talking about?

'I've heard her! Time and time again. On the telephone.'

'Don't be ridiculous.' I tried a light laugh. 'That's a client.'

'Rumpole! I've lived with you for a good many years.'

'Man and boy.'

'And I've never known you to be telephoned by a client. At home!'

'I usually have quiet, undemanding clients. Murderers don't fuss. Robbers can usually guess the outcome, so that they're calm and resigned. Divorcing ladies are different. They're inclined to telephone constantly.'

'So I've noticed!'

'Also they're always on bail. They're not kept locked up in Brixton, pending the hearing.'

'More's the pity! I'm going to stay with Dodo.

155

I'm going to stay with Dodo and help her out with her business.'

'The tea shop?' I tried hard to remember this Dodo, who was coming to play a major part in our lives.

'It's far better I leave you, Rumpole! To enjoy your harem!'

'Listen, Hilda.' I did my best to remain calm. 'I have a client whose unhappy marriage may well provide you and Dodo with another tea in Harrods. That can't be why you're leaving.'

There was one of those silences that had become so frequent between us, and then she said, 'No. No, it isn't.'

'Then why?'

'You've changed, Rumpole. You don't go to work in the mornings. And as for the gin bottle!'

'You marked it! That was unforgivable.'

'Then don't forgive me.'

'An Englishman's gin bottle is his castle.'

At which point the phone rang. Hilda picked it up, apparently thinking it was a taxi she had ordered; but it was, of course, Mrs Thripp, the well-known married lady, who seemed to depend entirely on Rumpole. Hilda handed me the phone as though her worst suspicions were now thoroughly justified.

★   ★   ★

Hilda went while I was still pacifying the client. In the days that followed, I stayed later at Pommeroy's, got my own breakfast, had a poached egg in the evenings, and turned up alone and unaccompanied to have dinner with George

Frobisher at the Royal Borough Hotel in Kensington. We sat in a draughty dining-room, surrounded by lonely persons whose tables were littered with their personal possessions, their own bottles of sauce, their half bottles of wine, their pills, their saccharin, and their medicines. It was the sort of place that encourages talking in whispers, so George and I muttered over the coffee, getting such warmth as we could from our thimblefuls of port.

'I'm sorry it's not Thursday,' George told me sadly. 'They give us the chicken on Thursday. Tonight it was the veal so it must be Monday. Soup of the day is exactly the same all through the week. Enjoy your *pommes de terre à l'anglaise*, did you?'

'Boiled spuds? Excellent! Hilda'll be sorry she missed this.'

'Hilda cares for veal, does she? We always get veal on Mondays. So we know where we are.' George suddenly remembered something. 'Monday! Good God! I've got this divorce case tomorrow. The other side stole a march on us. They expedited the hearing!'

'George.'

'Yes, Rumpole?'

'What's your divorce about, exactly?'

'I told you. I'm a husband tomorrow.'

'It's just that, well. I've got one too, you know,' I confessed. 'I'm a wife.'

'Horrible case! I think I told you. We allege this monstrous female savaged my trousers. Furthermore, she hasn't spoken to me for three years.'

'*She* hasn't spoken to *you*?'

157

'She started it!'

'That's a damned lie, George!' I felt a sense of outrage on behalf of Mrs Thripp and raised my voice. A nearby diner looked up from his soup of the day.

'Oh really? And is it a damned lie about the bath water?'

'What about the bath water?'

'You ran off all the hot water deliberately. You put a note on the geyser, "Out of Bounds".'

'I haven't had a bath there for the last month. I have to go all the way to Ruislip, to my mother's.'

'Rumpole! You're against me?'

'Of course I'm against you. I'm the wife! You want to turn me out of the house—and my child!'

'*Your* child! You've alienated Norman's affections.'

'What?'

'You've turned him against me!'

It's no doubt a strange habit of barristers to identify themselves so closely with their clients. But by now we had both raised our voices, and the other diners were listening but looking studiously away, as though they were overhearing a domestic quarrel.

'That is the most pernicious rubbish I ever heard and if you dare to put that forward in Court I shall cut you in small pieces, George, and give you to the usher. I've behaved like a saint.'

'Oh yes, you. Joan of Arc!' George was becoming quite spirited.

'And I suppose you're Job himself.'

'I'd have to be. To put up with you.'

'You are nothing but a great big bully, George. Oh, you're all very fine and brave when you've got

158

someone weaker than yourself.'

'You! Weaker than me! I told you ... You're a Jezebel!'

'Bluebeard!'

'Lady Macbeth!'

'Let's just see how you stand up in Court, George. Let's just see how you stand up to cross-examination.'

'Don't rely on cross-examination. It's the evidence that matters. By the way, I'm making my evening trousers an exhibit!'

At this startling news the other diners had given up all pretence of not listening and were gazing at each other with a wild surmise. I wasn't taking these allegations against my wronged client lying down.

'Anyone, George, can lacerate their own evening trousers with a pair of nail scissors. It's been done before! Thank you for the dinner!'

'Rumpole!'

'Perhaps in the long watches of the night, George. Perhaps as you are watching Match of the Day on your colour T.V. it may occur to you to do the decent thing and let this case go undefended. Hasn't an unhappy woman suffered enough?'

I left the dining-room then, with all the diners staring at me. When I got home, and poured myself an unlimited gin, I began to wonder exactly what they had thought of my relationship with my old friend George Frobisher.

*   *   *

When I had rashly advised Mrs Thripp that there

wasn't a man sitting as a judge who wouldn't be appalled at hearing of her treatment at the hands of Thripp, I had made a serious miscalculation. I had forgotten that Mrs Justice Appelby sat in the Family Division of the High Court of Justice, and her Ladyship was known as the only genuine male chauvinist pig in the building. They used to say that when she went out on circuit, to try murders, she used to put on a thin line of lipstick before summing up to the jury. That was the nearest Mrs Justice Appelby ever got to the art of seduction.

If the judge was an unpleasant surprise, Mr F. Thripp was a disappointment. He was hardly ideal casting for the part of Bluebeard; in fact he looked decidedly meek and mild, a small man in rimless glasses and a nervous smile; we could have hoped for something about twice the size.

The clerk called the case and we were off. I rose to open a tale whose lightest word would harrow up the soul and freeze the young blood. I weighed in on a high note.

'This is one of the strangest cases this Court may ever have heard. The case of a Bluebeard who kept his wife a virtual prisoner in their flat in Muswell Hill. Who denied her the simple comforts of biscuits and bath water. Who never gave her the comfort of his conversation and communicated with her by means of brusque and insulting little notes.'

'Mr Rumpole.' Mrs Justice Appelby's blood was no doubt frozen already. She looked unimpressed. 'May I remind you of something? The jury box is empty. This is a trial by judge alone. I don't require to be swayed by your oratory which no doubt is enormously effective in criminal cases. Just give me the relevant dates, will you?'

I gave her the dates and then I called my client. She had dressed in black with a hat, an excellent costume for funerals or divorces. After a gentle introduction, I put her husband's notes to her.

'You and your so-called son can be off to your mother's in Ruislip. Let her pay for the light you leave blazing in the toilet.'

'That was pinned up on my kitchen cupboard.'

'And what was the effect on you, Mrs Thripp, of that heartbreaking notice to quit?'

'She stayed for more, apparently.' It was Mrs Justice Appelby answering my question. She turned to the witness box with that cold disapproval women reserve especially for each other. 'Well, you didn't go, did you? Why not?'

'I didn't know *what* he would do if I left him.' Mrs Thripp was looking at her husband. I was puzzled to see that the look wasn't entirely hostile. But the judge was after her, like a terrier.

'Mrs...Thripp. You put up with this intolerable conduct from your husband for three years. Why exactly?'

'I suppose I was sorry for him.'

'Sorry for him. Why?'

'I thought he'd never manage on his own.'

When we came out for lunch I saw Norman waiting outside the Court. He had a brand new armoured car with flashing light, a mounted machine gun and detachable soldiers in battle dress. Someone was doing well from this case; apart from Rumpole and George Frobisher.

In the afternoon I cross-examined the

respondent, Thripp. Miss Trant, sitting beside me in her virginal wig, waited with baited breath for my first question.

'Mr Thripp. Is there anything in your conduct to your wife of which you are thoroughly ashamed?' In the pause while Thripp examined this poser I whispered to Miss Trant, my eager apprentice, 'Good question that. If he says "yes" he's made a damaging admission. If he says "no", he's a self-satisfied idiot.'

At which point Thripp said 'No', proving himself a self-satisfied idiot.

'Really, Mr Thripp. You have behaved absolutely perfectly?' Her Ladyship had the point. I made that fifteen love to Rumpole, in the second set.

' "I'm going out to my Masonic Ladies' Night. It's a pity I haven't got a lady to take with me." ' I was quoting from the Thripp correspondence. 'Is that the way a perfect husband writes to his wife?'

'Perhaps not, *but* ... I was ... annoyed with her, you see. I *had* asked her to the Ladies' Night.'

'Asked her?'

'I left a note for her, naturally. She didn't reply.'

'Tell me, Mr Thripp, did you actually *want* your wife to accompany you to your Masonic Ladies' Night?'

'Oh yes, indeed.'

'This inhuman monster who drains away your bath water and refuses to wash your shirts ... you were looking forward to spending a pleasant evening with *her*?'

'I had no one else to go with.'

162

'And would rather go with her than no one?'

'Of course I would. She's my wife, isn't she?'

'Mr Thripp, I suggest all your charges against her are quite untrue.'

'They're not untrue.'

'But you wanted her with you! You wanted to flaunt her on your arm, at the Café Royal. Why? Come, Mr Thripp. Will you answer that question? It can hardly have been because you love her.'

There was a long pause, and I began to have an uneasy suspicion that I had asked one question too many. Then I knew I had because Mr Thripp said in the sort of matter-of-fact tone he might have used to announce the annual audit, 'Yes I do. I love her.'

I looked across at Mrs Thripp. She was sighing with a sort of satisfaction, as if she had achieved her object at last.

'Mr Rumpole,' Mrs Justice Appelby's voice, like a cold shower, woke me from my reverie. 'Is it really too late for commonsense to prevail?'

'Commonsense, my Lady?'

'Could there not be one final attempt at a reconciliation?'

I felt a sinking in the pit of the stomach. Could it be that even divorce was slipping away from us, and George and I would both have to go back to the crossword puzzle?

'I have no power to order this.' The judge did her best to look pleasant, it was not a wild success. 'But it does seem to me that Mr and Mrs Thripp might meet perhaps in counsel's Chambers? Simply to explore the possibilities of a reconciliation. There is one very important consideration, of course, and I refer to young

163

Norman Thripp. The child of the family. I shall adjourn now until tomorrow morning.'

At which her Ladyship rose smartly and we were all upstanding in Court. Obedient to Mrs Justice Appelby's orders, the Thripps met in my room that afternoon. George Frobisher and I, our differences now sunk in the face of the new menace from the judge, shared my small cigars and our anxieties.

'They've been there a long time,' George was looking nervously at my closed door. 'I'm afraid it doesn't look too healthy.'

Just then the clerk's room door opened for Henry to come out about some business. I had a brief glimpse of Norman Thripp, the child of the family, seated at Dianne's desk. He was banging the keys of our old standard Imperial, no doubt playing at 'secretaries'.

'In my opinion,' George was still grumbling, 'they shouldn't allow women on the bench. That Mrs Justice Appelby! What does she think she's doing, depriving us of our refreshers?'

Before I could agree wholeheartedly, the door of my room opened to let out a beaming Thripp.

'Well, gentlemen,' he said. 'I think we'll be withdrawing the case tomorrow. We still have one or two things to talk over.'

'Talk over! Well, that'll be a change,' said Mrs Thripp following him out. Then they collected Norman, who was still happily playing with Dianne's typewriter, and took him home, leaving George and I in a state of gloomy suspense.

*　　　*　　　*

The next morning I got to the Law Courts early, climbed into the fancy dress and found Mrs Thripp and young Norman waiting for me outside Mrs Justice Appelby's forum in the Family Division.

'Well, Mrs Thripp. I suppose we come to bury Caesar, not to praise him.'

'What do you mean Mr Rumpole?'

'You're dropping the case?'

Mrs Thripp, to my surprise, was shaking her head and opening her handbag. She brought out a piece of paper and handed it to me, her voice tremulous with indignation. 'No, Mr Rumpole,' she said. 'I'm going on with the case. I got *this* this morning. Leaning up against the cornflakes packet at breakfast.'

I took the note from her.

'The old barrister you dug up's going to lose this case. I'll have you and your so-called son out of here in a week. Your so-called husband.' I read the typewritten document, and then studied it with more care.

'He's mad! That's what he is. I can't live with a maniac, Mr Rumpole!' As far as my client was concerned, the reconciliation was clearly off.

'Mrs Thripp.'

'We've got to beat him! I've got to think of Norman—caged up with a man like that!'

'Yes. Norman.' I pulled out my watch. 'We've got a quarter of an hour. I feel the need of a coffee. Do you think Norman would like a doughnut?'

'I'm sure we'd be glad to.'

'Not "we", Mrs Thripp. In this instance I think I'd like to see young Norman on his own.'

165

So I took Norman down to the café in the crypt of the Law Courts, and, as he tucked into a doughnut and fizzy orangeade, I brought the conversation round to the business in hand.

'Rum business marriage ... You've never been married, have you Norman?' I lit a small cigar and gazed at the young hopeful through the smoke.

'Of course not.' Norman found the idea amusing.

'No seriously. Married people have odd ways of showing their love and affection.'

'Have they?'

'Some whisper endearments. Some send each other abusive notes. Some even have to get as far as the Divorce Court to prove they can't do without each other. A rum business! Care for another doughnut?'

'No. No, I'm all right, thanks.'

He was eating industriously with sugar on the end of his nose as I moved in to the attack.

'All right? You were all right, weren't you, Norman? When they really looked like separating?'

'I don't know what you mean.'

'When they were both trying to win you over to their side. When you got a present a week from Mum and a rival present from Dad? Tanks, planes, guns, it's been a sort of arms race between them, hasn't it, Norman?'

'I don't know what you're talking about, Mr Rumpole,' Norman repeated, with rather less conviction.

166

'This mad impulse of your parents to get together again doesn't show much consideration for you, or for me either, come to that.'

'I don't mind if they get together. It's their business, isn't it?'

'Yes, Norman. Their business.'

'I'm not stopping them.'

I ordered the child another doughnut, he was going to need it.

'Really?'

'Course I'm not!'

The second doughnut came and I gave Norman a fragment of my autobiography. 'I don't do much divorce, you know. Crime mainly. I was in the "Great Brighton Benefit Club Forgery".'

'What's forgery?' The child was round-eyed with innocence. You had to admire the act.

'Oh, you're good Norman! You'll come out wonderfully in your interviews with the police! The genuine voice of innocence. What's forgery?' I whipped out the latest item in the Thripp correspondence. 'This is! Inspect it carefully, Norman! All the other notes were typewritten.'

'So's this.' Norman kept his head.

'The others were done on the old Olivetti your parents keep in Muswell Hill. This morning's note was typed on a standard Imperial with a small gap in the capital "S".'

I got out my folding pocket glass and offered it to him.

'Here. Borrow my glass.'

Norman dared to do so and examined the evidence.

'Typed on the Imperial on which Dianne in my Chambers hammers out my so-called learned

167

opinions. The typewriter *you* were playing with so innocently yesterday in the clerk's room. I put it to you, Norman—you typed that last note! In a desperate effort to keep this highly profitable divorce case going.'

Norman looked up from my magnifying glass and said, 'I didn't see any gap in the capital "S".'

'Didn't you, Norman? The judge will.'

'What judge?' For the first time he sounded rattled.

'The judge who tries you for forgery, a word you understand perfectly. I'll take the evidence now.' I retrieved the last incriminating note. 'Four years they gave the chief villain in the Brighton case.'

'They *wouldn't*?' Norman looked at me. I felt almost sorry for him, as if he were my client.

'As your lawyer, Norman, I can only see one way out for you. A full confession to your Mum and Dad.'

He bit hard into the second doughnut, seriously considering the possibility.

'And one more word of advice, Norman. Settle for being a chartered accountant. You've got absolutely no talent for crime.'

My old friend George was extremely angry with me when Norman confessed and the Thripps were re-united. We lost all our refreshers, he told me, just because I had to behave like a damned detective. I explained to him that I couldn't resist using the skills I had learnt in the great Brighton fraud case, and he told me to stick to crime in the future.

'You Rumpole,' said George severely, 'have absolutely buggered up the work in the Family

Division.'

★   ★   ★

Further surprises were in store. When I got back to the mansions in search of the poached egg and the lonely bed, I found Hilda's case in the hall and She, apparently just arrived and still in her overcoat, installed wearily in her chair by the simulated coals of our electric fire.

'Rumpole!'

'What's the matter? Fallen out with Dodo? Had a bit of a scene over a drop scone?'

'You're home early. Daddy was never back home at three o'clock in the afternoon. He always stayed in Chambers till six o'clock. Regular as clockwork. Every day of his life.'

'My divorce collapsed under me.' I lit a small cigar. Hilda rose and started to make the room shipshape, a long-neglected task.

'You're going to seed, Rumpole. You hang about at home in the mornings.'

'And you know why my divorce collapsed?' I thought I should tell her.

'If I'm not here to keep an eye on you, you'll go to seed completely.'

I blew out smoke, and warmed my knees at the electric fire.

'The clients were reconciled. Because, however awful it is, however silent and unendurable, however much they may hate each other's guts and quarrel over the use of the geyser, they don't want to be alone! Isn't that strange, Hilda? They'd rather have war together than a lonely peace.'

169

'If I'd stayed away any longer you'd have gone to seed completely.' She was throwing away *The Times* for a couple of weeks.

'*O Woman! in our hours of ease.*' I got to my feet and gave her the snatch of Walter Scott again. '*Uncertain, coy and hard to please!*'

'You'd have stayed home from Chambers all day. Doing the crossword and delving into the gin bottle.'

'*And variable as the shade By the light of quivering aspens made.*' I moved to the door.

'If you're going to the loo, Rumpole, try to remember to switch the light off.'

'*When pain and anguish ring the brow, A ministering angel thou.*'

I was half way down the passage when I heard She calling after me.

'It's for your own good, Rumpole. I'm telling you for your own good!'

RUMPOLE AND THE LEARNED FRIENDS

'Now more than ever seems it rich to die, To cease upon the midnight with no pain.'

'Doctor Hanson told you, Rumpole. You're not dying. You've got flu.'

I was lying on my back, in a pair of flannel pyjamas, my brow with anguish moist and fever dew, and Hilda, most efficiently playing the part of Matey, or Ward Sister, was pouring out the linctus into a spoon and keeping my mind from wandering. Whatever Doctor Hanson, who in my humble opinion would be quite unable to recognize a case of death when he saw it, might say, I felt a curious and trance-like sense of detachment, not at all unpleasant, and seriously wondered if Rumpole were not about to drop off the twig.

'Fade far away, dissolve and quite forget What thou among the leaves hast never known, The weariness, the fever and the fret.'

As I recited to her Hilda took advantage of the open mouth to slide in the spoonful of linctus. I didn't relish the taste of artificially sweetened hair oil. All the same little Johnny Keats, Lord Byron's piss-a-bed poet, had put the matter rather well. Then more than ever, seemed it rich to get away from it all. No more judges. No more bowing and saying 'If your Lordship pleases.' No more hopelessly challenging the verbals. No more listening to endless turgid speeches from my learned friends for the prosecution. *'To cease upon the midnight. With no pain.'* From my position

171

between two worlds I heard the telephone beside the bed ringing distantly. Hilda picked it up and told whoever it was that they couldn't speak to Mr Rumpole.

'Who? Who can't speak to me?'

'Well, he's busy at the moment.' Hilda lied to the telephone. In fact I had done absolutely nothing for the last three days.

'Busy? I'm not busy.'

'Busy dying.' Hilda laughed, I thought a trifle flippantly. 'That's what he says anyway. No, Henry. Well, not this week, certainly...'

'It's my clerk. My clerk Henry!' I returned to earth and grabbed the telephone from She.

'I'm sorry to hear you're dying, sir.' Henry, as always, sounded perfectly serious, and not tremendously interested.

'Dying, Henry? Well, that's a bit of an exaggeration.'

'There was a con for you, sir. At Brixton Prison. 2.30. The "Dartford Post Office Robbery". Mr Bernard's got the safe blower...'

A safe blowing in Dartford! I felt my head clear and swung my legs out of bed and feet to the floor. There's nothing like the prospect of the Old Bailey for curing all other diseases.

'I'll tell Mr Bernard you can't be there.'

'Tell him nothing of the sort, Henry. I'll be there. No trouble at all. I'll just fling on a few togs.'

As I made for the wardrobe Hilda looked at me as if my recent flirtation with the Unknown had been some sort of a charade.

'I thought you were dying,' she said.

Dying, as I explained to her, would have to be

172

postponed. Safe blowing came first.

✱   ✱   ✱

When I was dressed, wrapped in a muffler and buttoned into an overcoat by Matey, I set out for Chambers. And there I made two unpleasant discoveries, the first being that there were those who would not have regretted Rumpole's continued absence from Chambers by reason of death. At that time we were suffering from a good deal of overcrowding and Erskine-Brown's small room, which opened into the entrance hall, had to accommodate not only Erskine-Brown himself, but his ex-pupil Miss Phyllida Trant, and his two new pupils who sometimes dived into my room to borrow books and then shot out again like frightened rabbits. Also my old friend George Frobisher took refuge there whenever *his* old friend Hoskins, with whom George shared a room, was having an intimate conference with a divorcée.

As I passed Erskine-Brown's open door I could see his room was bursting at the seams, and, as I hung up my hat and coat in the hallway, I heard the voice of the Erskine-Brown say he supposed they'd have to hang on in that Black Hole of Calcutta a little longer. 'But,' he added, 'at least *he* can't be with us forever.'

'Who can't be with us forever?' It was Miss Trant's voice.

'Rumpole, of course. I mean, he's bound to retire sometime. He's a good age and Henry's been telling me he's not all that well.'

I chose that moment to stick my nose into the

173

Black Hole.

'Morning, Erskine-Brown. Nose to the grindstone, Miss Trant?'

Miss Trant looked up from the brief she was reading and gave me a smile. She really has decidedly pretty teeth; ever since I deceived her so heartlessly I have become almost fond of Miss Trant.

'Oh, hello, Rumpole. I thought you were off sick.' Erskine-Brown was trying to move George's particulars of nuisance off his statement of claim.

'Recovered now.' I sneezed loudly. 'Rumpole Resurrected. Sorry to disappoint you.'

'That's a nasty cold you've got. Oughtn't you to be in bed?' Miss Trant was solicitous. I looked at her brief, neatly underlined in red and green, points for and against.

'Women are such industrious creatures! Who's your client?'

'Oh, just a thief. He'll have to plead guilty. He's said such ridiculous things to the police.'

'You twist his arm, Philly. Judges don't like you wasting the Court's time with hopeless cases.' Erskine-Brown was one of nature's pleaders. I decided that the stage of her career had come when Miss Trant might benefit from some proper advice.

'Never plead guilty!' I told her. 'That should be written up in letters a foot high. In every room in Chambers.'

'A foot high! We haven't got the room for it.' Erskine-Brown was still sulking, and George looked up from the corner of the desk he was occupying as though he'd just noticed me.

'Hello, Rumpole. Haven't see you about lately.'

'I've been dying.'

'I say, don't do that. I should miss your help with the crossword.'

Thinking uneasily that the sole justification of my existence seemed to be helping George Frobisher with the crossword, I went into the clerk's room and Henry presented me with the brief in the 'Dartford Post Office Robbery'.

'You've got plenty of time, Mr Rumpole. They don't want the two of you down there till three o'clock now.'

'The *two* of us?' I was puzzled.

'The defendant Wheeler's got a certificate for two counsel.'

'Excellent! Giving me a junior, are they? Someone to take a note?'

'Well, not exactly, Mr Rumpole.' Henry had the grace to look embarrassed. 'You're being led. They're briefing a silk. You can take it easy for once.'

I was being led! I was a junior barrister, in the 67th year of my life.

'Easy! I don't want to take it easy!' I'm afraid I exploded at Henry. 'Haven't they heard? I'm out of rompers! I'm off the bloody leading rein. I managed the "Penge Bungalow Murder" alone and without a leader.'

I came out of the clerk's room clutching my junior brief and was met with a whiff of after-shave as the tall, elegant figure of Guthrie Featherstone, Q.C., appeared through the front door in his gent's natty velvet-collared overcoat and bowler hat, slumming down in Chambers after a triumph in the House.

'Hullo, Rumpole.' He greeted me affably. 'I'm

175

afraid you're going to see a lot of my back this week.'

'Your back? What do you mean, your *back*?'

'I'm leading you. In the "Dartford Post Office Robbery".' He smiled in a damnably friendly fashion and went into the clerk's room.

'*You're* leading *me*, Featherstone?' I called after him, but he affected not to hear. I went on towards my room but, as I passed her open door, I looked in once more on that tireless worker Miss Phyllida Trant.

'You were perfectly right, Miss Trant. I ought to have stayed in bed.'

*   *   *

I don't expect you've noticed Brixton Prison as you've driven down to Brighton on a sunny Sunday morning. The prison gates are down a long, extremely dreary street off the main road; you pass little knots of visitors, girl friends, black mums with their babies, and large screws going or coming from their time off. Being a screw has become something of a growth industry; I met one who gave up school teaching for wardering, the pay's so much better and you get free golf. No matter what the weather is like in other parts of London, a fine rain always seems to be falling on the long walk down to Brixton. That day Featherstone had parked his well-manicured Rover up in the main road and leader and junior walked together up to the gates of the prison house.

Our client was a well-known minor South London villain named Charlie Wheeler, a professional safe blower with a string of convictions going back to his childhood days, when Charlie forced the Dr Barnardo's box in the local church, and which included many notable exploits with safes. The evidence against him wasn't much, just Charlie's fingerprints found on a fragment of gelignite left beside the blown safe in the post office. It wasn't much; but it was quite satisfactory evidence provided you were appearing for the prosecution. If you were for the defence, well, you'd have to improvise. I explained this to Featherstone, but he looked gloomy and said,

'If you ask me this case is as dead as a doornail.'

'So are we all, eventually.' I tried to cheer him up.

'Two men in stocking masks hold up the post office, one has a shotgun and our friend Wheeler's fingerprints are on a lump of explosive!'

'I know. I know.'

We'd reached the prison doors and I rang the visitors' bell. Featherstone smiled faintly.

'I wonder why he didn't leave his visiting card?'

'I'll tell you, old sweetheart.' I was serious. 'Old cons like Charlie Wheeler don't have visiting cards.'

The small hole in the huge wooden doors rattled open. I waved Featherstone in.

'After you, my learned friend. Leaders always go into prison first.'

As soon as I get into a prison I become moody and depressed and have a strong desire to scream and fight my way out. If this is how a visitor feels, treated with respect, even deference, by the screws, I don't know how I could stand a five-year

177

sentence, and yet I've had clients who greet five years rather like a pound from the poor box. I have also been entirely convinced, since my seventh year, that I would land up in the Nick sooner or later, for some trivial reason or other, and fear it constantly. That wet afternoon in the inner courtyard at Brixton, with the killer Airedales sniffing around at the end of their leads, and the trusty boys planting out chrysanths in the sooty flower beds, the feeling came over me more strongly than ever, stronger than the fear of death. When they put me inside, I said to myself, I'll volunteer to be one of those trusties that plant out the chrysanths, at least I'll get to learn about horticulture. But before I could plan further we were in the neat, glass-panelled interview room. You could see through the walls to where, in a succession of similar rooms, cons were having meetings with their briefs. In the centre of the complex the screws sat by a table on which cacti grew in pots, among stones, providing half a dozen elegant and miniature Japanese gardens. I can tell you, it's really very cosy in Brixton.

So we all sat round, Charlie Wheeler's advisers, Featherstone the Q.C., Rumpole the junior, Bernard the solicitor and Joyce, his secretary, a jolly, fair-haired girl in jeans and a mac, dressed more for a wet weekend in Haslemere than the Nick, who clutched the file and was inclined to giggle disconcertingly during serious passages of the evidence. I once had her in Court in a murder, and she laughed so audibly at the pathologist's report that she had to be led out. Well, we were both younger then; now she seemed moderately composed as Charlie Wheeler held out his hand to me, as though we were alone in the room.

'I'm glad to see you, Mr Rumpole. It'd amaze you. The reputation you got in E Wing.'

I felt a dry cough coming on, and my head still swam a little. 'They can inscribe that on my tombstone. "He had an amazing reputation round E Wing".'

'You're not going to *die*, are you, Mr Rumpole?' Charlie seemed genuinely concerned.

'I was considering the possibility.'

'I'm that glad you're doing my case.'

'I'm not exactly doing your case, Charlie.' I hated to disappoint him. 'Your case is being conducted by Mr Guthrie Featherstone, Q.C., M.P. His name is constantly mentioned, Charlie, in the corridors of power!'

'I haven't heard much of you,' Charlie looked doubtfully at the Q.C., M.P. 'Not from the blokes in E Wing.'

'Rumpole. If I may...' Featherstone was apparently about to gather up the reins.

'Of course, of course, my learned leader. You want to conduct this conference? Well, it's your right.'

'Now then, Wheeler.'

'He means you, Charlie,' I translated.

'Rumpole ... please!'

'I shall make a note of all your words of wisdom from now on.' I got out a note book and pen. Featherstone went on with admirable calm.

'What I wanted to say, Wheeler, was...'

'Not too fast, if you don't mind.' I was putting him down at dictation speed.

'We're here to fight this case. We're going to

179

leave no stone unturned to fight it. To the best of my poor ability!'

'My poor ability.' I repeated what seemed to me to be a key phrase as I wrote.

'But Mr Bernard's no doubt told you who our judge is,' Featherstone went on, ignoring the interruption.

'I know.' Charlie sounded deeply depressed. 'Judge Bullingham.'

'So any sort of attack on the honesty of the police...' Featherstone went on, and Bernard raised a voice in warning:

'I told you, Charlie!'

'Would act like a red rag to a Bullingham. I suppose you told him that?' I supplied the thought for Charlie to chew over.

'Look, Mr Bernard's explained it to me. I don't want to lay into "Dirty" Dickerson.'

'Who's that?' Featherstone looked puzzled and I enlightened him from my memory of the brief.

'I imagine that is a reference to Detective Inspector Dickerson, the officer in charge of the case.'

'I mean, there ain't a whole lot of point...' Charlie seemed resigned, for which Featherstone was extremely grateful.

'Well, exactly! The evidence against you is undisputable. So what's the point of annoying the judge with a whole lot of questions?'

'I told you, Charlie.' Bernard nodded wisely.

'I mean, if I don't say nothing against Dickerson. If I keep quiet, like. Well ... How much, Mr Rumpole? I were hoping for ... an eight.'

'Hope springs eternal in the human breast!' I

could tell him no more.

'In my experience...'

'Listen. To the wise words of the learned leader!'

When they came the leader's words were by no means filled with original thought. 'Any sort of attack on the police, in a case like this, will add considerably to your sentence. So let's be sensible. I must warn you, Wheeler, the time may very well come when I have to throw in my hand.'

'You mean Charlie's hand, don't you?' I said and Featherstone looked at me as if he wished he'd been lumbered with any other junior counsel in the Temple, however old and near to death.

As we walked back to the main road and the parked Rover, Featherstone put his problem in a nutshell.

'I can't make bricks without straw, Rumpole.'

'Down the Bailey you have to make bricks without bricks. You never get the luxury of straw...'

'Of course I'll mitigate,' Featherstone said sportingly.

I tried to point out the hopelessness of this course. 'What could you say in mitigation? "My client only called in for a 7p stamp, my Lord, but as he was kept waiting behind ten old ladies with pension books, and a lunatic arguing over a dog licence, he lost his patience and blew the safe"?'

'Well, Rumpole. Hardly.'

We were standing on each side of the Rover, eyeing each other in an unfriendly fashion across the polished roof, as Featherstone unlocked the driver's door.

'Forget mitigation for a moment!' I told him.

181

'What's the use of spending your life in an attitude of perpetual apology? Do you think Charlie Wheeler's going to blow a safe without gloves—even in a sub post office in Dartford? Do you think he's going to leave a bit of spare gelignite around—with his trade mark on it? Is that the mark of a professional?'

Featherstone slid into the driver's seat and opened the passenger door.

'Think about it, Featherstone.' I bundled myself into the car beside him. 'It would be like you standing up in Court and mitigating in your pyjamas!'

*　　*　　*

I decided that evening to drown all uneasy thoughts as to the conduct of Wheeler's defence in three or four glasses of Chateau Fleet Street in Pommeroy's Wine Bar. I went there with my old friend George Frobisher and saw that the watering hole was well filled, barristers at one end of the bar, including Erskine-Brown, Miss Trant and Guthrie Featherstone going walkabout among his loyal subjects, journalists at the other, and myself and George at one of the crowded tables in the snug.

'They say Uncle Tom's not too well,' George told me about our oldest, no longer practising, member of Chambers.

'Who is nowadays?'

'They say old T. C. Rowley is distinctly seedy. Well, he's a good age. He's over 80.'

'What's good about being over 80?'

I really would have liked an answer to this

question. Does the pain of hopeless frustration in which we all live become, at such an age, a dull and bearable ache of resignation? Is the loss of hearing and eyesight compensated for by a palate more than ever sensible to the thin warmth of Chateau Fleet Street? Before I could press George further on the subject, however, a young man in a tweed suit with horn-rimmed glasses and a falling lock of fair hair, detached himself from the journalists' group and approached our table.

'Mr Rumpole?'

I admitted it.

'Philbeam. I write the "In Depth" column, in the *Sunday*...'

George stood. I don't believe he trusts journalists. 'Forgive me, Rumpole. I thought I'd call in on old Tom, on my way back to the hotel. Any messages?'

'Give him my love. Oh, and tell him we'll all be joining him eventually.'

'Really Rumpole!' George sounded shocked and he went, whereupon Philbeam sat opposite me and fixed me with his glittering horn-rims.

I made him welcome and ordered further clarets. 'A gentleman of the press! I'll always be grateful for the space you gave me, during the "Penge Bungalow Murder"!'

'I think that was before my time.'

'I rather think it was. Probably reported by your grandfather.' Philbeam, I could see by looking at him, had a point.

'I was in Court when you defended Ken Aspen. The rape case with the Member of Parliament.'

'Hardly one of my major triumphs.'

'Admired the way you cross-examined that girl.'

I was just wondering where all this chat with the smooth-talking Philbeam was getting us, when he leaned forward and said, 'What I wanted to ask you, Mr Rumpole, was...'

'Yes?'

'Have you ever run up against a Detective Inspector Dickerson round Dartford somewhere?'

'"Dirty" Dickerson?' I was interested.

'Have you heard that too?' Philbeam smiled. 'You know how he got his name?'

'No,' I said, 'I've no idea.'

So he started to tell me. Up by the bar I heard Featherstone say 'Santé' as he raised his glass to Erskine-Brown. I discovered later that Erskine-Brown had been picked to make one of his comparatively rare appearances at the Bailey in the role of prosecuting counsel in the Dartford post office case, and that Featherstone was drinking to what promised to be a most civilized occasion, with both sides being of the greatest possible assistance to each other, and prosecution and defence collaborating in seeing Charlie Wheeler put gently away for a very long time indeed. Whilst this was going on Philbeam was telling me of an investigation his paper was carrying out on Dickerson. There were the usual sort of allegations, villains verballed unless they paid up, money taken for not opposing bail and such like police procedure.

'I once did an interview with a man called Harris,' Philbeam told me. 'Minor sort of South London villain. Loads of convictions...'

'Sounds like my kind of criminal.'

'Never printed it, of course. But Harry Harris told me D. I. Dickerson once handed him a stolen cigarette case. Got his finger-prints all over it. Then he made Harris pay him 300 quid not to be prosecuted for the theft.'

'Glory Hallelujah!' I had my first hint then of how dangerously Charlie Wheeler might be defended. 'You are a blessing, Philbeam, in an excellent disguise. I trust this is not an isolated incident?'

'I've got a whole file on Dickerson. Of course, I can't use it. Yet. The Leading Lady likes to win his libel actions.'

'Leading Lady?'

'That's what we call our editor.'

I let that pass. I had an urgent mission for Philbeam. 'Can you find us Harris?'

'I know the pubs he goes to. Shouldn't be difficult.'

'Oh, please, I beg you, Philbeam. Find him! Leave no pub unturned! He sounds like a small straw, we might just make a brick or two with him.'

Until Harris was found I had really nothing to go on, nothing that I could make Featherstone use as ammunition in a fight. Even if I had Harris and a pile of similar cannon-balls I was beginning to doubt if I could ever get Guthrie to fire a shot. I looked across to my learned leader at the bar, and saw him get out a large silk handkerchief and sneeze. It was not, I feared, a signal to change, rather a trumpet call to retreat.

*   *   *

Lacking Harris, or any other tangible defence, I had to fall back on the flu as ammunition for my learned leader. Accordingly I brought to Court a throat spray, a pile of clean handkerchiefs, and a packet of cough drops which could be opened and noisily consumed during vital parts of the prosecution evidence. I ranged these weapons out in front of me on the first, remarkably uneventful, day in Court.

It was so uneventful, in fact, and so little was said on behalf of the defence, that his Honour Judge Bullingham became positively benign. One of the unsolved mysteries of the universe, and a matter I find it harder to speculate upon than such relatively straightforward problems as Free Will or Life after Death, is why on earth Ronnie Bullingham was ever made an Old Bailey judge. It's not his fault that he has a thick, heavily veined neck and the complexion of a beetroot past its first youth; his personal habits such as picking his teeth and searching in his ear with his little finger while on the bench I can forgive, and his unreasoning prejudice against all black persons, defence lawyers and probation officers I can mercifully attribute to some deep psychological cause. Perhaps the Bull's mother, if such a person can be imagined, was assaulted by a black probation officer who was on his way to give evidence for the defence. What I cannot forgive is his Honour's appalling treatment of the English language. His summing-ups have to be translated by the Court of Appeal like pages of Urdu, and all the jury get is a vague impression of a man so shaken with rage that some dreadful crime *must* have caused it. The only kind of sentence in which Bullingham never falters is one of seven years and up.

186

So there we were before this appalling tribunal, Charlie Wheeler resigned, Bernard tremendously anxious, his nice secretary blushing as the judge stared with undisguised hostility at her trousers, and Erskine-Brown taking Mr Fingleton, the fingerprint expert, through his predictably damaging evidence. It was a rare occasion, peace and tranquillity in Bullingham's Court.

'Mr Fingleton,' said Erskine-Brown. 'Do you produce enlarged photographs of the first, second and third fingers of the defendant, Wheeler?'

'Yes.'

I carefully unfolded the first of my pile of hankies and loudly blew the Rumpole nose, diverting the attention of some of the jury.

'Does the defence admit them?' The Bull glared towards us. Featherstone rose and bowed as if he'd been addressing the House of Lords.

'Those are admitted, my Lord.'

'Well, thank you,' said the judge in an unprecedented burst of good manners. 'I'm very much obliged to you, Mr Featherstone.'

'I bet you are, old darling!' I muttered as Featherstone sank gracefully back into his seat.

'And do you also produce enlarged photographs of the fingerprints on the small piece of gelignite taken by Detective Inspector Dickerson from the scene of the crime?'

'Yes.'

I could see it was time to use the throat spray. I lifted it to the open mouth.

'Now what do you say about those two sets of fingerprints?'

I puffed the throat spray, regrettably I couldn't drown the answer.

187

'I have found 32 distinct points of similarity.'

'And by points of similarity you mean ... ?' The Bull wanted it spelt out for the jury.

'The break in the first whorl on the index finger, for instance, my Lord, is exactly the same in both cases.'

The photographs were handed round twelve good jury-persons, who were flattered into becoming experts.

'Yes, I think the members of the jury can see that *quite* clearly. You can, *can't* you?' Bullingham's manner to the jury was a nice mixture of a creep and a crow.

'And so, Mr Fingleton, what is your conclusion? Just tell the jury.' Erskine-Brown's approach was more subtle, he simply wanted the witness to tell us his views, provided, of course, they were the views of the prosecution.

'My conclusion is ...' Fingleton was an experienced witness. He turned politely to the jury. But Rumpole was an experienced defender. He worked at the throat spray producing a cloud of medicated mist and created a genuine diversion. Even Fingleton paused and turned to look.

'This is *not* a hospital!' The judge's remark seemed painfully obvious. 'I would stress that. For the benefit of *junior* counsel for the defence. Yes, Mr Fingleton?'

In the enforced silence that followed Fingleton struck. 'The fingerprints are identical, my Lord.'

'Thank you very much, Mr Fingleton.' Erskine-Brown sat down with great pleasure. I don't know what I expected of the rustling silk in front of me. An attack on the whole theory of the fingerprint as first promulgated by Professor Purkinje of the University of Breslau? The classification into whorls, loops, arches and composites pioneered by Sir E. R. Henry of the Bengal Police? Something, anything, to puzzle the jury and infuriate the Bull. As it was the Q.C. rose in all his glory to deliver himself of his single *bon mot*:

'No questions, my Lord.' 'I can't do anything with this evidence,' Featherstone whispered to me as he sat down.

'No. *You* can't,' I told him. I gave out a final fusillade of coughs, the only effect of which was to drown the judge as he thanked my leader, with every appearance of delight, for his brilliant contribution to the trial.

★　　★　　★

That evening I was re-reading my brief in the living-room at Froxbury Court with a still slightly feverish eye. I came again to something in Charlie Wheeler's proof of evidence that had always puzzled me, a conversation he had had with D. I. Dickerson at about two in the morning in a police cell. Charlie's recollection of the event hadn't been particularly clear but it seemed there had been an offer of bail in exchange for a confession and it had ended in some sort of temporary agreement, because the officer had shaken Charlie's hand before leaving him for the rest of the night. I read the short, unilluminating paragraph through several times before something which could hardly be called an idea, more a vague hint of the possibility of some future thought, floated into my mind. I lit a small cigar, which considerably improved the quality of my cough, and gazed at the rising smoke.

Then the telephone rang, a most unexpected caller, none other than Mrs Marigold Featherstone speaking directly from the sick bed. She was heart-broken to tell me, but poor Guthrie had a temperature of 102. It had come at the worst possible time, what with the Foreign Office dinner next week and his speech on Devolution. She really couldn't let Guthrie risk all that by coming down to the Old Bailey...

'Of course not! Don't dream of it! You keep the old darling tucked up in bed.' Rumpole was extremely solicitous. 'And keep the hot-water-bottles going, and beef tea constantly simmering on the hob. The Old Bailey's a nasty draughty place.'

Marigold sounded grateful and passed the phone to her husband who croaked an apology and said did I mind holding the fort, and he was sure I agreed there was nothing to do but to mitigate in view of the evidence we had heard.

'Quite right, Guthrie,' I assured him. 'Of course we'll have to plead. No, I won't attack the officer in charge of the case. I'll adopt your technique. I admired it so much. "No questions, my Lord." That really endeared you to the old Bull. You had the old sweetheart purring. Now you stay in bed, Guthrie. Twenty-four hours at least. Don't you dream of moving.'

I was putting down the phone with a grin of pure pleasure when Hilda came in, flushed from the washing up, and asked who was on the phone. I stood and greeted her with words of delight.

190

'*Oh frabjous day*!, Hilda,' I said. '*Callooh! Callay! He chortled in his joy*!'

'What on earth's the matter with you, Rumpole?'

'The matter? Nothing's the matter! It's an occasion for rejoicing. I've given my learned leader the flu!'

Then I phoned the night editor of the prestigious Sunday paper which examines our lives in depth and left a message for the industrious Philbeam.

* * *

I got up early the next morning and was down at Ludgate Circus, as the all-night printers came off work, and indulged myself in the treat of breakfast in Jock's Café opposite the Old Bailey, a place patronized by the discerning coppers, reporters, and meat porters of Smithfield, where the two eggs, rashers and fried slice are the best in London, and where I have roughed out, over a third cup of coffee, some of my most devastating cross-examinations and most moving speeches for the defence. I was joined at breakfast by Philbeam, to whom I gave the glad tidings that the world's greatest mitigator was docked in bed for the remainder of the trial. My spirits were only a little dashed by the fact that Philbeam had, so far, failed in his search for Harris.

'I've been round twenty pubs,' he told me. 'No joy. But I've got a number to phone. Place where his sister works.' He looked at his watch. 'They won't be open till 9.30.'

'Oh, find him, Philbeam, old darling. We may

be all set for the unmasking of "Dirty" Dickerson.'

I sent Philbeam about his business and went over to the Palais de Justice. The dear old place was as I liked it best, quiet and peaceful with only a few tired cleaning ladies and sleepy attendants to greet me. I got changed into my working clobber, wig, gown and so on, at my leisure and went down to the lower ground floor. I had rung Bernard the night before and asked him to meet me for an early conference with the client. But when I got to the old battered Newgate door, which divides the safe sheep from the imperilled goats, I found only the secretary Joyce, looking harassed and with her arms full of files.

'Oh, Mr Rumpole,' she panted at me, 'Mr Bernard won't be with you this morning. A funeral.'

'Not his?'

'A client's.'

'That's all right then. I'm just going down the cells to see Charlie.'

'Oh. Oh, well. I'm with Mr Hoskins on a fraud in the West Court. We've got a conference over there and...'

'You run along, my dear,' I reassured her. 'I believe I can cope with a conference alone and without a leader.'

At which she went off gratefully and I went up to the iron gate to do what no sensible barrister ever does, see a client alone before a trial. Perhaps I was too full of my sudden freedom from the leading rein to be sensible at that moment, and I was still in a cheerful mood when the screw left his mug of tea and jam sandwich to open the door

192

to me.

'Got Wheeler, have you?' I asked him. 'Charlie Wheeler?'

'Well, I don't think he's gone out anywhere.' This screw was a wit. 'He don't get many invitations.'

'Not many invitations! That's rich, that is. Exceeding rich!' I laughed appreciatively.

You know what being an Old Bailey Hack over the years blunts? It blunts the sensitivity. The sensitivity comes out like hair on the comb, and when you go down the cells you're prepared to laugh at anything.

*   *   *

'You ever paid Dickerson money, Charlie?' Wheeler and I were *à deux* in the interview room, both smoking away at my small cigars.

'I'd never entertain it! Oh, I know some as paid him.'

'Including Harry Harris?'

'You knows a lot, don't you?' Charlie looked at me with some admiration.

'I try to keep abreast of the underworld. So you were known to the Detective Inspector as a dedicated non-payer?'

'You could say that.' There was a pause as I searched for Charlie's statement in the brief. Then he said, 'Mr Featherstone not here today?'

'We had a bit of luck with the flu. It says somewhere here that the D.I. was on the point of offering you bail...'

'That seemed funny to me, like.'

'Very funny. With your record.'

'Of course, he wanted something for it. He was asking me to put my hands up, like.'

'Sign a confession? You weren't going to?'

'I never done that, Mr Rumpole. It's not the way I work. All the same...'

'Yes?'

'I strung him along a bit. I let him think we might do a deal. We even shook hands on it like.'

'Yes. Tell me more about that.'

'Shook hands on the deal, like. Well, he put out his hand, like ... and took mine.'

'You ever had your hand taken by a police officer before?' This was the part that interested me.

'No! Only me collar.'

'Show me, how he shook hands with you. You be the Detective Inspector.'

Charlie took my hand, but only for a moment. 'It was all over in a second. And I never made no statement. It ain't in me character.'

'How did Dickerson look when he shook hands with you? Did he look pleased—triumphant?'

'I couldn't hardly see him.'

'What?'

'It was in my cell. In the Dartford Nick. I don't know ... about two o'clock of a morning. I was half asleep ... well, he was in the dark, like. He did seem that little bit nervous.'

'Nervous?'

'Well. You know what you expect from a man of his build. Good firm grip. Well, that hand of his felt a bit clammy and soft.'

I stood up, the vague thought had not only become an idea but a plan of attack, a series of questions for cross-examination.

194

'How do you feel about this case, Mr Rumpole?' Charlie looked up at me doubtfully.

'Feel? Like stout Cortez.'

'Who?'

'*When with the eagle eyes He stared at the Pacific—and all his men Looked at each other with a wild surmise.*'

'You got me there, Mr Rumpole.'

'Keats! It's been an autumn of Keats. "*To cease upon the midnight with no pain.*" Quite enough of that! We're recovered now. Rumpole resurrected!'

'You reckon we've got a chance, Mr Rumpole?'

'A tiny chance perhaps. Like a small electric light bulb in a dark cell. More chance than mitigating.'

I sat down again at the table and started to explain the position as clearly as I could to Charlie. 'I can't tell you, understand that? I can't put you in the box and let the jury have your excellent record as a safe blower read out to them. But I want your express instructions...'

'You 'ave them, Mr Rumpole. What you got in mind?'

'I think I ought to ask Inspector "Dirty" Dickerson a few impertinent questions. So this is what I'm going to ask him, with your kind permission...'

It was then that I got Charlie Wheeler's instructions to do exactly as I did in his trial. I think, in view of the following disastrous happenings, I should make that perfectly clear.

★   ★   ★

D.I. Dickerson was a large, smiling man with

greying hair which covered the top of his ears and a bright and expensive silk tie and matching handkerchief. He looked the sort of man who would be the life and soul of the office party, or the man on the package holiday to Ibiza you would be most careful to move away from. He was holding his prized possession, a small plastic bag containing a minute quantity of gelignite, labelled 'Exhibit 1', as Erskine-Brown came to the end of his questions.

'We have heard from the expert that Wheeler's fingerprints are on that small piece of gelignite. Where did you find it?'

'Beside the safe at the scene of the crime, my Lord,' Dickerson said respectfully.

'In the Dartford post office?' the Bull weighed in.

'Yes, my Lord.'

'Thank you, Detective Inspector.' Erskine-Brown sat down, his duty done.

'Have you any questions to ask the Detective Inspector?' the judge dared me.

'Just a few, my Lord.' Rumpole rose slowly to his feet.

'Well then, get on with it.' The judge was treating the defence with his usual courtesy.

'Do you know a man named Harris, Harry Harris?'

There are two ways to cross-examine, depending on the witness and your mood. You either start off politely, asking a series of questions to which the answer will be 'Yes,' gaining the subject's confidence and agreement, leading him gently up the garden path to a carefully planned booby trap, or you go in like an old warship, with all guns blazing. I had decided that the Bull's Court at the Bailey was no place for subtlety and I went in for the broadside approach. The D.I. looked somewhat taken aback, but answered with his usual bonhomie.

'I know a Harry Harris.'

'A friend of Charlie Wheeler's?'

'Yes.'

'How would you describe him?'

'You want me to describe him?'

'Mr Rumpole has asked the questions. The risk is on his head.' The Bull's image was imprecise but his knowing leer at the jury made his meaning plain.

'Harris is a minor villain, sir. Round the Dartford area.'

'You asked for it, Mr Rumpole,' the judge was delighted and the jury smiled. I battled on, ignoring the barracking from the bench.

'Have you had any financial dealings with Harris?'

'My Lord.' As if I hadn't got enough opponents, Erskine-Brown rose to interrupt.

'Erskine-Brown,' I muttered, 'will you not interrupt my cross-examination!'

'Can I ask how questions about this man Harris are in any way relevant to the case of Wheeler?' Erskine-Brown persisted, with a glare of judicial encouragement.

'Quite right,' the judge challenged me. 'What's this man Harris got to do with this case?'

'Not *this case*, my Lord, but...'

'Then your question is entirely irrelevant.' A simple mind, that of the Bull.

'My Lord, when the character of this officer is

197

called into question...'

'Oh, really? Are you attacking this officer's character?' The judge tried a voice of dangerous courtesy, but only succeeded in sounding ordinarily rude.

'I wasn't offering him a gold medal.' At this the jury laughed. Bullingham let that one go and then said:

'I can only assume you're making this attack on instructions.'

'I take full responsibility, my Lord.'

'I see your learned leader isn't in Court.'

'Unfortunately, my Lord, he is struck down by the flu.' I tried to sound depressed. Bullingham came insultingly to my aid:

'Perhaps you'd like me to adjourn this cross-examination. So it can be done properly. By learned leading counsel?'

'Thank you, my Lord. I am quite happy to proceed.' I had no time to lose, for God's sake! Guthrie's flu might be better by the next day. The judge tried a last attack.

'I hope you are not making this suggestion without being in a position to call Harris?'

I looked round the Court, and, at this moment my good angel Philbeam came bursting in through the swing doors. I put my stake on an even chance and said, 'Certainly I can call him.'

At this point the witness nobly volunteered to answer my questions, however objectionable they might be, and I beckoned Philbeam to my side. The news was not good. Harris's sister had been contacted, but hadn't heard of her brother for two years. Philbeam whispered:

'Shall I keep trying?'

198

'For God's sake!' I whispered back, and then straightened to hear D.I. Dickerson tell the judge that he never had any financial dealings of any sort with Harris. The Bull wrote this down carefully and said:

'Very well. Mr Rumpole has his answer, although it probably wasn't the one he wanted.' With this judge the rapier was always replaced by the bludgeon. 'Do you want to try your luck with any *more* questions, Mr Rumpole?'

'Just one or two, my Lord. Detective Inspector. When Charlie Wheeler was in the Dartford Nick...'

'Where?' the judge frowned.

'In the police cells. At Dartford Police Station,' I translated politely.

'There is such a thing as plain English, Mr Rumpole. Just as well to use it.' *Bullingham* said that to me. I had no time to lose my temper with him and I was off in pursuit of the D.I.

'Did you ever on any occasion at Dartford Police Station shake hands with Charlie Wheeler?'

There was a moment's hesitation, and the witness put his big hands in his jacket pockets.

'Is my English plain enough for you?'

'Shake his hand? I may have done.'

'Have you ever shaken a prisoner's hand before?'

'Not that I can remember.'

'So why should you have shaken hands with Charlie Wheeler?'

Suddenly the Court was quiet, the jury were paying attention. Dickerson took a long ten seconds to think of his answer.

'Your client told me he was about to make a

199

confession statement. I was congratulating him on showing a bit of sense.'

The silence was broken by a general giggle, led by the judge.

'Is that the answer you wanted, Mr Rumpole?' The Bull was positively beaming.

'Yes, my Lord, it is. I wished to establish that this officer took my client by the hand.'

'*As* he was prepared to make a confession,' the jury were reminded from the bench.

Once again I ignored the interruption and asked the witness, 'Did you discuss bail with him on that occasion?'

'Bail? No, sir. There was no discussion of bail whatsoever.' Dickerson looked pained at the suggestion.

'Did you say you wouldn't oppose bail if he made a confession?'

'I said nothing of the sort, my Lord.'

Bullingham sighed heavily, threw down his pencil and turned on me. 'Mr Rumpole, are there any *further* allegations of a serious nature to be made against this officer?'

'Only one, my Lord. May I have Exhibit 1, please?'

The usher brought me the little lump of gelignite in its plastic bag.

'That is the small piece of gelignite,' the judge took great pleasure in reminding the jury. 'With your client's fingerprints on it.'

'Exactly, my Lord. Who found this piece of gelignite, Detective Inspector?'

'I did. At the scene of the crime.'

'Did you show it to any other officer?'

'When I got back to the station.'

'When you got back to the station! So the jury must rely on your evidence and your evidence alone to satisfy them that this small piece of gelignite was ever at the scene of the crime.'

'If my evidence isn't good enough...'

'If your evidence isn't good enough, Detective Inspector, Charlie Wheeler is entitled to be acquitted.' I felt the quietness in Court again, the jury were listening. I leant forward and spoke to the witness as though we were alone in the room. 'Have you ever in your long experience known a safe blower to leave his gelignite with his fingerprints on it at the scene of a crime?'

At which, of course, the judge had to comment to the jury. 'If criminals never made mistakes, we would have no trials at the Old Bailey.'

However, I felt they were becoming more interested in the witness than the judge and I went on quickly, 'You see, there is another possibility the jury may have to consider...'

'Is there?' Dickerson smiled, politely interested.

'We have no idea when the fingerprints got on the gelignite.'

'Haven't we?'

'Or where. Is it just possible, Detective Inspector, that Charlie Wheeler only touched the gelignite in the Dartford Police Station?'

There was another, minute pause before he answered. 'I don't know what you mean.'

It was time to tell the jury exactly what I meant, and bring Charlie's defence out into the open. 'In that dark cell, at two o'clock in the morning, do you think *you* had the gelignite, this little piece of gelignite, concealed in your palm when you held your hand out to him. And shook hands. As you

201

had never shaken hands with any prisoner in your life before? Is *that* the only explanation of how Charlie Wheeler's fingerprints got on to Exhibit 1?'

I hadn't expected Dickerson to crumble and apologize, but I had hoped for a bluster, an outraged denial which might have said more than he intended. But he was too experienced a witness for that; he only smiled tolerantly and said, 'If that's what Wheeler told you. I mean *if* ... Then it's a load of nonsense. You know that, Mr Rumpole.'

'Is it all lies, Detective Inspector?' Bullingham asked.

'All lies, my Lord.'

The judge wrote that last answer down, in case he forgot it. Then he gave the jury one of his least lovable grins. 'It's always painful to watch an officer of this sort of length of service under attack, members of the jury. I expect we'd all be glad of a break. Back at ten past two, Mr Erskine-Brown.'

So, ignoring Rumpole, he bundled himself out of Court.

*   *   *

'Mr Featherstone heard from the doctor, sir.' Henry was waiting for me as I came out of Court. 'He's to stay in bed for the rest of the week. He was asking, is it all over?'

'Tell him it's all going according to plan. Nothing to send his temperature up.'

In the lift, on my way up to the robing room, I met Miss Phyllida Trant. She seemed in a mood of strange elation and told me that everything was going wonderfully.

'Everything?'

'I took your advice and I didn't plead.' She was positively glowing, the light of battle burning behind her specs. 'Now it seems that there's no note of some of the verbals and most of it was after he was charged anyway and...'

'Good news from somewhere!'

'You were right, of course. When you said, always fight everything.'

Fight everything; what else had we left to do? I called the Sunday paper again from the robing room. Philbeam had gone out again and left no message.

*   *   *

'Wheeler. You're a coward as well as a thief. You tied up this helpless sub Post Mistress and you robbed. What makes it all a great deal more grave. You deliberately chose, through your counsel, to attack the honesty and good name of someone of twenty-five years standing in the police force. I mean Detective Inspector Dickerson. I've had the misfortune to sit here and hear that fine officer subjected to a number of questions...'

We were at the last gasp of the Wheeler trial, a proceeding marked by the continued absence of any man called Harris ... Even so the jury had taken three hours to find Charlie guilty by a majority, a fact which had clearly displeased the judge. I waited for the Bull to finish the ill-phrased lecture and come to announce a figure, when, to the surprise of everyone in Court, there was a voice of protest from the dock.

'I never!'

'Silence!' The usher shouted, but Charlie battled on.

'I never wanted my barrister to ask them questions! I told him to keep quiet!'

I sat quite still. I couldn't blame Charlie; but I began to feel that we were at the start of something that could prove deeply embarrassing for Rumpole. Ignoring the interruption the judge went on.

'You have the most appalling record and it is clearly time that society was protected from you for a considerably long period. The least sentence I can pass is one of twelve years' imprisonment. Take him down.'

Charlie was removed from the dock. I levered myself to my feet and started to move out of counsel's row when Bullingham stopped me.

'Just one moment. I have something to add, Mr Rumpole.'

I stopped, rooted to the spot. The judge proceeded to sentence once more.

'Your attack on the integrity of Detective Inspector Dickerson was not only not backed up by the evidence. It's now clear it was an adventure of your own. Without instructions. I take a very serious view of it. Very serious indeed.'

Fourteen years, I wondered? But the judge contented himself with saying ominously:

'I intend to report the matter in the proper quarter.'

'If your Lordship pleases.'

I gave him my politest bow, a much-needed lesson in Courtroom manners and, perhaps,

Rumpole's last genuflection in front of the bench. What had I to look forward to now, except the end of life as I knew it? As I took off the wig and looked in the robing room mirror I seemed to see a new Rumpole, a man who might just possibly not be a barrister any more.

★   ★   ★

Featherstone, back in the land of the living, was pacing his room, I thought somewhat nervously, while I sat in his big leather armchair and smoked a small cigar.

'Reported to the Benchers of your Inn. A disciplinary hearing. Before the Senate! My dear Horace. I don't want to worry you...'

'On the contrary, you're having a most calming effect,' I reassured him. 'I've thought about retiring from the Bar for a long time. Perhaps I shall start a small market garden, behind Gloucester Road tube station?'

'I've had to write to the Senate myself about the case,' Guthrie looked embarrassed.

'To tell them that the attack on "Dirty" Dickerson was an escapade dreamt up by your learned junior. Yes, I'm sure you had to write and tell them that.'

'You'll confirm that, of course?'

'Don't worry, old sweetheart. You've got a perfect alibi.' I stood as if in Court. 'My Lord, I call Mrs Marigold Featherstone. She will prove conclusively that my client was flat on his back having his chest rubbed with Vick and chewing aspirin at the time of the dark deeds down the Bailey.'

205

'Rumpole, don't you wish...'

'He is entirely innocent of the attempted rape of D.I. "Clean Fingers" Dickerson.'

'Don't you wish you'd been laid up with flu? During R. *v.* Wheeler?'

I looked at him, astonished at his lack of understanding. 'You want to know the truth, Guvnor? All right. I'll come clean. You've got me bang to rights.'

'Rumpole!'

'I loved that cross-examination. I enjoyed every minute of it, and, what's more, I swear by Almighty God, I was onto something. If I'd only had a tiny bit of straw to make a brick with...'

'I hope you're not going to say *that*, in front of the Senate!' Featherstone looked so worried that I comforted him by asking his advice.

'What would you suggest I said ... As my brief?'

He took me quite seriously and gave my hopeless case his most learned opinion. 'I think,' he said at last, 'I'd put it in *this* way. In your enthusiasm, understandable enthusiasm, for your client's interests, you were carried away, Rumpole. In the heat of the moment you made an attack on the honesty of a senior police officer which you now deeply regret...'

'What do you think I might get? Probation?'

'The worst aspect of your case, in my opinion...' Featherstone was giving the matter judicial consideration now.

'In your *learned* opinion?'

'Is that you proceeded entirely without instructions.'

I looked at him with astonishment. 'Do you
206

think I'm totally insane?'

'I must say I was beginning to wonder.'

'Of course I had instructions.'

'But at the conference in Brixton we clearly decided...'

'I had another conference. Whilst you were tucked up with your hot-water-bottle.'

'Charlie Wheeler gave you instructions to put to this officer...?'

'That he handed him the gelignite! Yes, of course I got instructions.'

Of course Featherstone asked the question which they'd be bound to ask in the Senate. 'You made a note of them at the time?'

'A note! I've got too old for making notes, in or out of Court. I carry things in my head.' There's no fool like an old fool, of course I should have made a note.

'Our solicitor! Bernard will have a note of the conference. Or at any rate a recollection.' Featherstone was doing his best.

'Bernard was off enjoying himself at some funeral or other. He left me to the tender mercies of Joyce.'

'Then Joyce will remember. We'll get hold of Joyce.' He saw another ray of light and reached for the phone.

'Joyce wasn't there. Oh, she had some sort of fraud on with Hoskins in the West Court.'

'You mean you actually saw the client alone?' Featherstone was reduced to the unalterable fact.

'Oh, we live dangerously,' I told him, 'down the Old Bailey.'

'The trouble is...'

'More trouble?'

'Wheeler denied he'd given you instructions. He told the judge as much.'

'Wouldn't you have done that in his place, old darling?'

'As a matter of fact, Rumpole, I've never been on trial for safe blowing.'

I did my best to help Featherstone's imagination. 'You've just waited three hours for the jury to find you guilty. You've been told by learned leading counsel, no less, in Brixton Prison, that it's a few extra years for asking the "Dirty" D.I. certain rude questions. Wouldn't you deny you'd given any instructions? I'm too old to expect honour among safe blowers.'

'It's a problem!' Featherstone sat at his desk, temporarily bankrupt of ideas. I felt sorry for him.

'To me it seems perfectly simple.'

'I'll have to give it a good deal of thought.'

'Give what a good deal of thought?' I was on my way to the door. It was only then I realized that the old darling had actually briefed himself for my defence.

'Exactly what I'm going to say. On your behalf to the Senate.'

'*Say*? I don't want you to *say* anything. You'd only mitigate.'

*   *   *

Featherstone wasn't the only one who had been giving thought to the nature of Rumpole's defence. A few days later Hilda rang up Chambers and invited my old friend George Frobisher to dinner. She put on a very passable meal for us, and, as we sat over our apple pie and

208

cream, gave me some words of wisdom, apparently learned at her father's knee.

'Daddy always said, a man should stand up and admit he's in the wrong. He said that was by far the best way.'

'Hilda. What are you talking about?' I was puzzled by the relevance of the thoughts of Daddy.

'He always told his clients, "An apology costs nothing, but it can earn you untold gold in sympathy from the judge."' Hilda finished triumphantly.

'Old C. H. Wystan, your Daddy, was hardly one of the nation's fighters, was he, George?'

'A man with a good deal of wisdom, for all that.' George and Hilda seemed to be in agreement.

'I'll go and make some coffee.'

'All right. Quite all right.'

'I'll leave you two gentlemen to your wine.'

Hilda left us and I poured port for George. I meant to pluck out the heart of his mystery.

'George,' I said, 'how long is it since Hilda last asked you to dinner with us?'

'It must be a good few years now.'

'A good few years. Yes, it must be. So why do you think my wife felt this sudden longing to have you share our cutlets?'

'You know perfectly well Hilda's worried, Rumpole. And so am I. Very worried by the stand you're taking.'

'Stand, George? What sort of stand is that?'

'This wretched man, this Wheeler. How can he be worth risking your career over, Rumpole? Your wife can't understand that and I must say I have

209

considerable difficulty...'

'He was worth defending. Everyone's worth defending. That's what we're for, isn't it? Do we have any other function?'

'But Hilda says that you admitted to her that the man was a professional safe blower.' George looked at me, distinctly puzzled, but he had put his finger on the exact point.

'Professional? Of course! So he wouldn't have left fingerprints...'

'Do you honestly believe, can you put your hand on your heart, Rumpole, and tell me you really *believe* that this man Wheeler was innocent?'

'Oh, come now, George. How many of your clients can you swear were innocent?'

'So you don't believe he was innocent?'

'If you ask my view of the matter—and you know my view is strictly irrelevant...'

'All the same, Rumpole. I'd like you to answer my questions.'

I admired him then, a new George, quiet but firm and not to be put off. I told him he'd make a cross-examiner yet, and poured him another glass of port. Then I gave him his answer. 'No. No, I don't believe he was innocent. In fact I think Charlie Wheeler probably blew the safe in the Dartford post office.'

'So no injustice was done.'

'Probably not...'

George stood up then. He was beaming at me, apparently hugely relieved. 'So that *is* good news, Rumpole. You've seen sense at last.'

Hilda came in with the coffee tray and George gave her the glad tidings. 'I believe your husband's seen sense at last.'

210

'I knew you'd be able to talk to him.' Hilda smiled as she poured the coffee. 'You've always told me, Rumpole, "George is so sensible." Rumpole's always had a tremendous amount of respect for you, George.'

'Guthrie Featherstone agrees it can all be dealt with by way of an apology—and now you admit it was unnecessary to attack the officer!' George took his coffee and smiled at me. I hated to disappoint him.

'Unnecessary? Did you say unnecessary?'

'You said yourself, Wheeler was probably guilty.' George seemed to think that was an end of the matter.

'Guilty or innocent. What's it matter? What matters is—he may have been convicted on faked evidence.'

'But, Rumpole, if he'd done it anyway...' Hilda was as puzzled as George. I did my best to explain it to them both.

'We can't decide guilt or innocence. That's not for us, *you* know that, George. That's for twelve puzzled old darlings pulled off the street for three boring days with a safe blower. But we can make sure they're not lied to, not deceived, not tricked by some smiling copper who wants to take away their decision from them by a few conjuring tricks in a dark cell. Oh, for God's sake, have another glass of port.'

I felt he needed it, for he sat looking quite despondent and asked what on earth I thought I was going to do.

'Grow vegetables. We'll probably have to go to the country to do it.'

'Rumpole. They won't disbar you ...' George

211

did his best to sound comforting. I went over to the old desk in the corner and found a packet of small cigars.

'Suspend me, disbar me, I don't care. I shan't apologize for what I did for Wheeler.'

'Talk to him, George. Please talk to him.' Hilda sounded desperate. George did his best.

'Rumpole. Forget Wheeler for a moment. You've got yourself to think about.'

I found my cigars and lit one. I was still searching for something I had concealed in a drawer of the desk. 'Oh, I am thinking of myself. You see, Hilda, with the insurance policy and what we'd get for this flat, we could get quite a decent cottage and a small-holding.'

'A small-holding! Oh, George. Has he gone quite mad? You wouldn't know what to do with a small-holding, Rumpole!'

'Dig it and dung it! That's what I'd do. And grow the stuff I'm rather keen on. Artichokes and marrows and parsnips and, after a few years, perhaps asparagus ...' I had found what I wanted, a seed catalogue, full of fine colour photographs of prize vegetables. 'Look, Hilda. Do look at this. Please look at it.'

I took the catalogue over to Hilda and held it open at a particularly succulent row of runner beans. 'Don't you think it all looks rather splendid?'

She shook her head. Hilda Rumpole is incredibly urban, all her life has revolved round Law Courts and barristers' Chambers; she could only see a row of runners, or even a picking of early peas, through a haze of tears.

212

A man, under our system, is innocent until he's proved guilty, and in the time that elapsed before my case was due to be heard in the Senate, by the tribunal that decides matters of discipline at the Bar, I continued business as usual, although the briefs didn't exactly fall like summer rain onto the fertile soil of Rumpole's Chambers. However, I left home earlier than usual, largely to escape the sorrowful and rebuking eye of She Who Must Be Obeyed, often had breakfast on my own with *The Times* crossword at Jock's Café, and lingered late in Pommeroy's Wine Bar. I was sitting there at a lonely table with my head deep in the *Evening Standard* when I heard Erskine-Brown's voice ringing from the bar.

'Vegetables! Did you say Rumpole was going to grow vegetables?'

'He actually bought a catalogue. A list of seeds. With illustrations.' George sounded like a doctor, announcing the symptoms of a fatal disease.

'How *old* is Rumpole? Do you think he might be going a bit screwy?'

'Of course not!' The female voice was quite positive. 'The first thing I learned at the Bar was, never underestimate the cunning of Rumpole.' It was the clear and dulcet tone of Miss Trant.

For a while their voices were drowned in the general clatter of legal anecdotes, journalists' attempted seductions and cries for claret, which make up the full orchestra of the sound of Pommeroy's, and then I heard my old friend George booming sadly.

'Obstinate! Rumpole's incredibly obstinate.

213

You know what he's saying now? Even if they just suspend him—for a little while. Even if they censure him—he'll leave the Bar, and he won't apologize!'

'Then surely one thing's perfectly clear, George.' It was Erskine-Brown again.

'What's that?'

'Rumpole has absolutely no one to blame but himself. I'm going back to Chambers. Come on, Philly. I've just got to pick up a brief, and then we're off to the Festival Hall!'

'I'll catch you up.'

I sank my head deeper in the 'Londoner's Diary' and then looked up as Miss Trant's voice came again, from about three feet away. 'You going to send us up some nice fresh vegetables?'

As I lowered the paper Miss Trant sat down and joined me uninvited; it was amazing, the confidence she had developed since her baptism of fire in Dock Street. 'Peas and carrots. New potatoes! Sounds delicious.'

'I have been having doubts.' I suppose I needed someone to talk to at that moment, life with Hilda being then on the silent side. 'Looking back at my past life, hanging round Law Courts, I found absolutely no evidence for the proposition that I have green fingers.'

'Neither have I.'

'What?'

'My pot plants all go yellow.'

'It's only that, whenever I visit prisons and see the trusties planting out straight rows of chrysanths in the sooty soil, I think, yes. That's the job I'll choose when I'm in the Nick.'

Then an extraordinary thing happened. Miss

Trant actually seemed to lose her temper with me. 'Really! You're not going to the Nick. You told me never to underestimate your cunning—like the time when I was prosecuting you and you got me to bore the magistrate with a load of law—and you won the case!'

'Finally tumbled to that, did you?' I smiled, remembering the occasion.

'Well, if you can think of that in the Dock Street Mag's Court can't you deal with this little case of yours in the Senate?'

'I shan't apologize!' I told her that quite firmly, and another surprise: she didn't argue.

'Of course you won't. Why? Were you thinking of it?'

'Was I?'

'Creeping off to the country. To grow vegetables! It's like pleading guilty. Well, stuff that for a lark!' This slip of a girl had the spirit which was lacking in Featherstone, or Hilda, or even George; the courage of an advocate.

'Miss Trant,' I told her, 'I remember when you first came to the Chambers, you were a somewhat straight-laced young woman, only interested in law reports.'

'I've learned a lot since then.'

'From your pupil master, Erskine-Brown?'

'No, from you! What do you say we ought to have written up in Chambers, in letters a foot high? *Never plead guilty*!'

'Bricks without bricks, Miss Trant ... Bricks without the bloody shadow of a brick. Unless...'

'Well, go on. Unless?'

'Someone could lay their hands on a man called Harry Harris.'

215

When she had gone I sat on for a while alone. I thought of my hearing before the Senate of the Inns of Court. What would that august body do to me? Change me utterly? I might leave their presence as someone quite new, perhaps even as myself. It seemed to me that I had spent my whole life being other people, safe blowers, fraudsmen, a few rather gentle murderers. I'd had remarkably little time to be Rumpole. Would I have time now; and if I had time, hanging heavy on my hands forever, should I enjoy the experience of being my own, genuine, unadulterated Rumpole at last?

Jack Pommeroy broke in on this uncomfortable reverie. There was a phone call for me, from Philbeam. He wanted me to stay where I was, he was bringing a man round for a drink, a man called Harry Harris.

*   *   *

A few nights later Detective Inspector Dickerson was sitting in the corner of his favourite Chinese restaurant (The Garden of Delights, in Bromley) waiting. His eyes lit up when a tall, very thin man with grey hair came in, for had this man not arrived the Detective Inspector was in great danger of having to pay his own bill.

'Harris!' Dickerson waved a large hand at the empty chair at his table. 'Where you been keeping yourself, Harry?'

'I got word you wanted to see me, Dickerson.'

'You want to buy me a Chinese, do you? The A1 combination with the sweet and sour lobster.'

'I'd be glad to.' Harris smiled patiently.

216

'I thought you would. You been a bit late on your instalments, Harris.'

'Sorry, Dickerson. I've been travelling.' At this point Harris took a bulky envelope out of his breast pocket and handed it to the Detective Inspector, whose manner became, if possible, even more affable.

'Well, leave a forwarding address then. We'll get on much more nicely if I can bleed you regular. I think,' Dickerson consulted the wine list, 'a nice bottle of Chablis'd go well with the sweet and sour.'

When Harris had ordered the Chablis from the Chinese waiter he broached an awkward subject. 'Can we forget it now?' he asked, and his voice had, for the first time, a whining tone.

'Forget what, Harris?'

'A couple of fingerprints on a gold case.'

There was a long silence and then Dickerson said, 'You're so careless, Harris, where you put your fingers. You're as bad as your friend Charlie Wheeler.'

'I heard you fitted Charlie up nicely too.'

'Fitted him up? Who told you I fitted Charlie up? The jury convicted him, didn't they?' Dickerson sounded cautious, but Harris was laughing.

'Such a nice friendly lad, Charlie. He'd shake hands with anyone!'

It was a little while before Dickerson joined in the joke, but apparently he found it irresistible. 'All right, Harris,' he said through chuckles, 'Very funny. Very funny indeed. But let it be a lesson to you ... If you don't bleed regular I'll have your fingers round a lump of jelly. Just the way I did

217

with Charlie.'

There was an interruption then, when the waiter brought the Chablis. Dickerson turned his attention to the temperature of the bottle. If he hadn't done so he might have noticed the tip of a small metallic object, hidden in the breast pocket of Harris's jacket. The reason for that, and for my having a verbatim account of this conversation, is that it was being taken down for posterity, and the subsequent police inquiry, on a small but efficient tape recorder which was later delivered to Philbeam's car, parked outside the Garden of Delights.

*　　　*　　　*

Whilst I was explaining matters to the Senate the learned friends of No. 1 Equity Court were holding a Chambers meeting. I am grateful to George Frobisher for supplying me with a note of what was said during my enforced absence. The first item on the agenda was the question of accommodation in Chambers, and was raised by Erskine-Brown.

'It seems likely,' he began, 'that we will soon be having a vacancy in Chambers.'

'What do you mean exactly?' Miss Trant asked the question.

'Well, Philly. After today's hearing, Rumpole's made it quite clear. He intends to leave the Bar and grow vegetables.'

'Vegetables? I hadn't heard about the vegetables.' Featherstone was understandably puzzled.

'Shouldn't we perhaps wait?' George suggested,

but Erskine-Brown was not to be stopped.

'I think it's important,' he said, 'that we should decide what the policy is. As you know, my own room is impossibly over-crowded. George Frobisher is sharing with Hoskins, which isn't always convenient when it comes to conferences. I mean, do we take in another young man who could make himself useful and do a bit of paper work and so on?'

The door was behind him and he didn't stop immediately when I opened it. 'Or do we use Rumpole's room to relieve our acute accommodation problem?'

'Do you want to take over my room, Erskine-Brown?' I was back from my hearing, from Erskine-Brown's point of view like bloody Banquo at the dinner party. He stopped in full flow and George said:

'Rumpole! It can't be over?'

'Ah, Horace.' Featherstone pulled up a chair for the ghost of Rumpole. 'You can help us. We've just been discussing the possible future.'

'So have I, old darling, and I'll tell you what. The possible future is rather interesting.' I lit a small cigar. 'Remember Detective Inspector Dickerson? He's suspended, a full inquiry. When he heard that in the Nick, Charlie suddenly remembered giving me instructions. So, we're applying to the Court of Appeal, with fresh evidence. I was rather thinking of doing it alone—without a leader. I'm sorry, Erskine-Brown. The vegetables have been postponed indefinitely...'

I left them then, the learned and astonished friends, to sort out their accommodation problems knowing that Rumpole's room would not be available in the foreseeable future.

★   ★   ★

When I got home to the mansions I found Hilda sitting inert by one bar of a sullen electric fire. She looked up as I came into the living-room and said, 'Rumpole. Is it over?'

'I'm afraid so.'

'Oh, Rumpole. It's over!'

'I know, my dear. No peace. No quiet. No just being Rumpole. Above all, no vegetables. I'm doing rather a larky manslaughter tomorrow. At Chelmsford.'

'They let you off?' I couldn't imagine why she sounded so surprised. I filled in the details.

'Acquitted. By unanimous verdict. Left the dock without a stain on my character. In fact, I was commended for picking out one of the few rotten apples in that sweet-smelling barrow-load, the Metropolitan Police.'

'Oh, Rumpole!' It was an astonishing moment. She Who Must Be Obeyed actually had her arms round me, she was holding me tightly, rather as though I were some rare and precious object and not the old White Elephant that continually got in her way.

'Hilda. Hilda, you're not ... ?' I looked down at her agitated head. 'You weren't worried, were you?'

'Worried? Well, of course I was worried!' She broke away and resumed the Royal Manner. 'Having you at home all day would have been impossible!'

220

'Yes. Yes. I suppose it would.'

'Now we can go on. Just as before.'

'Just as before. I suppose ... it calls for a celebration.' I went to the drinks table and poured two Booths, taking care not to ruin them with too much tonic.

'Well, just a tiny one. I've got dinner to get and ...'

'I'm sorry to have to tell you this, Hilda. You know your old Daddy, old C. H. Wystan, was quite wrong.' I handed her a steadying G. and T.

'Wrong? Why was Daddy wrong?'

'Never plead guilty! Come on, old thing, bottoms up.'

I raised my glass. Hilda raised her's and we drank to a future which was going to be, thanks to the wonders of tape recording and the fallibility of human nature, as indistinguishable as possible from our past.

RUMPOLE AND THE HEAVY BRIGADE

The story of my most recent murder, and my defence of Petey Delgardo, the youngest, and perhaps the most appalling of the disagreeable Delgardo brothers, raises several matters which are painful, not to say embarrassing for me to recall. The tale begins with Rumpole's reputation at its lowest, and although it has now risen somewhat, it has done so for rather curious and not entirely creditable reasons, as you shall hear.

After the case of the 'Dartford Post Office Robbery', which I have recounted in the previous chapter, I noticed a distinct slump in the Rumpole practice. I had emerged, as I thought, triumphant from that encounter with the disciplinary authority; but I suppose I was marked, for a while, as a barrister who had been reported for professional misconduct. The quality of briefs which landed on the Rumpole corner of the mantelpiece in our clerk's room were deteriorating and I spent a great deal more time pottering round Magistrates Courts or down at Sessions than I did in full flood round the marble halls of the Old Bailey.

So last winter picture Rumpole in the November of his days, walking in the mists, under the black branches of bare trees to Chambers, and remembering Thomas Hood.

'No warmth, no cheerfulness, no healthful ease, No comfortable feel in any member, No shade, no shine, no butterflies, no bees, No fruits, no flowers, no leaves, no birds,—November!'

As I walked, I hoped there might be some sort of trivial little brief waiting for me in Chambers. In November an old man's fancy lightly turned to thoughts of indecent assault, which might bring briefs at London Sessions and before the Uxbridge Justices. (Oh God! Oh, Uxbridge Justices!) I had started forty years ago, defending a charge of unsolicited grope on the Northern Line. And that's what I was back to. In my end is my beginning.

I pushed open the door of my Chambers and went into the clerk's room. There was a buzz of activity, very little of it, I was afraid, centring round the works of Rumpole, but Henry was actually smiling as he sat in his shirt-sleeves at his desk and called out, 'Mr Rumpole.'

'Stern daughter of the Voice of God! Oh, duty! Oh my learned clerk, what are the orders for today, Henry? Mine not to reason why. Mine but to do or die, before some Court of Summary Jurisdiction.'

'There's a con. Waiting for you, sir. In a new matter, from Maurice Nooks and Parsley.'

Henry had mentioned one of the busiest firms of criminal solicitors, who had a reputation of being not too distant from some of their heavily villainous clients. In fact the most active partner was privately known to me as 'Shady' Nooks.

'New matter?'

'"The Stepney Road Stabbing". Mr Nooks says you'll have read about it in the papers.'

In fact I had read about it in that great source of legal knowledge, the *News of the World*. The Delgardo brothers, Leslie and Basil, were a legend in the East End; they gave copiously to charity,

223

they had friends in 'show business' and went on holiday with a certain Police Superintendent and a well-known Member of Parliament. They hadn't been convicted of any offence, although their young brother, Peter Delgardo, had occasionally been in trouble. They ran a club known as the Paradise Rooms, a number of protection rackets, and a seaside home for orphans. They were a devoted family and Leslie and Basil were said to be particularly concerned when their brother Peter was seen by several witnesses kneeling in the street outside a pub called the Old Justice beside the blood-stained body of an East End character known as Tosher MacBride. Later a knife, liberally smeared with blood of MacBride's group, was found beside the driver's seat of Peter Delgardo's elderly Daimler. He was arrested in the Paradise Rooms to which he had apparently fled for protection after the death of Tosher. The case seemed hopeless but the name 'Delgardo' made sure it would hit the headlines. I greeted the news that it was coming Rumpole's way with a low whistle of delight. I took the brief from Henry.

'"*My heart leaps up when I behold ... a rainbow in the sky.*" Or a murder in the offing. I have to admit it.'

I suddenly thought of the fly in the ointment.

'I suppose they're giving me a leader—in a murder?'

'They haven't mentioned a leader,' Henry seemed puzzled.

'I suppose it'll be Featherstone. Well, at least it'll get me back to the Bailey. My proper stamping ground.'

224

I moved towards the door, and it was then my clerk Henry mentioned a topic which, as you will see, has a vital part to play in this particular narrative, my hat. Now I am not particularly self-conscious as far as headgear is concerned and the old black Anthony Eden has seen, it must be admitted, a good many years' service. It has travelled to many far-flung courts in fair weather and foul, it once had a small glowing cigar end dropped in it as it lay under Rumpole's seat in Pommeroy's, it once blew off on a windy day in Newington Causeway and was run over by a bicycle. The hat is therefore, it must be admitted, like its owner, scarred and battered by life, no longer in its first youth and in a somewhat collapsed condition. All the same it fits me comfortably and keeps the rain out most of the time. I have grown used to my hat and, in view of our long association, I have a certain affection for it. I was therefore astonished when Henry followed me to the door and, in a lowered tone as if he were warning me that the coppers had called to arrest me, he said,

'The other clerks were discussing your hat, sir. Over coffee.'

'My God! They must be hard up for conversation, to fill in a couple of hours round the A.B.C.'

'And they were passing the comment, it's a subject of a good many jokes, in the Temple.'

'Well, it's seen some service.' I took off the offending article and looked at it. 'And it shows it.'

'Quite frankly, Mr Rumpole, I can't send you down the Bailey, not on a top-class murder, in a hat like it.'

'You mean the jury might get a peep at the titfer, and convict without leaving the box?' I couldn't believe my ears.

'Mr Featherstone wears a nice bowler, Mr Rumpole.'

'I am not leading counsel, Henry,' I told him firmly. 'I am not the Conservative-Labour M.P. for somewhere or other, and I don't like nice bowlers. Our old clerk Albert managed to live with this hat for a good many years.'

'There's been some changes made since Albert's time, Mr Rumpole.'

Henry had laid himself open, and I'm afraid I made the unworthy comment.

'Oh, yes! I got some decent briefs in Albert's time. The "Penge Bungalow Murder", the Brighton forgery. I wasn't put out to grass in the Uxbridge Magistrates' Court.'

*   *   *

The chairs in my room in Chambers have become a little wobbly over the years and my first thought was that the two large men sitting on them might be in some danger of collapse. They both wore blue suits made of some lightweight material, and both had gold wristwatches and identity bracelets dangling at their wrists. They had diamond rings, pink faces and brushed back black hair. Leslie Delgardo was the eldest and the most affable, his brother Basil had an almost permanent look of discontent and his voice easily became querulous. In attendance, balanced on my insecure furniture, were 'Shady' Nooks, a silver haired and suntanned person who also sported a large gold wristwatch, and his articled clerk, Miss Stebbings, a nice-looking girl fresh from law school, who had clearly no idea what area of the law she had got into.

I lit a small cigar, looked round the assembled company, and said, 'Our client is not with us, of course.'

'Hardly, Mr Rumpole,' said Nooks. 'Mr Peter Delgardo has been moved to the prison hospital.'

'He's never been a well boy, our Petey.' Leslie Delgardo sounded sorrowful.

'Our client's health has always been an anxiety to his brothers,' Nooks explained.

'I see.' I hastily consulted the brief. 'The victim of the murder was a gentleman called Tosher MacBride. Know anything about him?'

'I believe he was a rent collector.' Nooks sounded vague.

'Not a bad start. The jury'll be against murder but if someone has to go it may as well be the rent collector.' I flipped through the depositions until I got to the place where I felt most at home, the forensic report on the blood.

'Bloodstains on your brother's sleeve.'

'Group consistent with ten per cent of the population,' said Nooks.

'Including Tosher MacBride? And Exhibit 1, a sheath knife. Mr MacBride's blood on that, or, of course, ten per cent of the population. Knife found in your brother's ancient Daimler. Fallen down by the driver's seat. Bloodstains on his coat sleeve? Bloodstained sheath knife in his car?'

'I know it looks black for young Peter.' Leslie shook his head sadly.

I looked up at him sharply. 'Let's say it's evidence, Mr Delgardo, on which the prosecution might expect to get a conviction, unless the judge has just joined the Fulham Road Anarchists—or the jury's drunk.'

'You'll pull it off for Petey.' It was the first time Basil Delgardo had spoken and his words showed, I thought, a touching faith in Rumpole.

'Pull it off? I shall sit behind my learned leader. I presume you're going to Guthrie Featherstone, Q.C., in these Chambers?'

Then Nooks uttered words which were, I must confess, music to my ears.

'Well, actually, Mr Rumpole. On this one. No.'

'Mr Rumpole. My brothers and I, we've heard of your wonderful reputation,' said Basil.

'I did the "Penge Bungalow Murder" without a leader,' I admitted. 'But that was thirty years ago. They let me loose on that.'

'We've heard golden opinions of you, Mr Rumpole. Golden opinions!' Leslie Delgardo made an expansive gesture, rattling his identity bracelet. I got up and looked out of the window.

'No one mentioned the hat?'

'Pardon me?' Leslie sounded puzzled, and Nooks added his voice to the vote of confidence.

'Mr Delgardo's brothers are perfectly satisfied, Mr Rumpole, to leave this one entirely to you.'

'Now is the Winter of my Discontent, Made Glorious Summer by a first-class murder.' I turned back to the group, apologetic. 'I'm sorry, gentlemen. Insensitive, I'm afraid. All these months round the Uxbridge Magistrates Court have blunted my sensitivity. To your brother it can hardly seem such a sign of summer.'

'We're perfectly confident, Mr Rumpole, you can handle it.' Basil lit a cigarette with a gold lighter and I went back to the desk.

'Handle it? Of course I can handle it. As I always say, murder is nothing more than common assault, with unfortunate consequences.'

'We'll arrange it for you to see the doctor.' Nooks was businesslike.

'I'm perfectly well, thank you.'

'Doctor Lewis Bleen,' said Leslie, and Nooks explained patiently, 'The well-known psychiatrist. On the subject of Mr Peter Delgardo's mental capacity.'

'Poor Petey. He's never been right, Mr Rumpole. We've always had to look after him,' Leslie explained his responsibilities, as head of the family.

'You could call him Peter Pan,' Basil made an unexpected literary reference. 'The little boy that never grew up.'

I doubted the accuracy of this analogy. 'I don't know whether Peter Pan was actually responsible for many stabbings down Stepney High Street.'

'But that's it, Mr Rumpole!' Leslie shook his head sadly.

'Peter's not responsible, you see. Not poor old Petey. No more responsible than a child.'

★   ★   ★

Doctor Lewis Bleen, Diploma of Psychological Medicine from the University of Edinburgh, Head-Shrinker Extraordinaire, Resident Guru of 'What's Bugging You' answers to listeners' problems, had one of those accents which remind you of the tinkle of cups and the thud of dropped scones in Edinburgh tea-rooms. He sat and sucked his pipe in the interview room at Brixton and looked in a motherly fashion at the youngest of the Delgardos who was slumped in front of us, staring moodily at nothing in particular.

'Remember me, do you?'

'Doctor B ... Bleen.' Petey had his brothers' features, but the sharpness of their eyes was blurred in his, his big hands were folded in his lap and he wore a perpetual puzzled frown. He also spoke with a stammer. His answer hadn't pleased the good doctor, who tried again.

'Do you know the time, Petey?'

'N ... N ... No.'

'Disorientated ... as to time!' Better pleased, the doctor made a note.

'That might just be because he's not wearing a watch,' I was unkind enough to suggest.

The doctor ignored me. 'Where are you, Peter?'

'In the n ... n...'

'Nick?' I suggested.

'Hospital wing.' Peter confirmed my suggestion.

'Orientated as to place!' was my diagnosis. Doctor Bleen gave me a sour look, as though I'd just spat out the shortcake.

'Possibly.' He turned back to our patient. 'When we last met, Peter, you told me you couldn't remember how MacBride got stabbed.'

'N ... No.'

'There appears to be a complete blotting out of all the facts,' the doctor announced with quiet satisfaction.

'Mightn't it be worth asking him whether he was *there* when Tosher got stabbed?' I was bold

230

enough to ask, at which Nooks chipped in.

'Mr Rumpole. As a solicitor of some little experience, may I interject here?'

'If you have to.' I sighed and fished for a small cigar.

'Doctor Bleen will correct me if I'm wrong but, as I understand, he's prepared to give evidence that at the relevant moment...'

'So far I have no idea when the relevant moment was.' I lit the cigar, Nooks carried on regardless.

'Mr Delgardo's mind was so affected that he didn't know the nature and quality of his act, nor did he know that what he was doing was wrong.'

'You mean he thought he was giving Tosher a warm handshake, and welcome to the Rent Collectors' Union?'

'That's not exactly how I suggest we put it to the learned judge.' Nooks smiled at me as though at a wayward child.

'Then how do you suggest we tell it to the old sweetheart?'

'Guilty but insane, Mr Rumpole. We rather anticipated your advice would be that, guilty but insane in law.'

'And have you anticipated what the prosecution might say?'

'Peter has been examined by a Doctor Stotter from the Home Office. I don't think you'll find him unhelpful,' said Doctor Bleen. 'Charles Stotter and I play golf together. We've had a word about this case.'

'Rum things you get up to playing golf. It always struck me as a good game to avoid.' I turned and drew Peter Delgardo into the conversation. 'Well, Peter. You'll want to be getting back to the telly.'

Peter stood up. I was surprised by his height and his apparent strength, a big pale man in an old dressing gown and pyjamas.

'Just one question before you go. Did you stab Tosher MacBride?'

The doctor smiled at me tolerantly. 'Oh I don't think the answer to *that* will be particularly reliable.'

'Even the question may strike you as unreliable, doctor. All the same, I'm asking it.' I moved closer to Peter. 'Because if you did, Peter, we can call the good shrink here, and Doctor Stotter fresh from the golf course, and they'll let you off lightly! You'll go to Broadmoor at Her Majesty's Pleasure, and of course Her Majesty will be thinking of you constantly. You'll get a lot more telly, and some exciting basket-weaving, and a handful of pills every night to keep you quiet, Petey, and if you're very good they might let you weed the doctors' garden or play cricket against the second eleven of male warders ... but I can't offer you these delights until I know. Did you stab Tosher?'

'I think my patient's tired.'

I turned on the trick cyclist at last, and said, 'He's not your patient at the moment. He's my client.'

'Doctor Bleen has joined us at great personal inconvenience.' Nooks was distressed.

'Then I wouldn't dream of detaining him a moment longer.' At which point Doctor Lewis Bleen D.P.M. (Edinburgh) left in what might mildly be described as a huff. When he'd been

232

seen off the premises by a helpful trusty, I repeated my question.

'Did you do it, Peter?'

'I c ... c ... c ...' The answer, whatever it was, was a long time in coming.

Nooks supplied a word. 'Killed him?' but Peter shook his head.

'Couldn't of. He was already c ... cut. When I saw him, like.'

'You see, I can't let you get sent to hospital unless you did it,' I explained as though to a child. 'If you didn't, well ... just have to fight the case.'

'I wants you to f ... f ... fight it. I'm not going into any nut house.' Peter Delgardo's instructions were perfectly clear.

'And if we fight we might very well lose. You understand that?'

'My b ... b ... brothers have told me ... You're hot stuff, they told me ... Tip top l ... awyer.'

Once again I was puzzled by the height of my reputation with the Delgardos. But I wasn't going to argue. 'Tip top? Really? Well, let's say I've got to know a trick or two, over the years ... a few wrinkles ... Sit down, Peter.'

Peter sat down slowly, and I sat opposite him, ignoring the restive Nooks and his articled clerk.

'Now, hadn't you better tell me exactly what happened, the night Tosher MacBride got stabbed?'

*   *   *

I was working overtime a few days later when my door opened and in walked no less a person than

Guthrie Featherstone, Q.C., M.P., our Head of Chambers. My relations with Featherstone, ever since he pipped me at the post for the position of Head, have always been somewhat uneasy, and were not exactly improved when I seized command of the ship when he was leading me in the matter of the 'Dartford Post Office Robbery'. We have little enough in common. Featherstone, as Henry pointed out, wears a nice bowler and a black velvet collar on his overcoat; his nails are well manicured, his voice is carefully controlled, as are his politics. He gets on very well with judges and solicitors and not so well with the criminal clientele. He has never been less than polite to me, even at my most mutinous moments, and now he smiled with considerable bonhomie.

'Rumpole! You're a late bird!'

'Just trying to feather my nest. With a rather juicy little murder.'

Featherstone dropped into my tattered leather armchair, reserved for clients, and carefully examined his well-polished black brogues.

'Maurice Nooks told me, he's not taking in a leader.'

'That's right.'

'I know the last time I led you wasn't *succès fou*.'

'I'm a bit of a back seat driver, I'm afraid.'

'Of course, you're an old hand at crime,' Featherstone conceded.

'An old lag you might say.'

'But it's a question of tactics in this case. Maurice said, if I appeared, it might look as if they'd over-egged the pudding.'

'You think the jury might prefer—a bit of good plain cooking?' I looked at him and he smiled delightfully.

'You put things rather well, sometimes.'

There was a pause, and then the learned leader got down to what was, I suppose, the nub and the purpose of his visit.

'Horace. I'm anxious to put an end to any sort of rift between the two senior men in Chambers. It doesn't make for a happy ship.'

'Aye aye sir.' I gave him a brief nautical salute from my position at the desk.

'I'm glad you agree. *Sérieusement*, Horace, we don't see enough of each other socially.' He paused again, but I could find nothing to say. 'I've got a couple of tickets for the Scales of Justice ball at the Savoy. Would you join me and Marigold?'

To say I was taken aback would be an understatement. I was astonished. 'Let's get this quite clear, Featherstone.'

'Oh "Guthrie", please.'

'Very well Guthrie. You're asking me to trip the light fantastic toe ... with your wife?'

'And if you'd like to bring *your* good lady.'

I looked at Featherstone in total amazement. 'My...'

'Your missus.'

'Are you referring, at all, to my wife? She Who Must Be Obeyed? Do I take it you actually want to spend an evening out with She!'

'It'll be great fun.'

'Do you really think so?' He had lost me now. I went to the door and unhooked the mac and the old hat, preparatory to calling it a day. However,

235

Featherstone had some urgent matter to communicate, apparently of an embarrassing nature.

'Oh, and Horace ... this is rather embarrassing. It's just that ... It's well ... your name came up on the bench at our Inn only last week. I was lunching with Mr Justice Prestcold.'

'That must have been a jolly occasion,' I told him. 'Like dinner with the Macbeths.' I knew Mr Justice Prestcold of old, and he and I had never hit it off, or seen eye to eye. In fact you might say there was always a cold wind blowing in court between counsel and the bench whenever Rumpole rose to his feet before Prestcold J. He could be guaranteed to ruin my cross-examination, interrupt my speech, fail to sum up the defence and send any Rumpole client down for a hefty six if he could find the slightest excuse for it. Prestcold was an extra-ordinarily clean man, his cuffs and bands were whiter than white, he was forever polishing his rimless glasses on a succession of snowy handkerchiefs. They say, and God knows what truth there is in it, that Prestcold travels on circuit with a portable loo seat wrapped in plastic. His clerk has the unenviable job of seeing that it is screwed in at the lodgings, so his Lordship may not sit where less fastidious judges have sat before.

'He was asking who we had in Chambers and I was able to tell him Horace Rumpole, *inter alia*.'

'I can't imagine Frank Prestcold eating. I suppose he might just be brought to sniff the bouquet of a grated carrot.'

'And he said, "You mean the fellow with the disgraceful hat?"'

236

'Mr Justice Prestcold was talking about my *hat*?' I couldn't believe my ears.

'He seemed to think, forgive me for raising this, that your hat set the worst possible example to younger men at the Bar.'

With enormous self-control I kept my temper. 'Well, you can tell Mr Justice Prestcold—the next time you're sharing the Benchers' Vegetarian Platter ... That when I was last before him I took strong exception to his cuff links. They looked to me just as cheap and glassy as his eyes!'

'Don't take offence, Horace. It's just not worth it, you know, taking offence at Her Majesty's judges. We'll look forward to the Savoy. Best to your good lady.'

I crammed on the hat, gave him a farewell wave and left him. I felt, that evening, that I was falling out of love with the law. I really couldn't believe that Mr Justice Prestcold had been discussing my hat. I mean, wasn't the crime rate rising? Wasn't the State encroaching on our liberties? Wasn't Magna Carta tottering? Whither Habeus Corpus? What was to be done about the number of 12-year-old girls who are making advances to old men in cinemas? What I thought was, hadn't judges of England got enough on their plates without worrying about my hat! I gave the matter mature consideration on my way home on the Inner Circle, and decided that they probably hadn't.

*　　*　　*

A few mornings later I picked up the collection of demands, final demands and positively final demands which constitutes our post and among the hostile brown envelopes I found a gilded and embossed invitation card. I took the whole lot into the kitchen to file away in the tidy bin when She Who Must Be Obeyed entered and caught me at it.

'Horace,' She said severely. 'Whatever are you doing with the post?'

'Just throwing it away. Always throw bills away the first time they come in. Otherwise you only encourage them.'

'If you had a few decent cases, Rumpole, if you weren't always slumming round the Magistrates Courts, you might not be throwing away bills all the time.' At which she pedalled open the tidy bin and spotted the fatal invitation.

'What's that?'

'I think it's the gas.' It was too late, She had picked the card out from among the potato peelings.

'I never saw a gas bill with a gold embossed crest before. It's an invitation! To the Savoy Hotel!' She started to read the thing. 'Horace Rumpole and Lady.'

'You wouldn't enjoy it,' I hastened to assure her.

'Why wouldn't I enjoy it?' She wiped the odd fragment of potato off the card, carried it into the living-room in state, and gave it pride of place on the mantelpiece. I followed her, protesting.

'You know what it is. Boiled shirts. Prawn cocktail. Watching a lot of judges pushing their wives round the parquet to selections from *Oklahoma*.'

'It'll do you good Rumpole. That's the sort of

place you ought to be seen in: the Scales of Justice ball.'

'It's quite impossible.' The situation was becoming desperate.

'I don't see why.'

I had an inspiration, and assumed an expression of disgust. 'We're invited by Marigold Featherstone.'

'The wife of your Head of Chambers?'

'An old boot! A domestic tyrant. You know what the wretched Guthrie calls her? She Who Must Be Obeyed. No. The ball is out, Hilda. You and Marigold wouldn't hit it off at all.'

Well, I thought, She and sweet Marigold would never meet, so I was risking nothing. I seized the hat and prepared to retreat. 'Got to leave you now. Murder calls.'

'Why didn't you tell me we were back to murder? This *is* good news.' Hilda was remarkably cheerful that morning.

'Murder,' I told her, 'is certainly better than dancing.' And I was gone about my business. Little did I know that the moment my back was turned Hilda looked up the Featherstones number in the telephone book.

*   *   *

'You can't do it to Peter! I tell you, you can't do it! Fight the case? How can he fight the case?' Leslie Delgardo had quite lost the cool and knowing air of a successful East End businessman. His face was flushed and he thumped his fist on my table, jangling his identity bracelet and disturbing the notice of additional

239

evidence I was reading, that of Bernard Whelpton, known as 'Four Eyes'.

'Whelpton's evidence doesn't help. I'm sure you'll agree, Mr Rumpole,' Nooks said gloomily.

'You read that! You read what "Four Eyes" has to say.' Leslie collapsed breathless into my client's chair. I read the document which ran roughly as follows. 'Tosher MacBride used to take the mick out of Peter on account he stammered and didn't have no girl friends. One night I saw Peter try to speak to a girl in the Paradise Rooms. He was asking the girl to have a drink but his stutter was so terrible. Tosher said to her, "Come on, darling ... It'll be breakfast time before the silly git finishes asking for a light ale." After I heard Peter Delgardo say as he'd get Tosher. He said he'd like to cut him one night.'

'He's not a well boy,' Leslie was wiping his forehead with a mauve silk handkerchief.

'When I came out of the Old Justice pub that night I see Tosher on the pavement and Petey Delgardo was kneeling beside him. There was blood all over.' I looked up at Nooks. 'You know it's odd. No one actually *saw* the stabbing.'

'But Petey was there wasn't he?' Leslie was returning the handkerchief to his breast pocket. 'And what's the answer about the knife?'

'In my humble opinion,' Nooks' opinions were often humble, 'the knife in the car is completely damning.'

'Oh completely.' I got up, lit a small cigar, and told Leslie my own far from humble opinion. 'You know, I'd have had no doubts about this case if you hadn't just proved your brother innocent.'

'I did?' The big man in the chair looked at me in a wild surmise.

'When you sent Doctor Lewis Bleen, the world-famous trick cyclist, the head shrinker extraordinaire, down to see Petey in Brixton. If you'd done a stabbing, and you were offered a nice quiet trip to hospital, wouldn't you take it? If the evidence was dead against you?'

'You mean *Peter* turned it down?' Leslie Delgardo clearly couldn't believe his ears.

'Of course he did!' I told him cheerfully. 'Petey may not be all that bright, poor old darling, but he knows he didn't kill Tosher MacBride.'

★   ★   ★

The committal was at Stepney Magistrates Court and Henry told me that there was a good deal of interest and that the vultures of the press might be there.

'I thought I should warn you sir. Just in case you wanted to buy...'

'I know, I know,' I interrupted him. 'Perhaps, Henry, there's a certain amount of force in your argument. "Vanity of vanities, all is vanity," said the preacher.' Here was I a barrister of a certain standing, doing a notable murder alone and without a leader, *the* type of person whose picture might appear in the *Evening Standard*, and I came to the reluctant conclusion that my present headgear was regrettably unphotogenic. I took a taxi to St James' Street and invested in a bowler, which clamped itself to the head like a vice but which caused Henry, when he saw it, to give me a smile of genuine gratitude.

241

That evening I had forgotten the whole subject of hats and was concerned with a matter that interests me far more deeply: blood. I had soaked the rubber sponge that helps with the washing up and, standing at the kitchen sink, stabbed violently down into it with a table knife. It produced, as I had suspected, a spray of water, leaving small spots all over my shirt and waistcoat.

'Horace! Horace, you look quite different.' Hilda was looking at the evening paper in which there was a picture of Pete Delgardo's heroic defender arriving at Court. 'I know what it is, Horace! You went out. And bought a new hat. Without me.'

I stabbed again, having re-soaked the sponge.

'A bowler. Daddy used to wear a bowler. It's an improvement.' Hilda was positively purring at my dapper appearance in the paper.

'Little splashes. All over the place,' I observed, committing further mayhem on the sponge.

'Horace. Whatever are you doing to the washing up?'

'All over. In little drops. Not one great stain. Little drops. Like a fine rain. And plenty on the cuff.'

'Your cuff's soaking. Oh, why couldn't you roll up your sleeve?'

I felt the crook of my arm, and was delighted to discover that it was completely dry.

'Now I know why you didn't want to take me to the Scales of Justice annual ball.' Hilda looked at the *Evening Standard* with less pleasure. 'You're too grand now, aren't you Rumpole? New hat! Picture in the paper! Big case! "Horace Rumpole. Defender of the Stepney Road Stabber". Big noise at the Bar. I suppose you didn't think I'd do you credit.'

'That's nonsense, Hilda.' I mopped up some of the mess round the sink, and dried my hands.

'Then why?'

I went and sat beside her, and tried to comfort her with Keats. 'Look. We're in the Autumn of our years. *"Season of mists and mellow fruitfulness, Close bosom-friend of the maturing sun..."*'

'I really can't understand *why!*'

'*"Where are the songs of Spring? Ay, where are they? Think not on them, thou hast thy music too."* But not jigging about like a couple of Punk Rockers. At a dance!'

'I very much doubt if they have Punk Rockers at the Savoy. Doesn't it occur to you, Rumpole? We never go out!'

'I'm perfectly happy. I'm not longing to go to the ball, like bloody Cinderella.'

'Well, I am!'

I thought Hilda was being most unreasonable, and I decided to point out the fatal flaw in the entire scheme concerning the Scales of Justice ball.

'Hilda. I can't dance.'

'You can't what?'

'Dance. I can't do it.'

'You're lying, Rumpole!'

The accusation was so unexpected that I looked at her in a wild surmise. And then she said,

'Would you mind casting your mind back to the 14th of August 1938?'

'What happened then?'

'You proposed to me, Rumpole. As a matter of fact, it was when you proposed. I shouldn't expect

243

you to remember.'

'1938. Of course! The year I did the "Euston Bank Robbery". Led by your father.'

'Led by Daddy. You were young, Rumpole. Comparatively young. And where did you propose, exactly? Can't you try and remember that?'

As I have said, I have no actual memory of proposing to Hilda at all. It seemed to me that I slid into the lifetime contract unconsciously, as a weary man drifts off into sleep. Any words, I felt sure, were spoken by her. I also had temporarily forgotten where the incident took place and hazarded a guess.

'At a bus stop?'

'Of course it wasn't at a bus stop.'

'It's just that your father always seemed to be detaining me at bus stops. I thought you might have been with him at the time.'

'You proposed to me in a tent.' Hilda came to my aid at last. 'There was a band. And champagne. And some sort of cold collation. Daddy had taken me to the Inns of Court ball to meet some of the bright young men in Chambers. He told me then, you'd been very helpful to him on blood groups.'

'It was the year before I did the "Penge Bungalow Murder",' I remembered vaguely. 'Hopeless on blood, your father, he could never bring himself to look at the photographs.'

'And we danced together. We actually waltzed together.'

'That's simple! That's just a matter of circling round and round. None of your bloody jigging about concerned with it!'

It was then that Hilda stood up and took my breath away. 'Well, we can waltz again, Rumpole. You'd better get into training for it. I rang up Marigold Featherstone and I told her we'd be delighted to accept the invitation.' She gave me a little smile of victory. 'And I tell you what. She didn't sound like an old boot at all.'

I was speechless, filled with mute resentment. I'd been double-crossed.

★   ★   ★

My toilette for the Delgardo murder case went no further than the acquisition of a new hat. As I sat in Court listening to the evidence for the prosecution of Bernard 'Four Eyes' Whelpton, I was vaguely conscious of the collapsed state of the wig (bought secondhand from an ex Chief Justice of Tonga in the early thirties), the traces of small cigar and breakfast egg on the waistcoat, and the fact that the bands had lost their pristine crispness and were forever sagging to reveal the glitter of the brass collar-stud.

I looked up and saw the judge staring at me with bleak disapproval and felt desperately to ensure that the fly buttons were safely fastened. Fate span her bloody wheel, and I had drawn Mr Justice Prestcold; Frank Prestcold, who took such grave exception to my hat, and who now looked without any apparent enthusiasm at the rest of my appearance. Well, I couldn't help him, I couldn't even hold up the bowler to prove I'd tried. I did my best to ignore the judge and concentrate on the evidence. Mr Hilary Painswick, Q.C., the perfectly decent old darling who led for the prosecution, was just concreting in 'Four Eyes' story.

'Mr Whelpton. I take it you haven't given this evidence in any spirit of enmity against the man in the dock?'

The man in the dock looked, as usual, as if he'd just been struck between the eyes with a heavy weight. Bernie Whelpton smiled charmingly, and said indiscreetly, 'No. I'm Petey's friend. We was at university together.'

At which Rumpole rose up like thunder and, to Prestcold J.'s intense displeasure, asked for the jury to be removed so that he could lodge an objection. When the jury had gone out the judge forced himself to look at me.

'What is the basis of your objection, Mr Rumpole? On the face of it the evidence that this gentleman was at university with your client seems fairly harmless.'

'This may come as a surprise to your Lordship.'

'May it, Mr Rumpole?'

'My client is not an old King's man. He didn't meet Mr "Four Eyes" Whelpton at a May Ball during Eights Week. The university referred to is, in fact, Parkhurst Prison.'

The judge applied his razor-sharp mind and saw a way of overruling my objection.

'Mr Rumpole! I very much doubt whether the average juryman has your intimate knowledge of the argot of the underworld.'

'Your Lordship is too complimentary.' I gave him a bow and a brassy flash of the collar-stud.

'I think no harm has been done. I appreciate your anxiety to keep your client's past record out of the case. Shall we have the jury back?'

246

Before the jury came back I got a note from Leslie Delgardo telling me, as I knew very well, that Whelpton had a conviction for perjury. I ignored this information, and did my best to make a friend of the little Cockney who gazed at me through spectacles thick as ginger beer bottles.

'Mr Whelpton, when you saw my client, Peter Delgardo, kneeling beside Tosher MacBride, did he have his arm round Mr MacBride's neck?'

'Yes, sir.'

'Supporting his head from behind?'

'I suppose so.'

'Rather in the attitude of a nurse or a doctor who was trying to bring help to the wounded man?'

'I didn't know your client had any medical qualifications!' Mr Justice Prestcold was trying one of his glacial jokes. I pretended I hadn't heard it, and concentrated on Bernie Whelpton.

'Were you able to see Peter Delgardo's hands when he was holding Tosher?'

'Yes.'

'Anything in them, was there?'

'Not as I saw.'

'He wasn't holding the knife, for instance?' I had the murder weapon on the desk in front of me and held it up for the jury to see.

'I tell you. I didn't see no knife.'

'I don't know whether my learned friend remembers.' Hilary Painswick uncoiled himself beside me. 'The knife was found in the car.'

'Exactly!' I smiled gratefully at Painswick. 'So my client stabbed Tosher. Ran to his car. Dropped the murder weapon in by the driver's seat and then came back across the pavement to
247

hold Tosher in his arms and comfort his dying moments.' I turned back to the witness. 'Is *that* what you're saying?'

'He might have slipped the knife in his pocket.'

'Mr Rumpole!' Prestcold J. had something to communicate.

'Yes, my Lord?'

'This is not the time for arguing your case. This is the time for asking questions. If you think this point has any substance you will no doubt remind the jury of it when you come to make up your final address; at some time in the no doubt distant future.'

'I'm grateful. And no doubt your Lordship will also remind the jury of it in your summing up, should it slip my memory. It really is *such* an unanswerable point for the defence.'

I saw the Prestcold mouth open for another piece of snappy repartee, and forestalled him by rapidly re-starting the cross-examination.

'Mr Whelpton. You didn't see Tosher stabbed?'

'I was in the Old Justice wasn't I?'

'You tell us. And when you came out, Tosher...'

'Might it not be more respectful to call that good man, the deceased, "Mr MacBride"?' the judge interrupted wearily.

'If you like. "That good man Mr MacBride" was bleeding in my client's arms?'

'That was the first I saw of him. Yes.'

'And when he saw you Mr Delgardo let go of Tosher, of that good man Mr MacBride, ran to his car and got into it?'

'And then he drove away.'

'Exactly. You saw him get into his car. How did

248

he do it?'

'Just turned the handle and pulled the door open.'

'So the car was unlocked?'

'I suppose it was. I didn't really think.'

'You suppose the door was unlocked.' I looked at the judge who appeared to have gone into some sort of a trance. 'Don't go too fast, Mr Whelpton. Mr Lord wants an opportunity to make a note.' At which the judge returned to earth and was forced to take up his pencil. As he wrote, Leslie Delgardo leaned forward from the seat behind me and said,

'Here, Mr Rumpole. What do you think you're doing?'

'Having a bit of fun. You don't grudge it to me, do you?'

*   *   *

The next item on the agenda was the officer in charge of the case, a perfectly reasonable fellow with a grey suit, who looked like the better type of bank manager.

'Detective Inspector. You photographed Mr Delgardo's antique Daimler when you got it back to the station?'

'Yes.' The officer leafed through a bundle of photographs.

'Was it then exactly as you found it outside the Old Justice?'

'Exactly.'

'Unlocked? With the driver's window open?'

'Yes. We found the car unlocked.'

'Then it would have been easy for anyone to

have thrown something in through the driver's window, or even put something in through the door?'

'I don't follow you, sir. Something?'

I found my prop and held it up. Exhibit 1, a flick knife. 'Something like this knife could have been dropped into Peter Delgardo's car, in a matter of moments?'

I saw the judge actually writing.

'I suppose it could, sir.'

'By the true murderer, whoever it was, when he was running away?'

The usher was beside me, handing me the fruit of Mr Justice Prestcold's labours; a note to counsel which read, 'Dear Rumpole. Your bands are falling down and showing your collar-stud. No doubt you would wish to adjust accordingly.' What was this, a murder trial, or a bloody fashion parade? I crumpled the note, gave the bands a quick shove in a northerly direction, and went back to work.

'Detective Inspector. We've heard Tosher MacBride described as a rent collector.'

'Is there to be an attack on the dead man's character, Mr Rumpole?'

'I don't know, my Lord. I suppose there are charming rent collectors, just as there are absolute darlings from the Income Tax.'

Laughter in Court, from which the judge remained aloof.

'Where did he collect rents?'

'Business premises.' The officer was non-committal.

'What sort of business premises?'

'Cafés, my Lord. Pubs. Minicab offices.'

250

'And if the rent wasn't paid, do you know what remedies were taken?'

'I assume proceedings were taken in the County Court.' The judge sounded totally bored by this line of cross-examination.

'Alas, my Lord, some people have no legal training. If the rents weren't paid, sometimes those minicab offices caught on fire, didn't they Detective Inspector?'

'Sometimes they did.' I told you, he was a very fair officer.

'To put it bluntly, that "good man" Tosher MacBride was a collector for a protection racket.'

'Well, officer, was he?' said Prestcold, more in sorrow than in anger.

'Yes, my Lord. I think he was.'

For the first time I felt I was forcing the judge to look in a different direction, and see the case from a new angle. I rubbed in the point. 'And if he'd been sticking to the money he'd collected, that might have provided a strong motive for murder by someone other than my client? Stronger than a few unkind words about an impediment in his speech?'

'Mr Rumpole, isn't that a question for the jury?' I looked at the jury then, they were all alive and even listening, and I congratulated the old darling on the bench.

'You're right! It is, my Lord. *And for no one else in this Court!*'

I thought it was effective, perhaps too effective for Leslie Delgardo, who stood up and left Court with a clatter. The swing doors banged to after him.

251

By precipitously leaving Court, Leslie Delgardo had missed the best turn on the bill, my double act with Mr Entwhistle, the forensic expert, an old friend and a foeman worthy of my steel.

'Mr Entwhistle, as a scientific officer I think you've lived with bloodstains as long as I have?'

'Almost.'

The jury smiled, they were warming to Rumpole.

'And you have all the clothes my client was wearing that night. Have you examined the pockets?'

'I have, my Lord.' Entwhistle bowed to the judge over a heap of Petey's clothing.

'And there are no bloodstains in any of the pockets?'

'There are none.'

'So there can be no question of a bloodstained knife having been hidden in a pocket whilst my client cradled the deceased in his arms?'

'Of course not.' Entwhistle smiled discreetly.

'You find that a funny suggestion?'

'Yes I do. The idea's ridiculous.'

'You may be interested to know that it's on that ridiculous idea the prosecution are basing their case.'

Painswick was on his feet with a well-justified moan. 'My Lord...'

'Yes. That was a quite improper observation, Mr Rumpole.'

'Then I pass from it rapidly, my Lord.' No point in wasting time with him, my business was with Entwhistle. 'Had Mr Delgardo stabbed the

252

deceased, you would expect a spray of blood over a wide area of clothing?'

'You might have found that.'

'With small drops spattered from a forceful blow?'

'I should have expected so.'

'But you found nothing like it?'

'No.'

'And you might have expected blood near the area of the cuff of the coat or the shirt?'

'Most probably.'

'In fact, all we have is a smear or soaked patch in the crook of the arm.'

Mr Entwhistle picked up the overcoat, looked and, of course, admitted it.

'Yes.'

'Totally consistent with my client having merely put an arm round the deceased when he lay bleeding on the pavement.'

'Not inconsistent.'

'A double negative! The last refuge of an expert witness who doesn't want to commit himself. Does "not inconsistent" translated into plain English mean consistent, Mr Entwhistle?'

I could have kissed old Entwhistle on the rimless specs when he turned to the jury and said, 'Yes, it does.'

*   *   *

So when I got outside and saw Leslie Delgardo sitting on a bench chewing the end of a cigar, I thought he would wish to congratulate me. I didn't think of a gold watch, or a crinkly fiver, but at least a few warm words of encouragement. So I

253

was surprised when he said, in a tone of deep hostility, 'What're you playing at, Mr Rumpole? Why didn't you use Bernie's conviction?'

'You really want to know?' Other members of the family were thronging about us, Basil and a matronly person in a mink coat, dabbing her eye make-up with a minute lace hanky.

'We all want to know,' said Basil, 'all the family.'

'I know I'm only the boy's mother,' sobbed the lady in mink.

'Don't underestimate yourself madam,' I reassured her. 'You've bred three sons who have given employment to the legal profession.' Then I started to explain. 'Point one. I spent all this trial trying to keep your brother's record out. If I put in the convictions of a prosecution witness the jury'll get to know about Peter's stretch for unlawful wounding, back in 1970. You want that?'

'We thought it was helpful,' Basil grumbled.

'Did you?' I looked at him. 'I'm sure you did. Well, point two, the perjury was forging a passport application. I've already checked it. And point three.'

'Point three, Mr Rumpole. You're sacked.' Leslie's voice was high with anger. I felt grateful we weren't in a turning off Stepney High Street on a dark night.

'May I ask why?'

'You got that judge's back up proper. He'll do for Petey. Good afternoon, Mr Rumpole. I'm taking you off the case.'

'I don't think you can do that.' He'd started to walk away, but now turned back with a look of

254

extreme hostility.

'Oh don't you?'

'The only person who can take me off this case is my client, Mr Peter Delgardo. Come along Nooks, we'd better go down to the cells.'

*   *   *

'Your brother wants to sack me.'

Petey looked at me with his usual lack of understanding. Nooks acted as a smooth interpreter.

'The position is, Mr Leslie Delgardo is a little perturbed at the course this case is taking.'

'Mr Leslie Delgardo isn't my client,' I reminded Peter.

'He thinks we've got on the wrong side of the judge.'

I was growing impatient. 'Would he like to point out to me, strictly for my information, the *right* side of Mr Justice Prestcold? What *does* that judge imagine he is? Court correspondent for *The Tailor and Cutter?*' I stamped out my small cigar. 'Look, Peter, dear old sweetheart. I've abandoned the judge. He'll sum up dead against you. That's obvious. So let the jury think he's nothing but a personal anti-pollution programme who shoves air-wick up his nostrils every time he so much as smells a human being and we might have *got* somewhere.'

'Mr Leslie Delgardo is definitely dissatisfied. This puts me in a very embarrassing position.' Nooks looked suitably embarrassed.

'Cheer up, Nooks!' I smiled at him. 'Your position's nothing like so embarrassing as Peter's.'

255

Then I concentrated on my client. 'Well. What's it going to be? Do I go or stay?'

Peter began to stammer an answer. It took a long time to come but, when it did, it meant that just one week later, on the day of the Scales of Justice ball, I was making a final speech to the jury in the case of the Queen against Delgardo. I may say that I never saw Leslie, or Basil, or their dear old Mum again.

★　　　★　　　★

'Members of the jury, may I call your attention to a man we haven't seen. He isn't in the dock. He has never gone into that witness box. I don't know where he is now. Perhaps he's tasting the delights of the Costa Brava. Perhaps he's very near this Court waiting for news. I'll call him Mr X. Did Mr X employ that "good man" Tosher MacBride to collect money in one of his protection rackets? Had Tosher MacBride betrayed his trust and was he to die for it? So that rainy night, outside the Old Justice pub in Stepney, Mr X waited for Tosher, waited with this knife and, when he saw his unfaithful servant come out of the shadows, he stabbed. Not once. Not twice. But you have heard the evidence. Three times in the neck.'

The jury was listening enrapt to my final speech; I was stabbing violently downwards with my prop when Prestcold cleared his throat and pointed to his own collar meaningfully. No doubt my stud was winking at him malevolently, so he said, 'Hm! ... Mr Rumpole.'

I ignored this, no judge alive was going to spoil

256

the climax of my speech, and I could tell that the jury were flattered, not to say delighted, to hear me tell them,

'Of course you are the *only* judges of fact in this case. But if you find Peter Delgardo guilty, then Mr X will smile, and order up champagne. Because, wherever he is, he will know ... he's safe at last!'

Frank Prestcold summed up, as I knew he would, dead against Petey. He called the prosecution evidence 'overwhelming' and the jury listened politely. They went out just after lunch, and were still out at 6.30 when I telephoned Hilda and told her that I'd change in Chambers, and meet her at the Savoy, and I wanted it clearly understood that I wasn't dancing. I was just saying this when the usher came out and told me that the jury were back with a verdict.

★ ★ ★

After it was all over, I looked round in vain for Nooks. He had apparently gone to join the rest of the Delgardos in the great unknown. So I went down to say 'good-bye' to Peter in the cells. He was sitting inert, and staring into the middle distance.

'Cheer up, Peter.' I sat down beside him. 'Don't look so bloody miserable. My God. I don't know how you'd take it if you'd lost.'

Peter shook his head, and then said something I didn't wholly understand. 'I was ... meant to l ... l ... lose.'

'Who meant you to? The prosecution? Of course. Mr Justice Prestcold? Undoubtedly. Fate.

Destiny. The Spirit of the Universe? Not as it turned out. It was written in the stars. "Not Guilty of Murder. And is that the verdict of you all?".'

'That's why they ch ... chose you. I was meant to lose.'

What the man said puzzled me. I admit I found it enigmatic. I said, 'I don't follow.'

'Bloke in the cell while I was w ... w ... waiting. Used to be a mate of Bernie "Four-Eyes". He told me why me brothers chose you to defend me.'

Well I thought I knew why I had been chosen for this important case. I stood up and paced the room.

'No doubt I have a certain reputation around the Temple, although my crown may be a little tarnished; done rather too much indecent assault lately.'

'He heard them round the P ... P ... Paradise Rooms. Talking about this old feller Rumpole.' Peter seemed to be pursuing another line of thought.

'The "Penge Bungalow Murder" is in *Notable British Trials*. I may have become a bit of a household name, at least in criminal circles.'

'They was l ... looking for a barrister who'd be sure to lose.'

'After this, I suppose, I may get back to better quality crime.' The full force of what Peter had said struck me. I looked at him and checked carefully. '*What* did you say?'

'They wanted me defended by someone they could c ... count on for a guilty verdict. That's why they p ... p ... picked you for it.'

258

It was, appallingly, what I thought he'd said.

'They wanted to fit me up with doing Tosher,' Peter Delgardo went on remorselessly.

'Let me get this clear. Your brothers selected *me* to nobble your defence?'

'That's it! You w ... was to be the jockey like.' That pulled me back.

'How did they light on me exactly? Me ... Rumpole of the Bailey?'

My entire life, Sherlock Holmes stories, Law degree, knock-about apprenticeship at Bow Street and Hackney, days of triumph in murder and forgery, down to that day's swayed jury and notable victory, seemed to be blown away like autumn leaves by what he said. Then, the words came quickly now, tumbling out of him, 'They heard of an old bloke. Got p ... past it. Down to little bits of cases ... round the M ... M ... Magistrates Courts. Bit of a muddler, they heard. With a funny old broken-down hat on him.'

'The hat! Again.' At least I had bought a bowler.

'So they r ... reckoned. You was just the bloke to lose this murder, like.'

'And dear old Nooks. "Shady" Nooks. Did he help them to choose me?' I suspected it.

'I d ... don't know. I'm n ... n ... not saying he didn't.'

'So that's my reputation!' I tried to take stock of the situation, and failed abysmally.

'I shouldn't've told you.' He sounded genuinely apologetic.

'Get Rumpole for the defence—and be sure of a conviction.'

'Perhaps it's all lies.' Was he trying to cheer my

up? He went on. 'You hear lots of s ... s ... stories. In the cells under the Bailey.'

'And in the Bar Mess too. They rubbish your reputation. Small cigar?' I found a packet and offered him one.

'All right.'

We lit up. After all, one had to think of the future.

'So where does this leave you, Peter?' I asked him.

'I'd say, Mr Rumpole, none too s ... safe. What about you?'

I blew out smoke, wondering exactly what I had left.

'Perhaps not all that safe either.'

*   *   *

I had brought my old dinner jacket up to Chambers and I changed into it there. I had a bottle of rum in the cupboard, and I gave myself a strong drink out of a dusty glass. As I shut the cupboard door, I noticed my old hat, it was on a shelf, gathering dust and seemed to have about it a look of mild reproach. I put it on, and noticed how comfortably it fitted. I dropped the new, hard bowler into the wastepaper basket and went on to the Savoy.

*   *   *

'You look charming, my dear.' Hilda, resplendent in a long dress, her shoulders dusted with powder, smiled delightedly at Mrs Marigold Featherstone, who was nibbling delicately at an after-dinner mint.

'Really, Rumpole.' Hilda looked at me, gently rebuking.

'She!'

'She?' Marigold was mystified, but anxious to join in any joke that might be going.

'Oh "She",' I said casually. 'A woman of fabulous beauty. Written up by H. Rider Haggard.' A waiter passed and I created a diversion by calling his attention to the fact that the tide had gone out in my glass. Around us prominent members of the legal profession pushed their bulky wives about the parquet like a number of fresh-faced gardeners executing elaborate manoeuvres with wheelbarrows. There were some young persons among them, and I noticed Erskine-Brown, jigging about in solitary rapture somewhere in the vicinity of Miss Phyllida Trant. She saw me and gave a quick smile and then she was off circling Erskine-Brown like an obedient planet, which I didn't consider a fitting occupation for any girl of Miss Trant's undoubted abilities.

'Your husband's had a good win.' Guthrie Featherstone was chatting to Hilda.

'He hasn't had a "good win", Guthrie.' She put the man right. 'He's had a triumph!'

'Entirely thanks ... to my old hat.' I raised my glass. 'Here's to it!'

'What?' Little of what Rumpole said made much sense to Marigold.

'My triumph, indeed, my great opportunity, is to be attributed solely to my hat!' I explained to her, but She couldn't agree.

'Nonsense!'

261

'What?'

'You're talking nonsense,' She explained to our hosts. 'He does, you know, from time to time. Rumpole won because he knows so much about blood.'

'Really?' Featherstone looked at the dancers, no doubt wondering how soon he could steer his beautiful wife off into the throng. But Hilda fixed him with her glittering eye, and went on, much like the ancient mariner.

'You remember Daddy, of course. He used to be *your* Head of Chambers. Daddy told me. "Rumpole", Daddy told me. In fact, he told me that on the occasion of the Inns of Court summer ball, which is practically the last dance we went to.'

'Hilda!' I tried, unsuccessfully, to stem the flow.

'No. I'm going to say this, Horace. Don't interrupt! "Horace Rumpole", Daddy told me, "knows more about bloodstains than anyone we've got in Chambers."'

I noticed that Marigold had gone a little pale.

'Do stop it, Hilda. You're putting Marigold off.'

'Don't you find it,' Marigold turned to me, 'well, sordid sometimes?'

'What?'

'Crime. Don't you find it terribly sordid?'

There was a silence. The music had stopped, and the legal fraternity on the floor clapped sporadically. I saw Erskine-Brown take Miss Trant's hand.

'Oh, do be careful, Marigold!' I said. 'Don't knock it.'

'I think it must be sordid.' Marigold patted her

262

lips with her table napkin, removing the last possible trace of after-dinner mint.

'Abolish crime,' I warned her, 'and you abolish the very basis of our existence!'

'Oh, come now, Horace!' Featherstone was smiling at me tolerantly.

'He's right,' Hilda told him. 'Rumpole knows about bloodstains.'

'Abolish crime and we should all vanish.' I felt a rush of words to the head. 'All the barristers and solicitors and dock officers and the dear old matron down the Old Bailey who gives aspirins away with sentences of life imprisonment. There'd be no judges, no Lord Chancellor. The Commissioner of the Metropolitan Police would have to go out selling encyclopaedias.' I leant back, grabbed the wine from the bucket, and started to refill all our glasses. 'Why are we here? Why've we got prawn cocktail and *duck à l'orange* and selections from dear old *Oklahoma*? All because a few villains down the East End are kind enough to keep us in a regular supply of crime.'

A slightly hurt waiter took the bottle from me and continued my work.

'Don't *you* help them?' Marigold looked at me, doubtfully.

'Don't I *what*?'

'Help them. Doing all these crimes. After all. You get them off.'

'Today,' I said, not without a certain pride. 'Today, let me tell you, Marigold, I was no help to them at all. I showed them ... no gratitude!'

'You got him off!'

'What?'

'You got Peter Delgardo off.'

263

'Just for one reason.'

'What was that?'

'He happened to be innocent.'

'Come on, Horace. How can you be sure of that?' Featherstone was smiling tolerantly but I leant forward and gave him the truth of the matter.

'You know it's a terrifying thing, my learned friend. We go through all that mumbo jumbo. We put on our wigs and gowns and mutter the ritual prayers. "My Lord, I humbly submit." "Ladies and gentlemen of the jury, you have listened with admirable patience ..." Abracadabra. Fee Fo Fi Bloody Fum. And just when everyone thinks you're going to produce the most ludicrously faked bit of cheese-cloth ectoplasm, or a phoney rap on the table, it comes. Clear as a bell. Quite unexpected. The voice of truth!'

I was vaguely aware of a worried figure in a dinner jacket coming towards us across the floor.

'Have you ever found that, Featherstone? Bloody scaring sometimes. All the trouble we take to cloud the issues and divert the attention. Suddenly we've done it. There it is! Naked and embarrassing. The truth!'

I looked up as the figure joined us. It was my late instructing solicitor.

'Nooks. "Shady" Nooks!' I greeted him, but he seemed in no mood to notice me. He pulled up a chair and sat down beside Featherstone.

'Apparently it was on the nine o'clock news. They've just arrested Leslie Delgardo. Charged him with the murder of Tosher MacBride. I'll want a con with you in the morning.'

I was left out of this conversation but I didn't

264

mind. Music started again, playing a tune which I found vaguely familiar. Nooks was muttering on; it seemed that the police now knew Tosher worked for Leslie, and that some member of the rival Watson family may have spotted him at the scene of the crime. An extraordinary sensation overcame me, something I hadn't felt for a long time, which could only be described as happiness.

'I don't know whether you'll want to brief me for Leslie, Nooks,' I raised a glass to old 'Shady'. 'Or would that be rather over-egging the pudding?'

And then an even more extraordinary sensation, a totally irrational impulse for which I can find no logical explanation, overcame me. I put out a hand and touched She Who Must Be Obeyed on the powdered shoulder.

'Hilda.'

'Oh yes, Rumpole?' It seemed I was interrupting some confidential chat with Marigold. 'What do you want now?'

'I honestly think,' I could find no coherent explanation, 'I think I want to dance with you.'

I suppose it was a waltz. As I steered Hilda out onto the great open spaces it seemed quite easy to go round and round, vaguely in time to the music. I heard a strange sound, as if from a long way off.

'*I'll have the last waltz with you, Two sleepy people together . . .*' Or words to that effect. I was in fact singing. Singing and dancing to celebrate a great victory in a case I was never meant to win.